Windrunner

By

Lee McQueen

McQueen Press

Denver, Colorado

Published by McQueen Press
http://www.mcqueenpress.com

All rights reserved. No part of this book may be reproduced or transmitted in any form or by any means, electronic or mechanical, including photocopying, recording, or by any information storage and retrieval system without written permission from the publisher.

This is a work of fiction. The names, characters, incidents, and locations are the products of the author's imagination or used fictitiously and are not to be construed as real. No character in the book is based on an actual person. Any resemblance to persons living or dead is entirely coincidental and unintentional.

Cover photo by CreateSpace. Author photo by McQueen Press.

Cover design, interior design, and typesetting by Lee McQueen

Map courtesy of the U.S. Department of the Interior.

Logo is a registered mark of McQueen Press and should not be copied without permission.

Copyright 2012 Lee McQueen

Printed in the United States of America

Publisher's Catalog-in-publication

McQueen, Lee
Windrunner/Lee McQueen
p. cm.
ISBN 978-0-9798515-7-5
  1. African American women in fiction 2. Indians of North America—Fiction 3. West (U.S.)—Fiction 4. Renewable energy sources—Fiction

Works by Lee McQueen

Short Story Collection

Imaginarium

Poetry Collection

Things I Forgot to Tell You

Novels

Kenzi
Celara Sun

Screenplays

SUDAN: The Lion of Truth
Kindred

Non-Fiction

Writer in the Library! 41 Writers Reveal How They Use Libraries to Develop Their Skill, Craft & Careers

The Wind is an Eternal Searcher

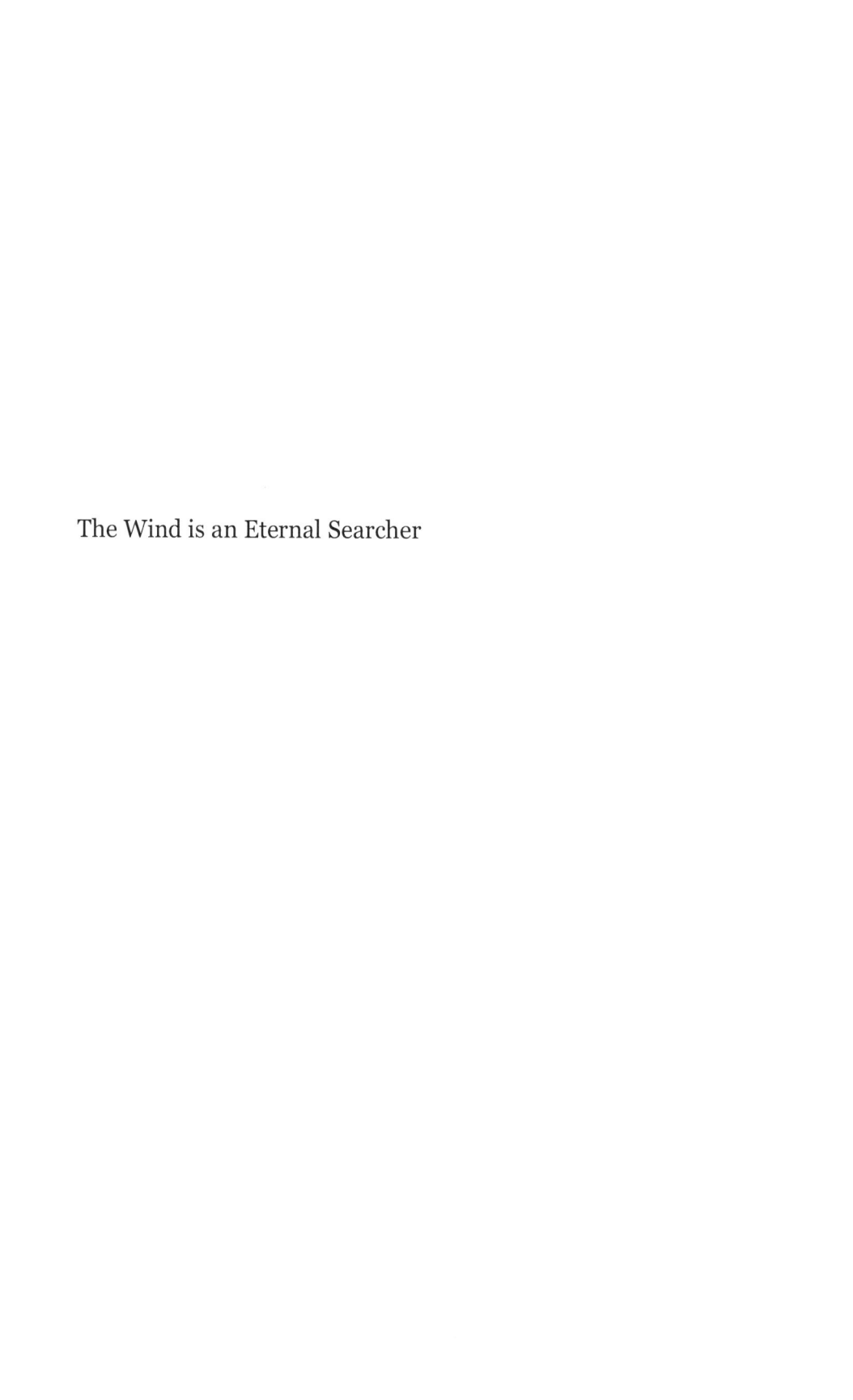

For the Optimists who Seek to Find

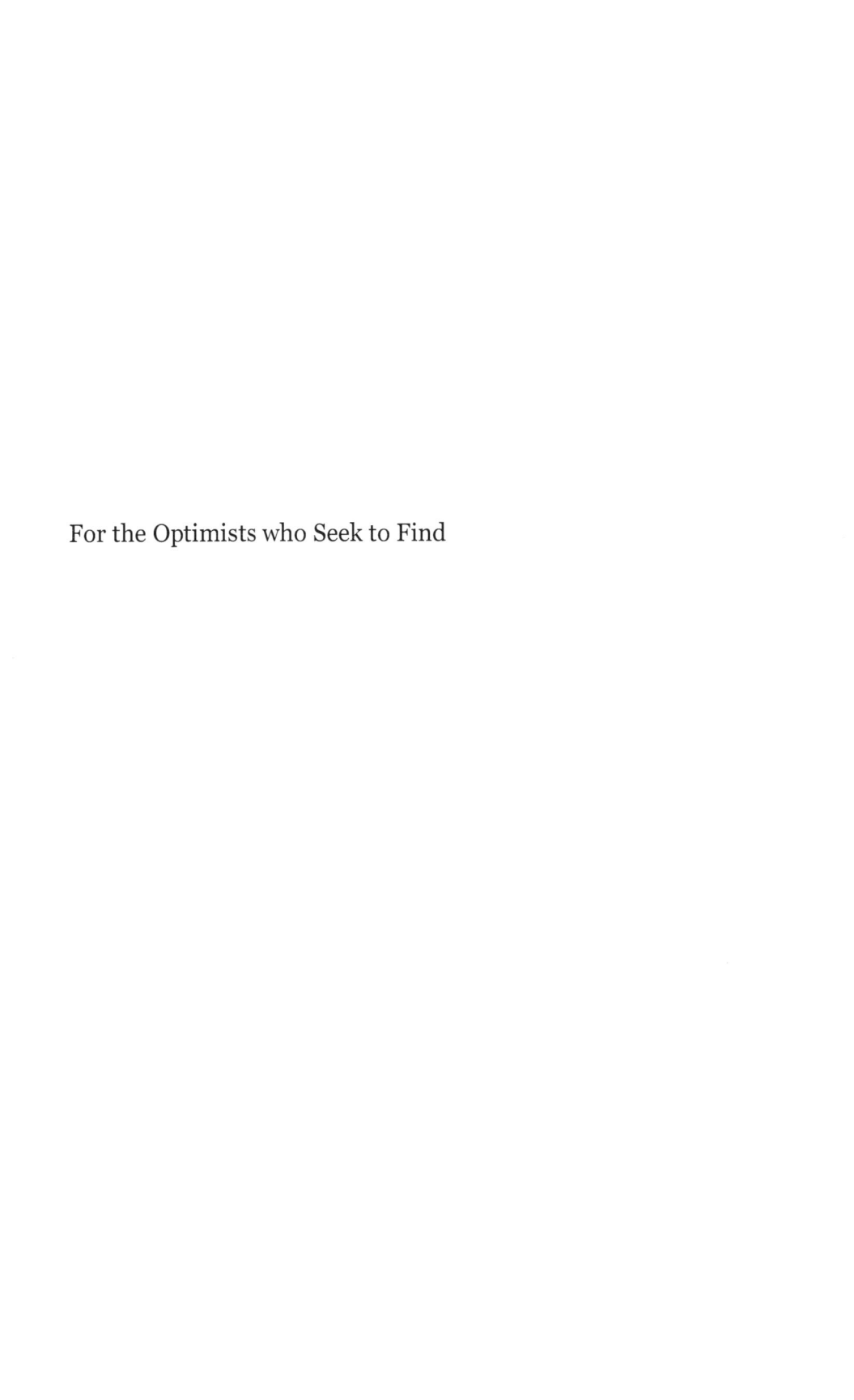

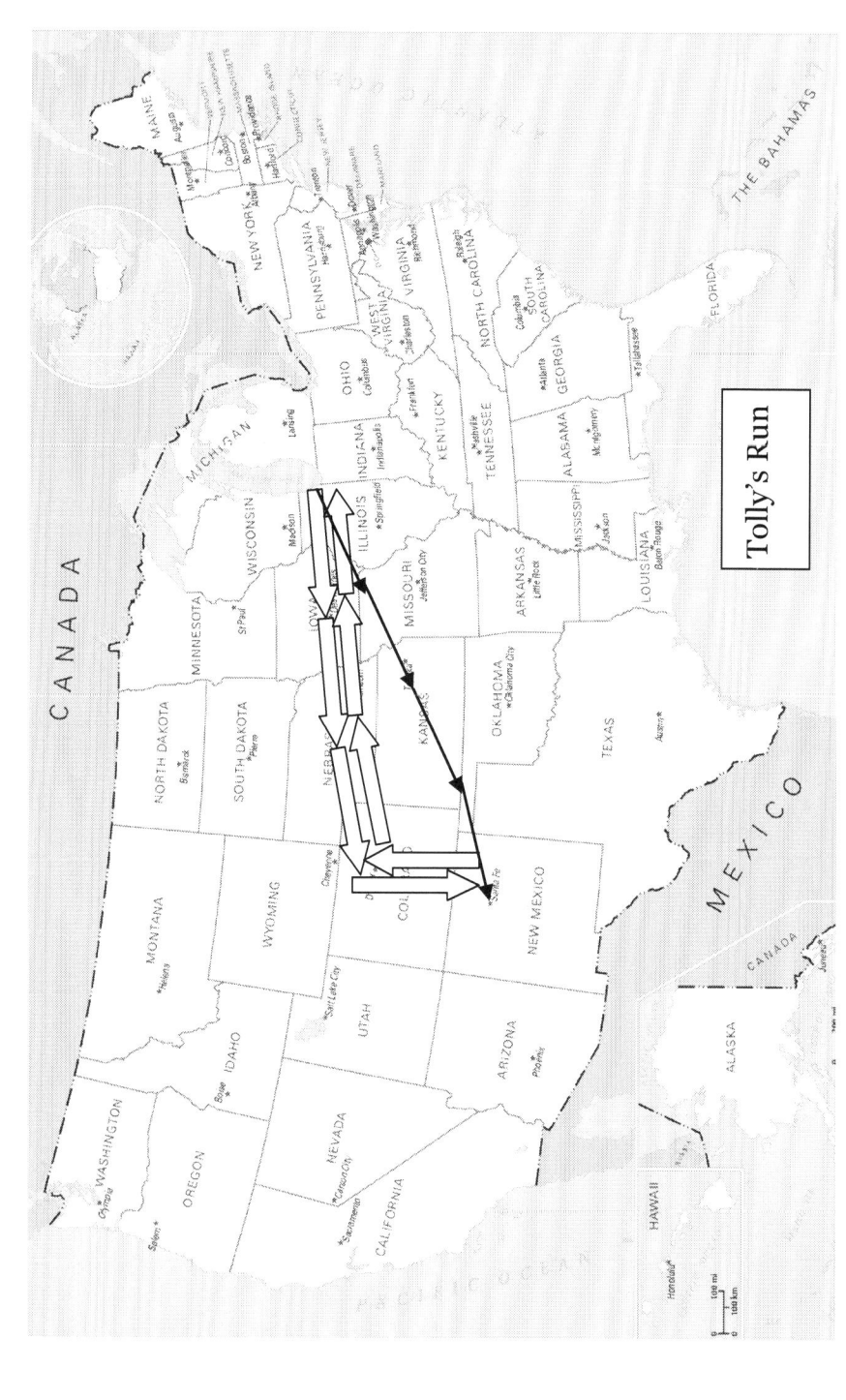

Chapter 1

The power and confidence of Alexander King's charm shone across Tolly like the rising sun splashed pink and orange into the eastern sky that stretched over the skyscrapers of Lake City in late August. He delivered a genius performance. The online viewers would go mad for him. Somewhat dazed, Tolly faced her camera to deliver closing remarks.

At 6:30 Monday morning, the Celara Wind industrial plant stood silent and alone in the midst of tall grass and cornfields, bypassed by a lonely road. The offices of the wind turbine manufacturer's headquarters had not yet opened for the day's business.

A trifle breathless, Tolly told King, "We'll get this edited and online as soon as possible."

Her interview subject delivered the goods and so would she.

"How long does it usually take?"

"Just a few hours."

King's handsome face belied impatient persuasion. "Yes, I hear my opponent's video has already received a lot of hits." Even, white teeth flashed.

"People in Lake City are very interested in green issues, especially energy resources."

King raised his eyebrows without a word. Here in front of Tolly stood a man used to getting what he wanted *when* he wanted it, a man who used the awkward moment, pregnant pause, even a long silence to dominate interactions.

The silence worked.

Tolly cleared her throat. "But I don't have to tell you that."

"Well, my campaign looks forward to the finished product. I'm sure it'll be just fine." King scanned her face for confirmation.

"It will," Tolly reassured him. "I'll see to that."

"Well, great!" Alex took a small step back.

Tolly exhaled with relief.

He looked at his watch. "I've got to get my family back home though. Apparently, the kids are a little fussy. And I do have a breakfast meeting and a few other media appearances. So..."

"Of course." Tolly glanced at his wife where she waited with their children. "I'll get to work on this."

She rushed through Celara Wind's front door at a near run. She still needed to record establishing shots of the industrial plant's exterior to the small handheld camera before the day shift began at eight o'clock. Soon, King's employees would fill the isolated parking lot surrounded by an emptier suburban expanse.

Once she located the best setting that included the company's brilliant blue sign in the background and bits of green shrubbery in the foreground, Tolly fixed the camera back to the tripod to record the introduction to King's interview.

She looked into the camera, confirmed the red light, and then pasted on a smile:

"Today, I visited with Alexander King, business man and leader in the green revolution, at Celara Wind to discuss his mayoral campaign. Full disclosure: Celara Wind, a wind turbine manufacturer, donates equipment and materials to the non-profit group that runs Lake City Balance..."

Profanity erupted over her shoulder. Tolly sighed. *Cut*. That would have been a good take. She would have to re-record.

She turned to peer through the shrubbery halfway between her and Celara Wind's front door. Alexander King, candidate for mayor, stood in the doorway. He struck his wife then yanked her arm. She stumbled forward. The two toddlers in the stroller cried.

Tolly stared in disbelief.

King shouted more expletives. His face was a bright, cherry red. He turned to lock the front door that he'd unlocked for Tolly no more than an hour ago.

Tolly's stomach churned the breakfast she'd eaten that morning in a mad dash to catch the bus to the northwest suburbs. The bus stop was half a mile down the road. No way for her to slip quietly away.

Finished with the door, King drew his right hand back to his left shoulder for a backhand hit. His wife shielded her face with her arm. She tried to cover the two toddlers in the stroller at the same time. The tiny woman looked unbelievably well-practiced at the defensive maneuver.

Hand still raised for the hit, King glanced up. Two pale blue lasers blazed thirty yards across the parking lot and through the shrubbery. Tolly's skin burned. But she felt no relief when the blue-white lights shifted their focus past her shoulder to the small camera that saw, heard, and filmed all.

"What the fuck do you think you're doing?" The King of the City shouted.

Tolly blinked. He apparently cursed *her* now instead of his tiny wife, sobbing over the stroller.

King stalked across the parking lot faster than Tolly expected. *Gym-training*, Tolly concluded. He reached past her to grab the camera. Tolly snapped out of her stunned reverie. She backed away, knocking the camera and tripod to the asphalt behind her. She looked around for help. There was no one in the vast stillness of suburban dawn.

"What are you trying to do here, Tolly?" he asked her. He stood so close that she could feel his breath on her face. "You realize you can't leave here with that footage, don't you?"

Tolly took a step back. King took a step forward.

"Hand it over," he told her. He held out his hand to her.

She shook her head. "I can't, Mr. King. I need the camera for work. I'll... I'll... edit the part..." Her voice trailed off.

King's eyes turned to solid steel. "Either you give me that camera, or I take it from you." He took another step towards her.

Tolly had nowhere to go. The shrubbery blocked her escape. "Mr. King, please. Don't do this. I'll take care of it. I won't..."

King yanked Tolly forward by the arm. He shook her until her teeth snapped together.

"Stop it!" Tolly's shoulder-length twists flew every direction. "Don't, don't!" She struggled to pull her arm away.

"Oh no you don't!" King changed tactics. This time, he tried to push past her to get to the camera where it lay on the ground. "Give me that!"

Tolly blocked him with her body.

He grabbed her by the arm again.

"No!" Tolly cried. She tried to twist away. "You're hurting me!"

"Give me that damn camera, Tolly." He ground the bones of her wrist against each other as though to break it. "You're not leaving here with that. Don't you dare try to fuck with me."

Tolly recognized that tone of voice. It was the same tone that Rafael used years ago to tell her she would be in for a bad night.

Tolly braced her feet against the ground. "Stop it! Please, Mr. King!" She shoved him away. She dove to pick up the camera and tripod.

"Bitch!" King grabbed her shirt tail. "Get back here!"

"Let go!" Tolly struck at his hands. "Let me go!" Again she searched the parking lot for rescue. There was no one except his wife frozen a crouch over the children. Over their screams Tolly heard a car door slam shut.

"What is going on here?" The new voice on the scene came from the road that led into the parking lot.

Chapter 2

Alex King released his hold on Tolly's shirt. Snorting like a ruby-faced dragon, he turned.

An older woman with brunette hair accented by a silver streak faced him. Her tailored navy suit screamed of a life enhanced by money. So did her leather shoes.

Tolly's heart beat fast. Her body shook and trembled from fear-induced adrenaline. The final humiliation would be to cry in public. She focused her energy on at least not breaking into tears. She attempted to slow her breathing the way her instructor at the local gym recommended.

The woman, about mid-sixties, wore violet-tinged designer sunglasses. Tolly felt self-conscious of her now-wrinkled shirt, her flustered expression, and the hard grip she still had on the camera and tripod. At seven-thirty in the morning, the woman looked ready for a fashion shoot. She turned her regal head back toward King.

"That's enough. I think you should leave." The woman's expression behind the sunglasses refused to yield.

"Now," she ordered.

Tolly held her breath, fearful King would renew his wrath.

To her surprise, King walked back across the parking lot to his wife without a word. Along the way, he smoothed his tailored suit and hair, still in place after his and Tolly's scuffle. Once he reached his family, he glanced over his shoulder at Tolly as though he blamed her for his children's tears.

"Miss," the woman looked from her to King then back again, "you seem terribly upset."

"I am." Tolly resisted tears, but she couldn't stop the tremble in her voice.

The older woman nodded in sympathy. "Can I call someone for you?"

"No." Tolly shook her head." There's... no one to call, really."

"Would you like a ride home?" Her rescuer nodded towards black Mercedes parked at the curb.

King led his family in the other direction towards a model of car too far away for Tolly to recognize. Whatever it was, it also looked expensive. He didn't look back again.

Tolly hesitated. "Yes, I think that's a good idea. I'm not up to walking to the bus stop by myself." Tolly didn't know whether King would circle the building to try to find her alone again.

"I understand." Both women glanced at the empty parking space abandoned by King and his family. "I wouldn't want to either."

"Just let me get my shoulder bag." Tolly took a few shaky steps to retrieve it. She shoved the camera, tripod, and notebook inside. She turned and let out a squeak.

The woman hovered over her. "Ready?" she asked.

They crossed the empty parking lot to the expensive sedan parked on the street. King's employees, the Celara Wind staff, had missed the entire episode. What would they have thought? Or would their boss's behavior have surprised them?

"I just can't believe that actually happened in broad daylight. Before when he..." She paused, unable to finish. "And then after he blew up at me, got so crazy. I didn't expect it. It came out of nowhere."

The woman allowed a small smile. She unlocked the car doors with a flick of her key ring. "Men are funny creatures sometimes." They got in.

"And sometimes they're psychopaths," Tolly declared.

The woman's smile disappeared. "So which way are we going, ah..."

"Tolly." Within the shelter of the expensive car, her voice steadied at last. "Henry."

"Tolly Henry." They shook hands. "Am I taking you home?"

"Oh yes." She shook her head as though to clear it. "Thanks. I'm still a little rattled, I guess." She gave the woman directions to her three-flat, a square building with apartments stacked one on top of another.

The sedan cut through traffic like a gunboat through water on the way towards Lake City's Central District. "So are you by yourself?" the woman asked.

"You mean..."

The woman's lifted her brows.

"Yes, I'm single."

The woman nodded as if to say, *I thought so.*

"I'm on the basement level. There." Tolly pointed out the three-story structure and the windows that peeked just halfway above the sidewalk. "I manage that building. Well, mostly, I keep things afloat."

Her driver signaled to make the turn onto Tolly's street. "That's wonderful to be so independent."

"Yes, I suppose. Building management's a lot of work, but then I like to work."

"Sometimes independence can be a problem."

"Problem how?"

"Most powerful men will stop at nothing to get what they want, when they want it." The woman pulled to the curb in front of Tolly's building.

"Yes. I know." She shivered remembering the bad nights with Rafael years ago and the encounter with King just minutes ago.

"Whatever it takes."

Another lick of ice slid down the back of Tolly's neck. She tightened her fingers on the passenger door handle. A polite way to end the conversation escaped her.

The woman persisted. "I mean, do you have a way to defend yourself if things become difficult?"

A long pause hung in the air.

"Difficult with Alex King?"

"He seemed to really want whatever it was that you didn't give him," the woman reminded her gently. "Was it the camera that you put inside your bag?"

Something... wasn't right. Tolly felt the base of the tripod press harder into her fingers.

She stared through the windshield. "Do you know him? Is he the type who'll... you think he'll pursue this?"

"Well," the woman laughed a little. "Everyone knows Alexander King, *Tolly Henry*."

Tolly listened to the deliberate pronunciation of her name and realized she failed to ask her driver's name. In the midst of rattled nerves that frazzled her common sense, she'd offered up too much information to a complete stranger, no longer so friendly.

"Maybe, just to make life easier, you should give him what he wants rather than make him take it from you," the woman suggested. She removed her sunglasses.

Tolly followed the woman's line of vision towards the address clearly marked on her building. She already knew Tolly's name. Her apartment number and phone number were listed in the directory behind protective glass. Tolly had put them there herself when she took over management from her father.

"Maybe." Tolly tried to think of something to counteract the woman's suggestion but came up blank.

"Lots of maybes in life." The woman's profile revealed the quiet, smug expression of the older, wiser person used to winning social interactions based upon experience. Tolly felt even more at a disadvantage, but the conversation remained far from over.

"Maybe he knows where you live. Alone." The woman's eyes slid across the building's worn facade. "Maybe he knows that you are... financially vulnerable."

Tolly's face heated. The building's exterior was clean and swept, but the distressed brick, crumbled around the edges and needed renovation.

Again, the woman smiled with quiet triumph at Tolly's embarrassment. "Lots of maybes."

Tolly reached her limit for being one-down that morning. "Who are you?" she demanded of the woman's profile.

"I'm Celara."

"That's the name of his company."

"And the name of his mother." The woman faced her at last.

For the first time, Tolly saw her eyes, hard and pale blue, an emptiness ringed by stark black eyeliner. She stuck out a well-maintained hand, the tips manicured, rings on several fingers.

"Celara King. Pleased to meet you, Tolly Henry."

Tolly stared into the black-rimmed vacant windows that should have contained a soul. She reached for the passenger door handle.

Click.

Celara King had engaged the child safety lock. "I'm very sure things will work out for my son in the primary, Tolly. And maybe things will work out for you. And maybe they won't. You see, we have many relationships and many resources in Lake City."

She looked at Tolly. "I'm sure you researched my son prior to your interview with him?"

Tolly didn't answer, spellbound by the silk-covered cruelty in Celara's voice.

"From your research," Celara continued, "you've probably already discovered that the police union supports his campaign. He's always been very supportive of their causes. Certainly not the campaign of that... *Yashuda woman.*"

"Tina Yashuda," Tolly corrected.

"Whatever. Lie after lie after lie, Tolly." Celara's cold smile turned snide. "She's desperate. She has reason to be and everyone knows it."

"Alex King doesn't like women, does he, Celara?"

Celara smiled into the rearview mirror. She smoothed back dark hair forced by what looked like rigor mortis into a sleek bun. Tolly wondered if the silver streak were real or added for effect.

"My son sometimes has trouble finding just the right words. Surely you can understand how things like that might happen." Celara's cold gaze, devoid of any understanding fell back upon Tolly.

"That's an excuse," Tolly responded in a quiet voice.

Celara ignored that. Tolly understood that her opinion mattered not a whit to King's mother.

"Alex knows that I'll always be here to do whatever it takes to make him the man he was meant to become."

Tolly shook her head in disbelief. How did a morning even turn out like this?

Celara continued her soliloquy. "You should understand that Alexander King does love women, Tolly Henry. No one can say that he doesn't. No one. Not Yashuda's campaign. Not you. Not *anyone.*"

Celara paused.

"Maybe you'll do the right thing." She glanced at the shoulder bag that Tolly clutched to her chest as a shield. "Maybe you won't make a mistake that might haunt you the rest of your life."

"Open this door."

Tolly didn't dare take her eyes off the older woman. If Celara reached for her glove box, then Tolly wouldn't just hold the tripod like a club, she would swing it like a club. Then she planned to break the passenger door window and scream for help.

"For instance," Celara released the passenger door lock, "now would be a good time for the right thing to happen."

Still monitoring Celara King's movements, Tolly opened the passenger door. She backed out and then slammed shut the door of the Mercedes—probably worth more than the sum total of her building. But the conversation still wasn't over. The window lowered.

"Maybe," Celara finished with a cold smile.

Tolly stood on the sidewalk in front of her three-flat. Celara's black chariot glided away to join the flow of Lake City's morning rush hour traffic.

Even though she felt like she'd just had her heart devoured by Snow White's step-mother, Tolly knew she had to make a decision on what to do with the film of King's physical assaults.

Chapter 3

Tolly's heart pounded. Still shaken by the morning's events, she lifted her head from her hands. She gasped for air. High anxiety made it hard for her to think.

She lived in Lake City in this manager's apartment on the basement level of her building her entire life. She didn't know any other existence. Her formal education stopped at the high school level as did that of her father and mother.

Her father, a carpenter and electrician owned his own small business because Lake City's unions didn't allow him as a member. He died of cancer when Tolly was in junior high school. Her mother cleaned homes, but died of diabetes complications just before high school graduation.

She loved her parents who taught her the skills that she needed to survive on her own. But nothing they taught her prepared her for Alex King or his mother. Rafael's abuse made her hyper-alert to danger, but his special conditioning also rendered her vulnerable and isolated. She felt very alone in the world, especially today. For instance, she couldn't think of a single person to call for help.

***

The large silver-haired man with a year-round tan shifted his six-foot, five-inch solid frame in the seat of his 4 x 4 black Chevy pickup truck. He turned down the bluegrass that blared from the stereo. His cell phone rang again.

"Windrunner," he snapped. His customary greeting invited the caller to get to the point.

"Scott, something's come up."

Scott twisted wide shoulders to look at the camping and fishing equipment in the bed of the pickup. He sighed. "Alex, one week before the primary I'd be surprised if something didn't come up." With a *what can you do* glance at his passenger, he listened for the inevitable.

"I need you to come in. It's an emergency."

***

The rumors she'd heard about King in the lead-up to the interview rang true. He was a dangerous man to cross. People in Lake City disappeared for days, weeks, sometimes months. Only after the ice and snow melted did they reappear on the river bed or crews dragged them from the lake on the eastern shore.

She'd stopped the anti-anxiety medication a year ago. She didn't like the side effects. Besides, the pills didn't make the problems go away.

But she could always swear at herself. "How could you let him do it? You just stood there and took it, Tolly. Why didn't you fight back? Why? You just let him mess with you the same way you let *him* mess with you."

She allowed herself a few more minutes to recover, but then her impatience grew. "You don't have time for this."

Precious time ticked away. "Cry later!"

Still she sat. "Get up and move," she insisted. She raised her voice. "Get up!"

***

Scott Windrunner preferred to apply his large build and quick reflexes to the great outdoors. If he couldn't get beyond the lights and traffic and noise of Lake City, he took in music and sports between short trips on his motorcycle. On this rare day off, he'd planned to show his younger brother, Jack, all the best places in the city and then the surrounding countryside.

Jack grinned at him now, reflecting the dark brown, almost black hair his older brother used to have and the strong cheekbones and chin they both still shared.

"Good thing we didn't stop to fill up the cooler." Jack, ever the optimist, always looked on the bright side.

"Yeah, real good thing." Scott shifted his monster pickup back into gear. So much for the barbecue, macaroni and cheese, and fish fry Scott planned in the back of beyond.

Besides Scott's lion-like mane of silver hair and five years of age, another characteristic that distinguished the brothers was Scott's intense gaze honed by years of military service. Jack's more relaxed demeanor served as a much-needed counter-weight to Scott's laser focus.

"So what now?" Jack asked him.

"Well, Jack, we skip orientation and training at Windrunner Security." Scott shook his head, rueful. "We saddle up to save Alexander King from reckless disregard of common sense and the job starts today."

For the past few years, Alex contracted Windrunner Security to perform a number of background check, surveillance, retail shrinkage, construction sabotage, and business intelligence jobs. With Jack's greater participation, Scott also manged to complete computer information salvage and worker's compensation investigations. Now, Alex needed Windrunner Security to handle indiscreet mayoral campaign moments.

"Let's do it," Jack said.

Scott swung the pickup north towards Celara Sun, Alex's main business headquarters.

***

Three months earlier, Tolly converted her basement apartment into a mini-studio filled with office and audio-visual equipment which she used to create webcasts for Lake City Balance, helping to make "renewable a reality."

She stared at the pictures on the wall opposite her desk and came to a decision. Stay under the radar until after the mayoral primary. Then return to the careful, normal, risk-free life she created for herself after the turbulence of Rafael.

"Calm down, Tolly. He won't take you seriously if you're hysterical. Be a professional and it will be all right." She picked up her cell phone from the desk and made the call.

"George. I'm... having a little problem with the, uh, green energy piece."

"What? Yashuda's? We looked at it. It's fine. Actually, it's great. You did a wonderful job. I can tell that you did thorough research. Plus we've been getting plenty of hits and comments from viewers. They like it."

"Good." Tolly forced a smile into her voice. "Thanks. I met with King today."

"And? How'd it go?"

"It..." Tolly cleared her throat. "I got the interview. I got all the shots."

"So what's the problem? Didn't he cooperate?"

"The interview is fine." Tolly unscrewed the small camera from the tripod. "It's just that he... I saw him..." She frowned when she saw the red light and the time that elapsed. She hit the OFF button. The camera stopped recording.

George waited a beat. "Tolly, what's going on? What happened?"

"I..." Shame filled her when she remembered how she smiled at King, nervous as a ten-year-old at her first spelling bee. "I didn't have time to record the intro."

Tolly pressed the phone to her ear. Alex must not have called Lake City Balance to report on what happened between him and her at Celara Wind. She still had a chance.

During the interview, she'd juggled the notebook and camera, anxious not to stumble or fall on flat on her face. She'd made her best effort to appear professional in front of the mayoral candidate. Again, she blinked back tears at the memory of the terrible way their meeting ended.

"I don't know..." With shaky fingers, Tolly connected the camera to her computer which housed editing software.

"Tolly, you sound really strange. If something's going on, we can finish production here at the office. But we have to get it online as soon as possible. Both campaigns demanded equal coverage and equal access to our base. We have to do our part not to appear partisan for tax exemption."

"I know." Her older-model computer groaned and growled when she awakened it from hibernation. Then she opened the video editing software.

"Look. It's one week prior to the primary so you know both campaigns are wound pretty tight. We told King and Yashuda that we'd get both pieces online this afternoon. It's in our best interests to maintain good will."

"Right."

"Tell you what. Just send raw footage as soon as you can."

"Tell you what, George. I can edit the main video. I just need a voice-over and intro."

Tolly blinked. Screenshots of Alexander King's wealth, power, and privilege danced across the monitor. She could start the edits in forty-five minutes. What would she keep? What would she leave out?

"You've been very reliable and we appreciate the productions you've been able to assemble for us. Look Tolly, after the election, I'm told that an infusion of funds will be headed our direction and we'll be able to get our staffing at even-keel. I'm not supposed to let you know, but you're at the top of the list."

Tolly's heart lurched. She wanted the job. It would mean a complete change in her lifestyle and income for the better. She would be a professional in a suit, no longer her building's janitor, maid, and secretary.

Serving as landlord for the building she inherited from her parents presented a somewhat stable existence, but the constant maintenance and paperwork consumed almost her entire life and left not a lot of time or energy for other pursuits.

With the Lake City Balance opportunity, she could sell the building. She could go out to eat, watch movies, and meet friends for fun events where she could afford the cover charge. All the sacrifices that her parents made so she wouldn't be stuck doing what they did would finally pay off.

"Thanks George. I'm so sorry about this. Some... unexpected family development. I just wanted to let you know." She held her breath and waited for George's judgment on the matter. He would decide whether she helped Lake City Balance to "make renewable a reality."

"I hear ya, Tolly. It happens to the best of us."

She exhaled.

"Tell you what," George continued. "Just send the footage, supporting materials, scripts, research—whatever you have. I can record the intro myself and edit it into the piece. Okay? Shouldn't take me more than an hour to get it up and running."

"Thanks, George, for understanding. I'll get everything assembled. You should see it within the hour."

***

Scott snapped his cell phone closed. He turned off the major thoroughfare that led to the northwest suburbs of Lake City and Celara Sun, about a mile away from Celara Wind and Celara Green Supply.

"That was Alex again. He just told me that this woman, Tolly Henry, is a thief." Scott stopped at a red light. "She stole a briefcase full of cash campaign contributions."

"Whew!"

"That's not all. The briefcase also contained strategy and other important documents."

"What does he want you to do?" Jack mostly handled the computer and administrative end of Windrunner Security. But this job, Scott already knew, would require street smarts—skills that Jack still needed to learn. Scott suspected that Jack finally joined him in Lake City from sheer boredom.

"Us," Scott reminded his brother. Both of them hailed from a small Colorado community. Between two stints with military service, Scott completed an MBA at a Colorado university. But after his last foray as a government gun, Scott left Calabasas for Lake City years to escape the gossip and whispers. Then he used his business skills and military earnings to start Windrunner Security Company.

"What does he want *us* to do?" For complicated reasons, Scott designated himself as silent partner, while his younger brother became the figurehead. The arrangement worked.

"Alex wants us to intercept the thief, and retrieve the materials, then return her and everything else to his campaign headquarters for a thorough talking to. This close to the primary, he doesn't want to involve the police. That would provide a distraction to the media that he doesn't want to deal with. Cut her a so-called break during these hard economic times, he says."

Scott pulled the pickup into Celara Sun's driveway. "He'll give us the specifics inside."

Chapter 4

The basement level of her building contained the plumbing, electrical, heating, and ventilation machinery. The constant hum of white noise meant she had relative privacy from the college-age renters on the third floor and the middle-aged couple plus their random family members who rented the first and second levels.

The files from her camera continued to download to her computer. Twenty minutes. A *lot* of edits.

Tolly shivered. From her computer screen, the cold fire from King's eyes tracked her across the room. She ascended to the first level to find Bill Martinez.

After a few quick knocks, she took another deep breath to settle her nerves.

"Mr. Martinez, I'm uh... Something unexpected happened. A family thing. And... I need to... leave for a while. It's a family thing, you see."

Mr. Martinez frowned. "You never take a vacation, Tolly."

"Yes, I know. I figured it was about time I did. For about a week. I know it's unexpected, but things happened all of a sudden."

Mr. Martinez smiled. "Say no more. With family, 'all of a sudden' is how it usually is. I should know with all my children and all of a sudden their children."

Tolly smiled.

"Look," he said. "I appreciate the fact that you let more of my family stay here. The job situation is so tough all over the country."

"It's not a problem. I know how it is. Everyone's been very respectful and helpful, so it's fine."

"Yes, we'll all help you when you need it. You need repairs, you need the front cleaned, then you ask us first before anyone else. We're happy to. We'll pick up trash and move furniture."

"I know you do."

But I'm hoping that the new mayor keeps their promise about more jobs. We need them."

"Right. I hear you."

"You know I don't mind paying extra. One by one, they find jobs. Then they go and find another place to live."

"Look, Mr. Martinez, we'll talk about that later, I promise you. But right now, I'm so sorry that I'm in a hurry. I really have to leave soon. Today."

"So I'll take care of the building?"

"Yes, if you could, for about a week."

"No problem. I used to do that for your father sometimes."

"I know."

"He was a good man, your father. A good friend to me when I first came here with my wife. You on your little bike, all the time, everyday."

Mr. Martinez laughed. "You remember that time, he took you all West? To the mountains, he told me. Then the Grand Canyon, driving around in that old truck."

Tolly gave up trying to end the conversation. "I remember."

"We like it here. That's why we never moved. Your father was a good man. Very good man."

"Thank you, Mr. Martinez. I appreciate that. Your family is fine. These old walls are so thick that I never hear anything from upstairs."

"Can't even hear the traffic except when the window is open. It's a good building."

"Thanks."

"Even those college kids on the third floor have people in and out all the time. All these parties."

"Well, you're only young once."

"I can't hear them either."

"This building's solid. Besides, I try to be flexible with the college students. That's how I make the most rent and that's why yours never goes up."

"Understood." Mr. Martinez laughed.

"Well, besides that, my father was very clear that you'd pay the same rent as long as you lived here."

"No problem. I've been here almost as long as you've been born. I know how to run things."

"All rent under the door like usual," Tolly told him as she tried to back away. "And remind the students to get their payments in on time. Water the plants. Watch the trash. And then take an extra week off your own rent for the work, okay?"

"No problem. I did it before for your father, God rest his soul. He took that trip out West with you and your mother, and I watched the building."

"I know." Tolly eased another step back.

"Now you're going somewhere all by yourself."

"I'll be all right."

"Okay, no problem."

Tolly walked back to the basement level. She needed the rent money now, but she had to be fair to her tenants. She would just take what she had with her on the road, which wasn't a lot. She'd try to ride out the next week until life returned to normal.

***

Jack stopped Scott before he got out of the truck. "I still don't know how you manage to stomp with the big dogs without a gun."

Scott shook his head. "Jack, we've been through this. No guns at Windrunner. I promised myself after... all that psychodrama I'd never carry a gun again."

"And the King of the City is okay with that?"

"He's okay with me getting the job done. Which I do. Every single piece of strange and twisted... *whatever*. I get it done."

"And it's never been a problem?"

Scott laughed. "Not for me. Actually, it makes things easier."

"How?"

"Lower insurance rates. Which means higher pay." He clapped Jack on the back. "For you, little brother."

"Then it's a great idea."

"Figured you'd feel that way." Scott refocused on business. "You already know the last jobs for Alex because you handled the closing paperwork and processing. But now you get to see how Windrunner handles a case from beginning to end and what happens in the field."

Scott got out of the pickup and slammed the door shut. Jack followed.

"Look Jack. I'm always going to be grateful that you allowed me to operate Windrunner Security under your name. Alex knows that I need extra hands to handle his campaign. He's okay with you because you're my brother and he's been working with you through me anyway." Scott ran a distracted hand through his silver hair. "The job is a rundown."

"Bounty hunting?"

"Not quite that messy. Something a little more subtle. This is Alex after all. We'll find out after we get inside."

***

Still a few minutes until the downloads finished. Tolly sat at her desk and stared straight ahead again.

She refused to give in to panic. "Get your head together, and keep it together!"

If Alex King won the primary, she would have nothing to worry about. Life would go on. She would take the job with Lake City Balance.

But if Alex King lost the primary... *if he lost...* Celara's silky, cruel voice and Alex's cold, dead-eyed stare crept in despite her best efforts to block them.

Tolly shivered again.

Deep down, she knew something was wrong with her. While she made steps to render herself physically invulnerable with martial arts classes at the local gym, she still hadn't resolved the negative thoughts Rafael left inside her head.

Tolly practiced her breathing. Her heart slowed. When she focused on the solution, her anxiety and tension eased. She had a problem. She would solve it.

The downloads waited for her next move.

His eyes ranged from pale blue, to icy grey, to steely flint depending upon his mood. Alexander King looked into Tolly Henry's own brown eyes with a steady intensity.

"You know, I've come up against opposition in the past—particularly, fear of the unknown. While the current mayor has done well to keep Lake City afloat, during this time of economic turmoil, term limitations dictate that the next mayor will need to move in a different direction—towards the future. I fully intend to do just that."

"Get started, Tolly," she ordered.

Chapter 5

Alex King's father, who passed away a few years ago, created Celara Electric, as a construction company. Well-known as a visionary, Alex King developed his father's company into Celara Solar, then added Celara Wind and Celara Green Supply into the fold. The latest project, the Midwest Consortium, provided the powerful springboard from which Alex ran for mayoral office.

Celara Sun's receptionist was a pill popper. Scott knew this from past investigations. Alex also knew because Scott reported what he discovered after weeks of surveillance. True to form, Alex did not reprimand his receptionist.

One, she was a functional addict, so Alex could still use her. Two, Alex preferred to wait until she caused him problems. Then he would use the information Scott provided to rid himself of her presence quickly and quietly. Until that day of reckoning arrived, the receptionist escorted the Windrunners in slow motion from the lobby to Alex's office.

The king himself sat surrounded by black décor, metallic and mirrored surfaces, as well as various comforts that included an espresso machine, air filter, humidifier, and computer equipment. The office walls displayed photos of Alex's favorite activities—

skiing, scuba diving, and hunting. In another photo Alex shook hands with the outgoing term-limited mayor and governor.

New to Scott was the stocky, medium-sized man with dark skin who sat in the rear corner of the office. The Windrunners exchanged polite nods with him.

Before any conversation began, Alex waved Scott and Jack to the chairs in front of his desk. Scott introduced Jack and Alex. The men shook hands.

Alex didn't bother to introduce or explain the new guy in the room. Instead, he sat back in his chair and surveyed the two men in front of him.

"So this is the famous Jack I've worked with all these years."

"It is," Jack answered.

"Doing a heckuva job, by the way," Alex said.

Jack acknowledged that with a slight smile. Scott's younger brother had a quiet, reassuring manner. In fact, he remained one of the very few people in whom Scott confided.

Alex turned to Scott. "So do I get a two for one deal, or what?"

"Double or nothing, Alex," Scott replied. "Especially since your campaign is on some kind of runaway rollercoaster lately."

Scott knew better than anyone to underestimate Jack, his secret weapon. Everyone trusted him and as a result, lowered their guard. Then Scott would move in to drop the hammer.

"That bitch, Yashuda," Alex bit out. "Good thing my wife is Asian too or I'd have trouble neutralizing her accusations. Anyway, fuck her. Time is money." Alex put on a grim smile. "Especially your time, Scott."

Scott smiled, undisturbed. "You get what you pay for, Alex."

He spoke that way because only the strong survived encounters with the forceful business executive. The king consumed, absorbed, excreted, and then never thought about again everyone and everything not tough enough to deal.

Alex came back with the expected, "I make sure I do."

***

Her research on his background indicated that he'd been groomed in the knock-down drag-out world of construction by his father.

"My Celara companies plus the Midwest Consortium have revolutionized renewable energy, infrastructure, and manufacturing. Each new project, especially the supergrid has created thousands of jobs and put Lake City on the national map in terms of economic development, industry, and labor. That's what it's all about."

A natural storyteller with charismatic delivery, King nodded and smiled to indicate he was ready for the next question. Then he took a step closer to her.

***

Scott shrugged. "Who the fuck is this?" He indicated the man seated in the far corner of the room.

"I'll get to that," Alex snapped back.

Scott shifted his large body in the chair, impatient. "So what about this woman?" *Get to the point, Alex.*

"We have a photo from the security camera and her home address." Alex tossed a file folder Scott's direction. "We think she's with Yashuda."

Scott passed the folder to Jack to peruse. "Who's we? Who knows about this?"

"Just me and my mother. She gave the subject a ride home this morning after... our encounter."

"How do you know she's with Yashuda and not freelancing?"

"Just a feeling," Alex answered.

Scott raised his eyebrows at that. Alex didn't have any feelings.

"Anyway," Alex continued, "Isn't that why I hire you?"

Scott didn't miss the defensiveness. "You seem really spooked." He eyed Alex. "What exactly did she do?"

***

Tolly cleared her throat. "So you see the office of mayor as another step forward?" she asked.

"Tolly, I see the office of mayor as a way to push Lake City many steps forward onto the world stage."

He'd introduced his wife and their fraternal twin two-year-olds on-camera at the beginning of the interview. Then she and King began the question and answer portion. Across the lobby, his children started to cry. Tolly noted another small flicker in King's eyes.

"Where Tokyo, Beijing, London, New York, Paris, and Los Angeles are now, we want to be."

Tolly flipped through her notebook not wishing to try his patience.

"It's our time."

He ended the statement on a radiant smile. However Tolly, late-thirties and not unfamiliar with the instability of the male ego, sensed a need to tread with care. She shifted again under his gaze. The crystal and gray flecks in his amazingly bright eyes flicked again over her dark skin, the color of chocolate spiced with cinnamon. He returned focus to her face so quickly that she thought she might have imagined the scrutiny.

Tolly finalized the video edits.

Since her truck was still in the shop, she knew five ways to travel under the radar—walk, bike, bus, stowaway, or hitchhike.

She considered each possibility while she packed.

***

Alex indicated Scott's brother with narrowed eyes. "Is he okay?"

"He's fine, Alex. C'mon. He knows the deal. We're exclusive to the King campaign and Celara companies. Like I already said, I need the extra hands and he needs to know what's going on in the field to better manage computer security and accounting forensics. I told you all this last week before he even got to the city. Now *you're* the one wasting time."

"Yashuda set me up."

"How?"

Alex leaned back in his chair. Scott recognized his employer's challenge position.

"My... weakness has always been women," Alex admitted.

And money and power, Scott added.

"Yashuda got this girl. This, 'Tolly Henry, to... seduce me. She compromised me and my campaign. And my marriage." Alex slammed his palm flat on his desk. "She filmed it."

***

From her periphery, Tolly saw King's wife try to soothe the children with treats. That distracted King again. Tolly decided to lob a softball.

"You sound very proud of what you've accomplished at Celara and the Midwest Consortium, Mr. King. How could becoming the next mayor of Lake City possibly compare with your success in the private sector?" she asked.

King radiated the confidence of a well-groomed, well-maintained forty-nine-year-old man without a single doubt of his place in life—King of the City.

"Here's the important thing, and let's get on a first-name basis, Tolly. I keep looking around for my father every time I hear 'Mr. King.'"

Tolly saved the edited video to her hard drive then emailed the same to George at Lake City Balance.

She downloaded the raw footage first to a flash drive, then a DVD. The multiple computer windows combined with her panic to disorient her.

She practiced her breathing again.

Chapter 6

Scott closed his eyes. "Are you fucking kidding?"

"Do I look like I'm kidding?" Alex stood up and stalked back and forth behind his desk like a predator confined to a cage. "Yashuda's desperate to run me off the rails. You've seen the polls. I think its blackmail."

"You think?" Scott quizzed his employer. "What do you mean you think? Has anyone made a demand?"

Alex stopped pacing and crossed his arms. "I'm not sure, but I'm not going to let either of those bitches take me down. No sir! I want Tolly Henry brought back to me." He pointed to Scott. "I want you here with her to discuss the illegality of her actions, the consequences, and all remaining options for her future."

Scott didn't let up. "Well, what's illegal about it?"

Alex counted the ways on his fingers. "Blackmail. Seduction." He flung out an arm out for emphasis. "Filming me without my consent."

"She asked you for money?"

"Not yet. But she will. Either that or she'll sell it to Yashuda. Or a newspaper."

"But you said Yashuda sent her. That means she's already been paid."

"Maybe." Alex sat down again. "I wouldn't fucking know how blackmail and bribery and extortion work, Scott, now would I?"

Scott decided not to answer that. Jack kept his mouth closed too. The unknown man in the corner had nothing to say either.

"It's not my thing," Alex continued. "I tried to run a clean campaign, but these bitches keep fucking with me. Trying to embarrass me and harass my family. Making the Lake City voters pay for their greed."

"I'm not going to allow it." He pointed. "You're not going to allow it. Get that girl and that video back. I want Tolly Henry to understand that her crimes do not and will not pay."

"We talk to Tolly Henry. We get the film." Scott cleared his throat. "And the documents and cash that she stole. If she hasn't sold the information and already spent the money."

"She hasn't sold it. We'd have heard something by now. The money, I don't know. Maybe she's holding everything, probably as a last-minute surprise right before the primary. Don't forget. I need for you to return Ms. Henry to my office. I want to explain it straight to her face myself."

"Okay."

"And if it takes a finder's fee or reward..."

"Bribe."

"Whatever. Do it only as a last resort. My mother said that she seemed the greedy type." Alex waved his hand. "Bruce will work with you."

Scott didn't take his eyes off Alex. "Who the fuck is Bruce?" he asked again.

Alex sighed with exasperation. "You just sat there and told me that you needed extra hands for all the extra security work that you can't handle alone." He waved Bruce's direction. "Well there you go."

"I told you that the extra hands would be attached to the arms of my brother." Scott pointed for clarity. "Jack, right here."

"Scott, look, we need all bases covered." Alex shuffled through a few papers on his desk. "I don't want you to forget about the bonus coming your way after I'm elected mayor, and more jobs to come."

***

Tolly left the camera, empty of all files, in a desk drawer. She held the flash drive and DVD in the palm of her hand. Once again, She faced the wall opposite her desk. Determined, she returned to the computer.

***

"I haven't forgotten. I'm counting on it."
"Maybe an official position with the King administration."
"No thanks."
"Well anyway… now you have four extra hands."
"Bruce what?"
"What do you mean?"
"Does he have a last name?"
"Not really."
Scott frowned. He didn't like any part of this new deal.
"Well, if you like," Alex conceded, "Bruce Wayne."
Scott paused. "Batman?"
Bruce spoke at last, "Black man."
That cut the tension in the room. The four men laughed together.
"He's a former middle-weight boxer, Scott." Alex announced with glee. "You can tell by the ugly face!"
At least Bruce could take a joke, Scott noticed. Alex waved the men out, cheerful once again.

***

All packed up, all planned out, Tolly made her move.

***

Scott told Jack and Bruce that they would pick up the official Windrunner Security car so that they could cover more ground in the Central District.
"Then what?" Jack asked.
"Look, when we get back to the office…"

Scott's cell phone rang. James Windrunner's resonant voice echoed through the receiver loud enough for both Jack and Bruce to hear.

"Scott. Been a while."

"Sorry about that, Pop. Been busy. But Jack's here now to help me get a handle on things. What's going on?"

"Nellie."

"The same situation?"

"It's worse."

"Sonny Youngbear," Scott guessed.

Jack sighed and shook his head from the passenger seat.

"Sonny Youngbear," his father confirmed. "When you left, Jack was still here and he held Sonny somewhat at bay. But now with both her older brothers gone, Sonny's gotten bolder, meaner."

Scott felt incredible guilt. Once again, he let his family down.

"He doesn't hide the marks anymore. My daughter walks around with bruises on her face and scratches on her arms where she tried to defend herself. I can't convince her to leave. She says she can't afford to. She says I don't have the ability to care for her and my grandchildren. I guess I'm kind of an old man and she doesn't trust an old man to defend her against Sonny if he comes after her and the kids. She's afraid and I'm afraid for her."

Scott sighed. "Okay, I'll call her. But I can't think of anything to tell her that I haven't said before. You know she doesn't listen to anyone but Sonny."

"She might listen to you this time."

"Hang on a second, Pop." Scott parked the truck in front of the small, non-descript, glass-fronted office that housed Windrunner Security Company. "I'll see what I can do, okay?"

He disconnected.

"I've got to find out what's going on with Nellie," he told his younger brother. "This job for Alex is pretty straightforward. You and Bruce take our badges and the company car to talk to her." He tossed Jack the file folder.

"See if you can persuade her to come back to Windrunner first for a friendly conversation. Be official. Be professional. We'll try to reason out her situation or whatever she thinks she's trying to do here before we take her to Alex. Get all copies of the film, the campaign documents, and any cash she stole, if there's any left. Just bring it all back here so we can work out something simple."

"Okay."

"I've got to call Nellie. Just keep everything on the level, okay?"

Jack and Bruce got out of the pickup. Scott watched Jack drive away while Bruce, more familiar with Lake City's complex system of neighborhoods, navigated.

Inside Windrunner Security, natural wood, sunlight, and area rugs created a kaleidoscope of tans, oranges, and yellows. Various office machines populated the small space. It was a traditional but functional design, similar to his condominium which Jack shared.

Scott switched his cell phone to speaker, then made the call to Nellie. While he waited for her to pick up, he walked around the office to check mail, messages, and various drawers and files. Jack usually did that as his assistant, but the time had come for Jack to start field work. The call connected.

"Nellie, what's going on with you and Sonny? Pop's worried about you. I'm hearing a bunch of crazy stuff."

"It's nothing, Scott. Just the same old, same old. Sonny got laid off. Being out of work gets to him."

"And then he gets to you?"

"It's complicated."

"There's nothing complicated about drinking too much."

"Scott..."

"I mean, you're having a tough time of it too, right? Do you smack him around?" Scott didn't wait for her answer. "No, you don't. Look, Nellie, you know you could still come to Lake City. You and the kids can stay with me and Jack."

"Wait, Scott..."

"I can find you work here. As a matter of fact..."

Nellie overrode him at last. "Sonny is my husband. My life is here. My children are in school here. Dad's here. Who's going to look after everyone?"

"Who's going to look after you?"

"I am." His younger sister sounded as defiant as ever.

***

Tolly glanced right and left. She dropped the DVD into a mailbox on the sidewalk in front of her building.

"Calm down. Breathe. Deep breath. Deep breath." Traffic eased enough for Tolly to cross the street. "Don't run."

She slipped away to the coffee shop across the street to watch her apartment and check her paranoia at the same time.

***

Scott confirmed that nothing in the Windrunner office required his immediate attention. He decided to follow Jack and Bruce to Tolly Henry's address in the Central District.

Just in case.

Chapter 7

"Chamomile tea, right?" the coffee shop's barista, greeted Tolly with a smile.

Tolly found a seat near the window, but not in front of the window, her normal routine. This time, she wanted to see, but not be seen so she hid behind a plant.

"I'm just going to hang out for a while. I'm waiting for someone."

"Aren't we all?" the barista laughed.

Tolly tipped her in better times, but not today. Today, her money ran way short.

She examined the coffee shop inhabited by the hip crowd of the Central District. Mascara, tattoos, and piercings competed with caps turned backwards, saris, and scarves. Some customers wore pants slung as low as the law would allow. Others wore three-piece suits—job hunters. In better economic times, Lake City attracted an amazing kaleidoscope of immigrants from around the world and migrants from across the United States.

She enjoyed the coffee shop's affordable prices and close proximity to her building. But there was another reason. She didn't have deep emotional ties. She didn't have a best friend. So she maintained pleasant acquaintances with the multitude of people she knew from the neighborhood. If anyone ever asked, they would have described her as reserved, cautious, and practical. But then, no one ever asked.

Across the street, Bill Martinez piled his entire family into a station wagon on an errand of some kind. She smiled as she stirred her tea. On some occasions, the Martinez family invited her to participate in their family events. But she didn't like to intrude.

***

"She's not gonna answer."

"See anything?"

Jack glanced through the window that faced the street.

"She might be in there waiting to see if we'll go away."

Jack buzzed the ringer at the front door, then knocked. Still no answer.

***

Multiple ethnicities, accents, and languages served as a magnet for multiple lifestyles. Tolly liked the swirling potpourri. Somehow amongst the guttural German, rapid-fire Spanish, and musical Arabic, she felt that she fit in. However, the colorful atmosphere often caused Tolly to long for a different life for herself someplace different.

She looked through the coffee shop window again. Two men she didn't recognize stood at the front door of her building. They wore badges. A security car, Windrunner, it said, sat at the curb.

Her stomach churned, but she waited.

She had to be sure.

Tolly knew everyone in her building and their visitors. She knew most of the delivery guys in the area.

These two on her doorstep did not belong.

***

"Let me try the other door." Bruce walked to the rear. Soon, Jack heard footsteps inside. Then Bruce opened the front door for Jack.

"What're you doing, man?"

"We don't have all day to wait while she finds a buyer."

"You heard Scott say keep it on the level."

"It's on the level, man. Basement level," Bruce pointed to the stairs. "See there?"

"It's breaking and entering."

"It's broken and entered. It's already done, Jack. We're here. Let's look around."

They entered Tolly's building, then her apartment.

***

Her worst fears confirmed, Tolly threw away her paper cup and napkins. She walked back towards the women's restroom. Then she looked over her shoulder. The barista bussed tables in the lobby amid shouts of laughter and British-accented English.

Head down, Tolly took a sharp turn behind the coffee shop's counter. Then she kept going through the back door.

***

Monday afternoon, Bruce surveyed the living area of Tolly's apartment. "God, look at this dump. You know how rich people pretend to be poor so they buy old shit that's actually worth a bazillion dollars?"

Jack had a bad feeling that he and Bruce really screwed up. Scott would have plenty to say about that. "No, I don't know."

"Well, this bitch is actually poor. All this looks like something her grandmother died on."

Jack didn't bother with an answer. Instead, he headed straight to his area of expertise. A computer perched on the desk surrounded by peripheral equipment. The computer felt warm to the touch.

"Yeah, you do that," Bruce told him. "I'll check out the rest."

Jack ignored that too. He turned on the machines and got to work.

"I mean, look at this crap in her closet," Bruce called from her bedroom. "Wow, what should I wear today? Gray? Or brown. Or gray? Well it's springtime now. Guess I'll switch to beige."

Jack waited for the computer, an older model, to come to life. It protested through the entire start-up process with loud groans.

Bruce's voice sounded muffled. "Goddamn! Not one high heel to save her life. Flats."

A pause.

"Bag of something from the thrift store. Well, what do you know? It's the long sleeve version of all that gray and brown and beige shit." Bruce knocked something over. "There's nothing here, man."

Jack heard heavy footsteps.

"Nothing in her bathroom. Not a speck. OCD."

Jack opened desk drawers with one hand and lifted the keyboard with the other. He located the digital camera in the top drawer, empty of files. He made short guesswork of Tolly's passwords. Her obsessive-compulsions, whatever they were, no longer mattered.

Bruce stomped across the living room. "Let's see what's in the kitchen."

Jack heard the sound of various cabinets and drawers thrown open, then closed with short *bangs*.

"Makes my skin crawl," he called. "Labels, labels, labels... on everything!"

Bruce continued to toss Tolly's apartment. He insulted everything he found including the fact that she had no pets.

Jack got busy on the keyboard.

"These are cooking herbs! This bitch is stupid. With a grow light and the right kind of seed, she wouldn't have to blackmail to make money."

More mutters from Bruce. "Jalepenos, wasabi, ginger, garlic, onions, pepper. Damn, her breath must really stink after a meal."

Jack heard the squeak of a styrofoam container. Bruce was eating something.

"Vegetarian." The container hit the floor.

Jack was tired of the whole routine. "Stop making so much noise!"

"First and second floor tenants went off somewhere. You saw them—Mom, Pop, all fifteen children. Top floor can't hear us over the machines."

Jack discovered that Tolly's last activities were to edit video, send video, and then delete video. She made copies and searched bus schedules. She also stored research on Alexander King.

Jack played the video files.

***

Tolly rolled her suitcase down alleys and across parking lots. She remembered being in another hurry about a year ago.

That time when she ordered her chamomile tea, she felt an attraction, a pull from a man across the café.

Silver hair topped black brows and black eyes that snapped and sparkled when they looked her way. She pushed her response to him down. As she'd reminded herself then, she needed to take a break so she could get her head clear of the shadows and echoes left by Rafael.

The one date she'd had since Rafael left her ended badly. The man she met while on a job for Lake City Balance told her that she was "boring with nothing of interest to talk about." After she refused to sleep with him on the first date, he berated her refusal of his advances. Tolly shriveled up inside. Ever since then, she threw her energy into running her building.

Once in a while, she wondered whether she'd see the mystery man at the coffee shop again. Maybe she'd be better prepared next time. Maybe he'd make a move. Maybe she'd make a move.

But that remained yet another lost opportunity in her life.

***

Still en route, Scott called his younger brother for an update.
"Was she there?"
"No."
"Where are you now?"
"In her apartment."
"You just said she wasn't there."
"She's not."
"Tolly Henry invited you in then left? That doesn't make sense."
"Ah, no."
"Jack." Scott slowed his voice. "Was she there?"
"No."
"Then how did you get in?"
"Well, Bruce..."
Scott blistered Jack's ears with a string of curses. "Stay right there. I'm just around the corner."

He yanked the pickup to a stop behind the security car then laughed aloud. No need for discretion now. Scott banged on the front door. His brother opened it with an anxious look, then guided Scott downstairs.

"Scott, real quick. She was working on video, alright. She sent it to someone called George at Lake City Balance. But the videos were straight-forward interviews with Alex King. I looked at them. There's nothing more."

Scott surveyed the jumbled state of Tolly Henry's apartment in silence. Jack waited.

"What are you talking about?" Scott asked.

"Nothing out of the ordinary. Nothing like what Alex described. Just an interview."

Bruce emerged from the kitchen with a proud look. Scott glared at him.

"Play it again," he ordered Jack.

I'm a developer. That's who I am and what I do. I develop projects. I develop business. I develop opportunities and I develop people."

Alex mirrored Tolly's movements with a brush of the hand to his own black hair, edged with white at the temples. He pressed into her space. Then he drew down matching brows in a thoughtful frown.

"The time and energy and focus I poured into myriad projects have paid off in the form of strong teams of people with the training, skill, talent, and expertise to move the green revolution forward. I hope the people of Lake City also see the benefit of developing more business in this region. I am definitely proud of that. Very proud."

"Did she send anything else?"

"That was it."

Scott thought for a moment. "So... she's holding back the rest—the parts that got edited out—for blackmail or another reason. What else did you find?"

"Her camera's empty."

"Bruce?" Scott looked at Alex's hire with expectation. "Anything?"

"I agree with Alex she's the blackmailing kind."

Scott allowed him another hard look. Then he looked around the living area. He saw soul, jazz, and funk CDs on a shelf. Below that shelf he saw a record collection which appeared to be her father's and a series of scrapbooks, probably her mother's.

Scott nudged Jack from Tolly's computer. Open drawers revealed neat rows and piles of pens, pencils, paperclips, and other administrative accoutrements. He saw financial paperwork related to the building that dated back years. One glance told him that she wasn't rolling in the dough.

"Scott, she searched bus schedules," Jack told him.

Finally.

Scott spoke over his shoulder. "Bruce, in your rampage of destruction, did you find a suitcase?"

"No."

"Cosmetics in the bathroom?"

"Not a whole lot. But she seems like the granola type anyway and..."

Scott ignored the rest. He looked up. Across the room from Tolly's desk, a series of photographs hung in a straight line on the wall. A young girl, Tolly at the age of four or five, held the hands of a man and woman, her mother and father. They stood in front a mountainous western landscape. Colorado or New Mexico. Maybe even Arizona.

Then he knew. "She split. She must have the damage with her since it's not on the computer."

Scott looked at the photographs again.

"Or it's already online," Jack suggested.

"No. We'd know already if she released it. She's smart. If she wants to stick Alex hard, she'll contact him just before the primary. Probably the night before." Scott looked at Jack and Bruce. "Our goal is to get to her before she makes her move."

"How?"

Scott spoke to the photographs across the room. She must have looked at them while she worked on the video edits.

"Jack, the bus schedules she searched... the next bus leaves when?"

Jack checked his watch. "Five minutes."

Scott swore. "You guys lock up here." Scott headed for the front door. "There's no time to clean up. Both of you meet me at the station."

***

Monday evening, Tolly stood in line behind college students, mothers with small children, and scruffy men who reeked of alcohol.

"So, Ms. Larimer, all the way to Patina, Colorado?"

Tolly allowed her eyes to go vague and blank. "Patina." She nodded and smiled. "Yes. Patina."

"Okay." The bus driver waved her on, assuming she didn't speak English.

Tolly learned that trick years ago when she cleaned hotel rooms for a labor agency. The language barrier helped her fit in with the other workers who often asked her to repeat what the hotel managers wanted them to do. It also kept perverted men, young and old, at bay.

On the bus, the language barrier would protect her privacy in case anyone else asked her questions.

Tolly kept her head low. She huddled under a blanket.

The sun crawled behind the skyscrapers that dominated the cityscape. The bus pulled out of the station.

Chapter 8

In the blackness of Tuesday morning before dawn, Scott barreled down eighty as fast as he dared. The pickup truck's headlights searched for taillights on the bus that carried Tolly Henry towards her destiny—a long layover at an Omaha truckstop.

Jack sat next to him. Bruce followed the Windrunner brothers in the security car across rolling prairie dotted by corn silos, decrepit barns, and windmills. Endless rows of yellow-green cornstalks walled-in the road on both sides.

Alex had been furious that Tolly slipped through all of their fingers. Jack remained silent in the passenger seat even though he overheard the pure rage that emanated from Scott's cell phone. Scott took full responsibility. Earlier, he acknowledged to Jack that his distraction with their sister allowed Tolly to make her getaway.

Scott knew all too well from past experience that Alexander King used the dreams, secrets, and desires of others as levers to manipulate their vulnerabilities, to humiliate them, and to break down anyone who threatened his supremacy. The hard knock business executive used money to buy love, respect, and loyalty. He never lost focus on the bottom line.

For instance, the pill-popping receptionist at Celara Sun would enjoy her blissful, slow motion existence until the day she made a very wrong move. Then Alex would fire her. Or, more likely, he would demand her total submission to his will until she retired or dropped dead from stress on a level beyond which the pills couldn't alleviate.

However, this latest episode with Tolly Henry was Scott's first time on the receiving end of Alexander King's wrath. Usually, he and Alex played the same team.

After he disconnected the call with Alex, Scott called Bruce in the Windrunner Security car behind them. On the speaker, Bruce still refused to be shy with his opinions.

"Stands to reason. It's not that far a stretch from drug mule to blackmailing grifter whore. Jamming up rich guys probably pays better."

Scott looked at Jack. "Not helping, Bruce."

"I'm just saying, that's Lake City. It's like that."

"You speak from experience?" Scott inquired.

Bruce didn't answer. Scott disconnected.

"Jack, use your laptop to do a full security profile on Tolly Henry. You've done those before, so you know what we need."

Jack, relieved to have something to do to make up for the blunder at Tolly's apartment yesterday, opened his laptop. "I'm on it."

They'd already passed through Iowa City and Des Moines. There remained only a narrow window to catch Tolly's bus in Omaha. Before Tolly continued on the slow road west to Patina, Scott needed to know more about her in order to convince her to return to Lake City with total strangers, three men at that.

"Okay," Jack announced. "I've got it all here."

Jack narrated a pretty sad story. Tolly's ex-boyfriend, Rafael, went to prison on a drug charge. Lake City police questioned her and nearly charged her as an accessory. Nothing much after that, although her current financial situation seemed pretty precarious.

"Nah," Bruce declared over the speaker with confidence. "That bitch won't snitch. She wants money. That's all she ever wanted."

"Wow," Jack responded with sarcasm.

Scott broke in. No time for argument. "Both of you, she's wary of police because she had a bad experience with them. That means you and Bruce lucked out this one time breaking and entering her apartment and leaving your fingerprints everywhere, but don't make the same mistake again."

Chastened, the men fell silent. The sun rose behind them. They drew closer to Omaha.

***

Tolly purchased the *Lake City Tribune* at the truck stop's front counter. In the bathroom stall, she found an article that provided a still shot from her video interview with King.

Tolly remembered that moment in the interview. King moved into her personal space. He overwhelmed and flustered her—a specialty of his she knew now.

The news article lifted a quote from her interview:

> Certainly, Lake City has received kudos for riding out a harsh economy where other cities have struggled. I continue to give credit to the current administration for keeping us all, and I include myself in that, above water. But now it's time to take the wheel, press the accelerator to the floor, and drive forward to the future.

The article declared him a hero to Lake City, especially when he talked about his philanthropic dedication:

> The advances made by the Celara companies in research and business development made it possible for us to give back to the community with job growth and training, scholarships, and solar and wind installations for low-income housing.

***

They spotted the bus parked in the midst of a crowd of eighteen-wheelers. The bus would leave the truck stop for Patina in a matter of minutes. They didn't see Tolly Henry anywhere, but Scott trusted his intuition. She was still inside. She would wait until the last minute to board within a crowd of people.

Bruce's voice squawked through the cell phone. "How do you know? She might be on the bus."

Scott negated that. "She has to get off in Omaha. No one can sit that long and not go crazy. Bruce, you said yourself that she was a clean freak. She's not going to use the bathroom on the bus."

"Maybe."

"Watch," Scott told him.

"For what? We can't see anything. The trucks block everything."

Scott opened the door to the pickup and grabbed his cell phone. "I'll go inside."

"How do you know she's inside?" Bruce's tone challenged again.

Scott raised his eyes to the heavens. "You guys watch the bus and the front door. No. Flash the badges and then walk the bus." He strode towards the truck stop entrance.

"Well, if she's inside, she's probably trying to make some extra cash off these truckers in the showers."

"Bruce."

"I'm just saying."

***

The supergrid contract to construct, install, and maintain the Midwest region was just a start, King said in the article.

Jobs, jobs, jobs.

He went on to describe his wish to leave a positive legacy for his children. His spokespeople described the Yashuda campaign as foreign, strange, and sinister. Even the *Lake City Tribune* branded Tina Yashuda's policies as unreliable and dangerous. A photo of King and his Indonesian wife, the one that he struck after Tolly interviewed him, served as a shield from criticism on the cultural disconnect.

According to the writer, King pressed endless flesh, doled out hugs, told inside jokes, stroked egos, posed for pictures, and agreed to every interview. The press reveled in his public relations.

***

"Look, Bruce." Scott stopped with his hand on the truck stop's front entrance. "She watched you and my brother break into her apartment from the coffee shop."

"How do you know this shit, man? Cause you're Indian? Did you find some broken twigs and shit leading to the coffee shop, or what?"

Scott felt somewhat guilty for forcing Jack to work with Bruce, but then someone had to. "Exactly, Bruce. Because I'm an Indian and I found some broken twigs."

Scott turned toward the Windrunner Security car to point.

"Bus," he ordered. He snapped his cell phone closed. He didn't bother to see whether Alex's idiot hire or his brother obeyed.

Neither did Scott tell Bruce the real reason he knew how Tolly made her escape. He remembered her. He'd seen her in the coffee shop before while he worked another job for Alex. And she'd seen him.

He wondered whether she would remember their near meeting from a year ago. Only one way to find out.

He entered the truck stop.

Tolly emerged from the women's restroom. The bus would continue its long trek from the Midwestern cornfields to southwestern Rocky Mountains any minute.

Lake City Tribune's fluff piece would boost King's position in the polls. And that would be a good thing for her, right? If Alexander King got what he wanted, that would mean a full-time job for her with Lake City Balance. She could make "renewable a reality" too.

She folded the newspaper. She had a lot to think over on the way to Patina. And she had to answer the questions she couldn't ignore.

Was she a coward?

Was King's political dominance her fault?

Something acrid bubbled in the back of her throat. She felt nauseated and would have returned to the bathroom stall to deal with the guilt except the bus would pull out of the truck stop with or without her. Her suitcase, filled with clothing and food, had to sustain her for a week. Once Alex King won the primary, she could return to Lake City.

She squared her shoulders.

The other bus passengers milled back and forth in the truck stop's retail area. Some concluded candy and potato chip purchases. Most edged with reluctance towards the door to cross the parking lot and re-board the bus for the ride west.

Scott's cell phone rang. It was Jack, who he could see through the plate glass window walking away from the bus with Bruce following.

"She's not on the bus, Scott. She's somewhere in the store."

Scott eased past aisles of car accessories, candy, and cleaning products. "I don't see her yet. I'll have to check near the restrooms."

He snapped the cell phone closed. He made his way to the rear of the store.

A large form loomed over her. The hollow feeling inside Tolly's stomach turned into a quiver. A large hulk decked out in black leather from head-to-toe blocked the narrow hallway.

She stared, amazed at the unexpected apparition. He stared down at her from six feet and change with dark eyes that snapped and flashed beneath black brows and a mane of silvery-white hair.

She and he did the little back-and-forth dance that people do when they tried to pass each other but misinterpreted body language.

He found her.

Scott didn't need to verify her photo in the file. He remembered her from the coffee shop a year ago—smooth, toffee-colored skin, chocolate eyes, full mouth curved into a bow. He'd been in her apartment yesterday and seen photos and intrusive evidence of her everyday life.

Fluffy, dark brown hair twisted into ropes hung to her shoulders. She wore a white cotton shirt and khaki pants.

Tolly Henry.

The biker stared down at her with what looked like amusement. Beyond embarrassed, Tolly tried to sidle past, but the passage was so small or he was so large that she felt his body heat rise off the black leather.

He smelled like sunshine, wind, and masculine skin.

She exhaled. "Excuse me."

He smiled down at her.

She jerked away. Then she looked back. He still watched her. Her face heated. Rescues by Mr. Wonderful only happened in movies. She was on her own now.

Tolly quickened her pace. She had to get back on the bus.

Scott made as if to enter the men's room, next to the women's bathroom. From the corner of his eye, he watched his quarry walk towards the front of the truck stop. She said something to the guy at the counter.

The truck stop jockey responded, flattered by the attention. She looked through the glass front of the store then froze.

Scott knew she must have spotted the same Windrunner Security car near the bus that she saw outside her three-flat from the coffee shop. She probably even recognized Jack and Bruce.

She didn't move.

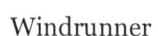

Chapter 9

How did they find her?

Tolly's cell phone vibrated again in her pocket. She ignored it, too preoccupied to have a conversation with anyone.

She knew they hadn't followed her from the coffee shop. She also knew that she could not board that bus without discovery. The two men—one dark, one tan—who broke into her apartment building stood next to the Windrunner Security car. The dark-skinned man crossed muscular arms across his chest.

Just steps away, the driver boarded the bus. Tolly looked from the men, who didn't appear to have anything to do but wait, back to the bus. She could not board.

Her cell phone vibrated again. She backed away from the glass. She turned back to the man behind the counter.

"Can I help you with anything?" he asked her, hope in his voice.

"Um, no," she replied. "I was just trying to think of what else I might need here."

"Okay," the guy shrugged. Another day, another dollar. "Let me know."

Tolly pulled the cell phone from her pocket. Bill Martinez had sent her four text messages. Someone trashed her apartment. Tolly looked through the plate glass window at the two men. They must have used her cell phone to trace her. They waited for her.

"Oh, you know what?"

The guy behind the counter shrugged.

"Now I know what I'm trying to remember. I think I left my newspaper in the bathroom." Tolly walked towards the back of the store.

Too late, Tolly realized she still held the newspaper under her arm.

Oh well.

When Scott saw Tolly's act, he decided upon a performance of his own.

He made a slow, casual walk towards the front of the store. He smiled at her again when he passed her. He also read her face, pretty sure that he knew what was about to happen.

Sure enough, she skipped out the back of the truck stop. Scott nodded at the truck stop's counter jockey who shook his head at weirdness of customers.

Scott followed Tolly out the back door, but he didn't see her anywhere. She dodged and hid amongst the parked eighteen-wheelers.

Scott whipped out his cell phone. "Jack, the security car spooked her. She ran out the back of the store. Watch for her!"

Jack snapped to attention. "Where is she now?"

"Somewhere in the parking lot. Watch the bus!"

"Where?" Jack demanded. "I don't see her. All these trucks."

"The bus is pulling out!" Bruce yelled.

"Jack! Do you see her?" Scott started a systematic search of broken cars and rusted trucks. He looked underneath, in the back seats... it took too long. "Talk to me."

"I don't know, man!" Jack replied. "I don't see her."

Scott swore. He scanned the dense cornfields that surrounded the truck stop. He still didn't see her. There were too many places to hide.

"If she's not on the bus, then she's got to be here somewhere."

Scott spun in a circle trying to think. Not this again. They had to intercept her without causing a ruckus. He was pretty sure the counter jockey was armed and would take Tolly's side if it came down to a choice.

"Okay Jack, dismount my bike off the pickup. Use the pickup to follow the bus. Bruce, go back to Lake City to see if she tries to double back."

"Go back with what?" Bruce asked.

"Take the security car."

"Now wait just a minute."

"Bruce, we need you back in Lake City. One, to clean up the mess you made of her apartment so it doesn't come back on your boss. Two, to see if you find anything that we may have missed the first time. Three, to watch her apartment from the coffee shop across the street. See if anyone tries to make contact with her."

"But..."

"Bruce, come on! There's no time for this. We need to cover ground. She's getting away either direction and we can't have this same screw up again."

Crouched between the back wheels of an eighteen-wheeler, Tolly saw the legs of a man in dingy tennis shoes stop next to a suburban van. He unlocked the driver side door. Tolly heard the engine start.

She emerged from her hiding place to wave him down.

A pudgy man with a scraggly beard, mustache, and earrings looked her over with interest. Through the window, she saw a baby seat amongst clutter.

Tolly glanced over her shoulder, but she and the driver were hidden from view by the eighteen-wheeler. The driver unlocked the passenger door.

"Hey, thanks!" Tolly walked over then gave him her best normal person smile.

"No problem." He rubbed his half-beard and waited to see what she wanted.

"So," Tolly asked, her hand on the door handle. "Are you headed towards Lincoln by any chance?"

"Ye-e-es. I can go to Lincoln."

Tolly hesitated. Something in his wording wasn't right. Was he on his way to Lincoln or not? But she didn't have a whole lot of options. The bus made its way to the road that accessed eighty..

She got in the passenger seat and slammed the door shut. The driver swung around the eighteen-wheeler.

She recognized the Windrunner Security car as it zigzagged towards the truck stop exit ahead of them. A pick-up truck followed close behind it. She couldn't go back to Lake City to face either Alex King or his hired minions. In light of his open-air physical assault of her from yesterday, who knew what he would do or have done to her if he got her alone?

Tolly dropped the *Lake City Tribune* on the floor of the van. She spent a few moments bent over to retrieve it. She peeked through the bottom edge of the passenger window. She didn't see the security car. She held up the newspaper in triumph.

"Got it!"

The driver viewed her with uncertainty, but made the proper turns towards Lincoln.

"What do you do?" she asked her rescuer.

He smiled at her. "I'm a silversmith."

"Oh." Tolly tried to think of something polite. After all, he'd helped her. "Silver's nice. I actually prefer it to gold. It's prettier."

"Mmm. Yes, it's very pretty."

Tolly felt the driver's gaze on her profile. His eyes traveled lower. She fought the instinct to cross her arms over her body. She looked at the road signs to confirm that he headed the right direction towards Lincoln. Maybe if he drove fast enough, she could reboard the bus to Patina.

The driver interrupted her planning. "So, can I undo my pants while we talk?"

"What?"

He gestured downward. "They're a little tight on me."

Tolly looked to the heavens for an answer because, Holy God, she got into the wrong van. But then again, maybe she heard him wrong. Maybe they just spoke differently in Nebraska. Maybe it was a type of local slang and he really meant something else.

"So..." he wanted an answer.

"I'd... rather you didn't."

"Just a little," he pleaded with another smile. "Halfway," he bargained.

Tolly kept her voice neutral. "Would you pull over please?"

"What?"

"Pull over!" she shouted. "I'm getting out!"

"Right now?" he seemed surprised.

"Yes!" Tolly raised her voice to full shriek. "Pull over right now!"

Scott spotted her two miles west from the truck stop. She emerged from a van.

Clever girl.

The van pulled away. She stuck her thumb out. Eighteen-wheelers roared past her. Their tailwinds blew her back from the road pavement.

Scott slowed his motorcycle to ride the shoulder. Then he stopped beside her.

"Yeah. I saw you back at that truck stop, didn't I?" Sunglasses afforded him the opportunity to watch her expression without her notice. He wanted to see how she'd answer.

"Yeah." She looked a little dazed.

In the pause, the suburban van passed on the opposite side of the road. The driver glared at them with outraged betrayal.

"Lost your ride?" Scott asked her.

"Yeah." She shivered a little.

"Where you headed?"

"North Platte. Nebraska." Not a good liar, Scott concluded.

"Get on." Scott indicated for her to mount behind him with his head. "I'll take you."

"Where are *you* going?"

A hard lesson she learned from the van driver, Scott decided.

"Calabasas." He shrugged, a study in nonchalance. "I got family there."

"I've never heard of Calabasas," she responded, suspicion in her voice.

Scott shrugged again, but this time he smiled to indicate they were in on the same joke. "It's a small place in Colorado. Not hardly on any maps."

"Colorado. Oh." Tolly Henry looked at the road behind. Not a lot of traffic. Not much choice. "So you can drop me in North Platte?" she asked with obvious reluctance.

Scott didn't take it personally. He did have an agenda, after all. Just not the agenda she assumed.

"Happy to," he told her. "There or further. Long as it's on the way."

Tolly still wasn't sure.

The man shifted his large leather-clad body on the bike. He gazed further down the road at the western horizon. The morning sun glowed an intense yellow-orange over their negotiation.

"I don't have a lot of extra gas." He gunned the engine.

"I... can pay." Tolly reached into her pocket. There actually wasn't a whole lot there for her to reach for.

"Nope. Don't want your money. Just need you to keep me from falling asleep."

"What!" Tolly amended her tone. "I mean... how do I do that?"

"Scream in my ear if the bike wobbles." He grinned. "Which is what most of you women like to do anyway."

Again, she scanned the road behind them. His firm lips parted in another amused smile. He pushed his mirrored sunglasses to his forehead. Tolly flushed.

She didn't like him. He was too good-looking. He knew it. In fact, the pure masculine beauty of his face made her head whirl. That meant she couldn't think straight around him and that scared her. Not thinking straight got her involved with another good-looking man—Rafael. She barely survived him with her sanity intact.

The gears in Tolly's head slowly ground it out. This motorcyclist was rude, yes. Impatient, yes. But he wasn't crazy. Besides, if he did decide to go nuts, she had the advantage. His back would be exposed, his hands occupied steering the bike. She could hit him in the head with her purse. She could bite him then hop off the bike and run away. Maybe she'd hit him again with a rock if he came after her.

In total, she choreographed three escape plans in her head. Meanwhile, she could take the ride or leave it. The bus would stop in North Platte. Maybe they could catch it.

"Time's wasting." The man gunned his engine again.

Satisfied that she'd given each option fair consideration, Tolly nodded.

She mounted the bike behind him.

Chapter 10

Midday Tuesday, Tolly couldn't stop the excitement that thrilled through her. A wide open expanse of road, sky, grass, and sunset rushed to greet her in ribbons of gray, blue, green, and yellow.

The man's wavy white hair blew back against her cheek and neck. It smelled clean and brisk. It smelled like wind. It felt silky soft and strangely comforting on her face. Her own rope twists flew back in the wind.

Tolly tied her shoulder bag over one arm and her purse over the other arm. That left her hands free to hold on to her driver (in case she had to hit him in the head). His back flexed now and then beneath the sun-warmed black leather jacket as he handled the bike. It was mostly straight road, but once in a while they rounded a curve or had to pass a tractor.

Two hours later, dark green, grey, then smoky black thunder clouds boiled across the western horizon. They rode into the smudge of humidity. Rain pattered down. The man surged faster on the bike. Out here in the great wide open, there wasn't much shelter. She'd wrapped the flash drive in plastic before she wedged it into her front pocket, so it should stay dry. At least she hoped so.

But she and her driver got drenched before they reached Kearney. He pulled into a motel, diner, and gas station triplex. Then he parked underneath the motel's canopy.

Underneath the curtain of rain, Tolly saw that the motel's tan exterior peeled back to reveal gray primor. An ancient soda machine displayed a handwritten out-of-order sign. Random tires and rusted car parts dotted the nooks and crannies of the gas station. But the diner was open twenty-four hours, so the neon blinked.

"Wait here," her driver commanded. He jogged into the motel's office without a backward glance. He moved fast for a man his size, Tolly noted.

"Okay, I got us a room." Mission accomplished, Scott tossed the motel key into the air. He snapped the key back into his fist. Fast reflexes.

"A room?"

"Yeah." Scott didn't elaborate. He watched Tolly Henry shift her bag to the other shoulder.

"How much did it cost?" she asked.

"Not much, but just like the gas, I don't have extra to pay for another room." Scott had plenty. But he needed to keep track of his quarry. He already knew she had a good disappearing act. "You can bunk with me." He tried on a magnanimous smile.

"We're not that far from North Platte, are we?" she asked. "It's barely noon."

The violent rush of wind from the motorcycle made it hard for new riders to judge speed compared to enclosed vehicles. He couldn't believe she still hadn't caught on to his deliberate slowdown.

"Lady, look." He pointed. "You see that?"

He stretched out a long arm with a large hand cupped to catch the rain. "You feel that? Our deal was that I'd take you to North Platte, but do you expect me to ride in that? That's not stopping anytime soon. For all we know, a twister's on the way."

Time to put the screws to her. He gestured again to the thunderstorm that whipped the countryside. "You're almost there, but I just assumed you wanted to get to town without road burn from us sliding into a ditch."

She waited a beat. "I have a little money. Maybe I could talk to the hotel manager and he'd make a deal for an extra room for me."

"Well," Scott inside the motel office. "Good night and good luck."

Her eyes followed his gaze. Behind the well-lit plate glass, the tattooed manager drank something out of a dark brown bottle. He laughed at a wrestling match on television. Then he lifted a dingy wife-beater to scratch his pot belly.

She shuddered a little. Scott hid a small smile. Tolly Henry would not appreciate the details of any deal the motel manager would present to her.

He waited to see what she would do.

Tolly didn't move. In the silence, her stomach growled. For a long while neither she nor the man acknowledged the noise. Even though his hair and black leather were soaked, he seemed to feel no need to rush to his room. Their room.

"I guess you heard that," Tolly told him.

"Heard what?"

Tolly sighed.

"Oh. The chainsaw?" He raised his eyebrows.

"Yes, the chainsaw."

"Nah." Then he laughed.

This time Tolly's stomach roared.

He laughed harder. "Now that, I did hear. What've you got an alien about to burst out of you?"

"Okay, I'll share the room," she told him. The words came out as if he held a gun to her head.

"Gee, would you please?" he mocked.

Embarrassed, Tolly laughed with him. "By the way, what should I call you?"

"Scott."

"Scott what?"

"I don't know." He shrugged. "Scott Dreamcatcher."

What an ego. Tolly's mouth dropped open. "Dreamcatcher? My God. You really think I'm going to call you that?"

"No. I'm not a god," Scott explained with patience. "But I am a dream, so I'm told. Catch me while you can."

Tolly sighed. "Time's wasting," she reminded.

"Time is wasting," he agreed. "And you are?"

"Hungry."

"Your mother named you that?"
"Funny," Tolly acknowledged. "No. It's Tolly."
"Let me guess…" he started.
"No, please don't."
"Tolly… Chocolate Toffee."
"This is going to be a long ride," she sighed.
"Yeah, I get that too. A lot."
Tolly giggled despite herself. "Stop it!"
"Come on," Scott told her. "Follow me."

They dumped their luggage inside the motel room but Tolly kept her purse with her. He took her hand, then pulled her at a run through the rain.

He would buy Tolly's dinner which would obligate her and put her further under his control. He fully intended to use the payment for Tolly's rundown to retire, buy land, and to help his family. She was a paycheck. He would need to learn more about her in order to convince her to return to Lake City willingly.

To conceal the interrogation, Scott would confide in her somewhat. However, something didn't add up in this scenario. He'd challenged her to buy her own room. She declined. Either she didn't have Alex's money with her, or she refused to display it. Or Jack might find large bills in her suitcase once he met the bus in Patina. Scott thought it would be unusually stupid of her to hide cash inside checked luggage.

She'd been pretty smart so far.

They found a booth next to the window. The harsh drum of cold rain against the glass created an aura of intimacy around their table. Tolly surveyed the empty diner. She cleared her throat.

"You know, this is the American gothic I've always heard about."

Travel outside Lake City was something she'd always dreamed about but never really had time to do. Her building and its tenants, paperwork, and operations didn't leave much time for recreation. She barely had time to finish her reports for Lake City Balance.

"What do you mean?" her dinner companion asked. He'd slicked his wet hair back with a careless hand.

Scott had been right to come off the road when he did. They wouldn't have made it to North Platte through the dark, dreary afternoon without damage.

"In here. Out there." She gestured with a hand. "The rolling prairie, the yellow and green corn, all those windmills spinning. It's amazing."

"It is?" he raised his eyebrows. "In that case, prepare to be amazed all the way to North Platte."

"I hope so! I mean, it's no longer a backdrop. I'm part of the scene now." She couldn't disguise the excitement in her voice.

"Yeah, I guess." Scott gestured for someone to take their orders. A waitress headed towards their table.

"All those rows of corn, mooing cows, red barns, those enormous silos, the fences that stretch to forever, and then *me* on the back of a motorcycle!"

Scott burst into laughter, then asked for a cheeseburger for him, tuna melt for her.

Tolly giggled a little. Maybe she weirded him out a little, but she didn't care. He deserved it for the jokes he made earlier.

"Do you have children?" she asked him.

"No." He winced as if from a bad memory.

"You?" he asked her in return.

"No." Tolly looked down at the table top.

She noticed that he seemed curious. "How'd you manage that?" he asked her.

"Just lucky, I guess." Tolly attempted to keep her tone light but the bad memories came back.

Rafael hadn't wanted children. And she'd always given Rafael what he wanted, nothing he didn't. The one time she did, he made her pay a steep price. Tolly felt a little queasy from the memory of her subjugation to Rafael's will.

She looked up to see that Scott watched her face closely. "Let's get dessert," he suggested over her protests. Then he told her all about the Harley, his bike of choice. Together, they made short work of a huge slab of chocolate cake topped with ice cream.

Tolly searched her purse for a few careworn bills to leave for the tip and then excused herself to the restroom to splash water on her face.

Scott made a mental note. Children weren't good conversation topics for either of them.

He walked to the register to pay the check, then tossed a five dollar bill on top of the three singles that Tolly left. He killed time chatting up the waitress while he waited for Tolly. He didn't think she'd try to skip out the back again.

Would she?

He frowned, uneasy. No. Her shoulder bag was in the hotel room and he had the only key on him. Though she might try to persuade the hotel manager...

Tolly joined him at the diner's front door. She wouldn't go anywhere this evening. The storm to end all storms thrashed against the buildings, isolated by distance from the nearest town. Hitchhiking prospects would prove slim.

She let him take her hand. They ran back to the motel room together.

"You don't have a lot," he commented eyeing her shoulder bag.

"No?"

"Most women would have a suitcase to go with the shoulder bag."

Tolly didn't respond. Instead, she picked out the toiletries that she needed and headed for the bathroom. She locked the door with loud purpose behind her, as if to tell Scott, whatever he hoped would happen tonight, in fact, would not. On top of that, she rattled the door knob as if to test whether he could break in on her if he succumbed to an unexpected fit of madness.

However, she left her purse and shoulder bag next to the bed. Scott searched them as soon as she finished her show with the bathroom lock.

He found a bus ticket under a name that didn't match her identification (Tolly Henry, brown eyes, brown hair, thirty-eight, 5'6, 140 lbs), eight dollars, and empty granola bar wrappers. He didn't find Alex's money, campaign documents, or a video file.

Scott had his second inkling that something didn't fit in the scenario. Tolly may have passed the information and money on to a confederate before she boarded the bus. Or her blackmail kit lay under the bus to Patina in her suitcase.

Too soon to hear from Jack.

Chapter 11

In the bathroom, Tolly removed the flash drive still wrapped in plastic from inside her pocket with care. Thankfully, the plastic kept the device from getting wet in the downpour. She laid the flash drive on the bathroom counter.

She removed the hair clip that kept her twists from swinging across her face whenever she moved her head or the wind blew. She set the hairclip next to the flash drive.

She removed every stitch of clothing. She washed all that she wore—cotton overshirt, knit undershirt, khaki pants. She scrubbed each piece clean with the motel's soap then hung everything on the bathroom's heater, including her underwear.

Then she showered.

Scott called his younger sister. "Nellie, I'm on my way to Calabasas."

"I thought you had to work."

"I am working. The job's taking me to Patina. I'll swing by to see you and the kids and Pop before I head back."

"Scott, I know what Pop must have told you. You don't have to come all the way out here. You're overreacting as usual."

"Nellie, I just said I'll be in the area. It's only twenty minutes from Patina. Can I at least get one home-cooked meal before I head back to the Lake City grind? I'm your brother!"

"Okay, okay!" Nellie laughed. "But look, Scott, I'm just trying to let you know that I'm okay."

"You didn't sound okay yesterday."

"That was yesterday. Today, I'm fine."

"Great! Then I'll see you for dinner tomorrow."

"Scott." Nellie hesitated. "You know not much has changed since you left. People still think their thoughts."

"Nellie, you're my favorite sister."

"I'm your only sister."

"Which is why I love you like you're my favorite sister." Scott hung up on her before she could raise further objections. He hated that he wasn't there to protect her the way he used to when they were younger.

Time to get back to work. He made another call. "Jack, where are you?"

"Still following the bus. We're three hours from Patina. But that depends on how many more stops the bus makes."

"I have her."

"What? You have Tolly Henry with you?"

"I picked her up near the truck stop, hitchhiking. I'm going to try to get the real story out of her. We're overnight in a motel in Kearney."

"I see." Jack chuckled. "I guess that's why you're the boss."

"Alex's money has to be in her luggage. She barely has anything on her."

"I thought that's how you liked your women."

"Now you sound like Bruce."

"Ugh, don't say that."

"Look, I'll work it from this end. Call me when you have her luggage from the Patina bus station."

"I'll call you from Calabasas."

"You bunking with Pop?"

"Just like old times. He knows to expect me."

"I'll meet you there tomorrow."

Tolly slathered on the tiny bit of lotion portioned out by the motel. She paused when she overheard Scott through the bathroom door.

I'll meet you there tomorrow.

Could be a girlfriend. Could be business. Oh well. Not any business of hers.

She picked up the flash drive again.

"I have Tolly Henry with me," Scott told his boss.

"That's why I pay you the big bucks, Scott."

"Yeah, right." Scott replied. "Bruce is on his way back to Lake City."

"For fucking what?"

"To clean up her apartment." Scott cocked his head toward the hotel's bathroom. He heard running water and the sound of teeth being brushed. Still, he lowered his voice and switched on the television.

"He broke into her apartment and trashed it before we left. He needs to clean that up and take care of all the fingerprints he left. I can't have that come down on Windrunner Security. Besides that, I need him to watch her building to see who comes and goes. That's how we'll figure out whether she's working for Yashuda or flying solo. If anyone from Yashuda's campaign shows up, then we'll know."

"What the fuck? That's not how I..."

"Exactly, Alex. That's not how. Which is why you hired a professional. Where did you find that guy, anyway? Another thing," Scott overrode Alex's attempt to interrupt. "She's not spending money and she's not carrying documents that I can see."

"Well, then she's being careful, isn't she?"

"Too careful."

Alex didn't respond.

"Is there anything else about this situation I need to know, Alex? Anything you need to tell me?"

"Yeah. You have the bitch. Find her shit. That's all you need to know." Alex disconnected.

Scott didn't like the tone. That type of aggression disguised defensive double talk. He remembered the days of lies and omissions by his superiors prior to violent confrontations in a foreign desert. Out of a sense of duty and honor, he'd passed those lies and omissions on to the men underneath his command.

The bathroom door opened. Tolly emerged from a cloud of steam. She wore only a towel which interrupted his meditations on past clusterfucks.

Scott stared at her too long. He covered with an irritated growl. "What took so long?"

"I had to wash my clothes. I've been in them for almost two days."

Scott continued to stare.

"Uhm so, perhaps you could..." Tolly gestured towards the carpet.

Scott looked to where she pointed in disbelief. "That carpet happens to be dirty."

"Not that dirty."

"No," he replied. "Actually it's filthy."

"Maybe if you put a towel down..."

"You sleep on it."

Tolly looked at the floor. The carpet was filthy.

"But..."

"But what?" Scott laughed. "I give you a ride. I pay for the room. I buy dinner. I even throw in witty repartee."

She lifted her chin in defiance.

"So *kind* of you to throw in your stand-up comedy along with the tuna melt." She tried to illustrate her sarcasm with air quotes around 'stand-up comedy,' but then the towel slipped down.

Scott couldn't stop the swift flick of his eyes over her exposed damp skin. The velvety-soft brown covered slender limbs wrapped by smooth lengths of muscles. She had the body of a dancer. Like that of a fawn.

He cleared his throat.

"Yeah, it was kind of me, wasn't it?" he agreed. "But my reward is to sleep on a filthy carpet? Not very likely."

"Well then," Tolly hitched the towel tighter. She took a step back towards the bathroom. "I'll sleep in the bathtub. I'll just need that blanket off the bed."

"Fine. But the bathtub's wet. From your shower, remember?"

"I know. I'll dry it."

"But not until after I shower too, right?"

She sighed.

Scott knew he was being difficult. In fact, he did it on purpose. Aggravating her was the only way to keep him from pulling her into his arms in order to protect her because he saw something else when the towel slipped.

Dark bruises marred her upper arms and wrists. She'd been handled by a man as recently as yesterday.

The television muttered, "Alex King," into the silence. She flinched. They both eyed the news update on Lake City's mayoral race that dominated current events across the Midwest.

To hide his preoccupation and to throw her further off her step, Scott stood to pull off his black leather jacket. Then he pulled off his shirt. An enormous chest and massive arms flexed. Tolly's mouth dropped open.

He snorted.

"If you could see the look of complete horror on your face." He stepped into the bathroom. Then he clicked the bathroom door knob lock back and forth. He tugged the doorknob with loud rattles, in case she tried to break in while he showered.

Tolly stared at the bathroom door, red-faced.

But the real horror she experienced was not the news update on King. She didn't expect her physical response to Scott's muscled bare chest and stomach to be so strong.

Her body still remembered hugging his on the back of the motorcycle. She felt him flex underneath her arms and hands... and legs. She didn't like for her body to tremble this way.

He started the shower. She tried not to think of a cool cascade of water that spilled over the hard planes of his bare body.

Years had passed since the last time she touched a man with that degree of intimacy—Rafael, her one and only intimate partner. That memory shook her out of her distraction. She switched off the television.

Tolly frowned. She'd left her purse and shoulder bag unguarded. Not like her to do that. Scott and his jokes. She counted the money. Eight dollars remained in her possession, nothing missing that she could see.

Quicker than quick, Scott emerged from the bathroom. He'd wrapped the other large towel tight to his waist. She pretended to rearrange her toiletries in her shoulder bag. Then she focused on the dirty carpet.

Just inside her peripheral view, he made a big show of unlocking his own leather bag, which seemed to take forever.

Tolly scowled. It was still early evening. They had a long night ahead of them. She cleared her throat, trapped by a raging torrent inside a tiny room with a circus clown who liked to tease.

"I'm going to go ahead and... spend the night in the tub."

"Oh!" he started as if he'd forgotten she sat right behind him.

Then he shrugged as if it meant not a thing to him.

Yeah. Okay.

After the usual coughs and blanket tugs, their motel room became silent except for the spray of water on the window... and the drips of water on Tolly's feet.

Drip. Drip. Drip.

It wasn't fair.

Tolly stood by the motel bed wrapped in the blanket, now damp near her feet. Scott groaned, then turned away from her so that she faced his backside, a smooth, tanned expanse that narrowed at the waist. She couldn't see what he wore underneath the blanket.

But, damn him, he knew she was there!

"Are you going to move over or not?" she finally asked, beyond annoyed. She didn't wait for an answer. Instead, she got into the bed, then nudged him further over.

"Don't touch me!" she ordered.

The bed shook beneath her. Again, he laughed at her expense. Tolly threw part of the blanket over him. She muttered for about another minute. Then she fretted and tugged at the blanket. At long last, dreamland carried her away.

Chapter 12

Wednesday morning arrived without Tolly's notice because she sailed across a wondrous dreamscape. She swam across a kaleidoscope of red mountains, blue skies, and mauve sunsets. She chased a silver fox who dodged back-and-forth. The warm haze around her cooled to violet and then moonlight blazed across a field of stars.

She shivered with excitement. The silver fox turned, and then chased her in return. A whirlwind circled around them, pushed them together.

The fox grew larger then folded its body around her in a rough, warm embrace.

She groaned aloud.

The sound woke her from sleep.

She froze.

Scott's arms and legs wrapped around her. She couldn't run from him if she wanted to. His heavy chest and arms felt as strong and heavy as logs.

And yes, his mouth rested against her neck. His open mouth. She knew that because she felt warm breath slide across her hair while he snored in and out.

She felt something else too. Tolly stiffened with shock. She dug an outraged elbow into his chest.

Scott snapped awake. "Lady, what're you trying to do here?" he demanded.

"Will you please get off?" Tolly asked through clenched teeth.

He hesitated.

"Get the hell off me!"

Tolly soon regretted her demand. In order for Scott to disentangle his limbs from hers, he had to touch her in other places. The hard friction of his muscular legs and arms slid across her body until he freed her. She wanted to scream. She refused to look at him.

"I'm going to take another shower," she told the dirty motel carpet.

"To cool down?" Scott asked with innocence. From the corner of her eye, she saw that he wore black boxer briefs.

"No! To wake up!" she snapped.

This time, she remembered to snatch up her shoulder bag and purse. The shower steamed most of the wrinkles out of her cotton shirt and khakis. When she emerged from the bathroom, fully-dressed, Scott stepped inside the motel door with his cell phone. At least he'd put on his jeans. She assumed he'd concluded another mysterious phone call. Then he showered, but with much less drama than the night before.

While he did that, Tolly tried to search his leather bag. She had to do it for her own safety, she decided. But he'd locked it against her intrusion. She tried to feel offended by that, but couldn't. She did look.

Scott finished in the shower in what seemed like seconds. He announced that they both needed to eat breakfast before they hit the road. Tolly didn't have the heart to dispute his takeover of her itinerary. She was too hungry.

The waitress in the diner seemed extra glad to see them. Or him.

"Hey baby!"

"Hey yourself!"

Tolly scowled at the salt and pepper. She felt furious that not only had 'Ethel,' her name badge said, called Scott 'baby,' but that

Scott had answered. For all the waitress knew, Scott was her boyfriend. He could even have been her husband. They could be on their honeymoon. Yes, in an all-night diner next to a cheap motel on their damn motorcycle honeymoon adventure.

Well why not?

Scott ordered pancakes, eggs and ham, plus coffee for himself. Tolly asked for eggs, hash browns, toast, and orange juice.

"Sugar?" The waitress smiled at Scott while she poured his coffee.

He smiled back, pleased. "Why thank you, Ethel. I'd love some."

Tolly imagined herself using one of Scott's syrup-covered pancakes to gently wash the smile off his face. She laughed a little to herself. Ethel the Waitress flashed a knowing look her direction then switched away.

Scott shrugged at Tolly as if to say, *what can you do?*

"I'm surprised she didn't offer to cut your ham for you and feed it to you herself."

"Maybe I'll ask her."

"Why don't you ask her to stir your coffee too?"

"What a great idea!" Scott beamed his approval.

"Oh, you'd like that." Tolly laughed.

"In fact, I'd *love* that." Scott joined the joke with chuckles.

Their orders arrived. Tolly sighed and got to work. Well aware of her budget, she decided to eat while she had the chance. After the first few hungry nips to take the edge off, she also decided that the least she could do was give her driver some conversation. Keep him from falling asleep. Early-morning physical reactions aside, that was all he'd asked of her.

"I'm getting a military vibe," Tolly probed.

"Fighting terrorism since 1492," he quipped back.

"Funny," Tolly said. "Are you still?"

"Years ago. You can tell?"

"I can tell you like to give orders."

"I do." Scott laughed. "What would be even more fun is if a certain person who shall remain nameless had the good sense to follow them. Now wouldn't that be special?"

"It would certainly be something."

"I guess we'll soon see."

"Not this lifetime."

"Pass the salt."

Tolly passed the salt to Scott. He held her hand still cupped around the shaker in his large, warm fist. He wagged his dark, black brows at her.

"Wait a minute!"

Scott laughed at her. She eyed Scott's remaining pancake dripping with syrup. Fast on the reflex, Scott speared it with his fork and knife. She missed her chance to snatch it up and smash it into his face.

"Oh, you're good, Scott. So very good."

"That's what I'm…"

"I know, I know. That's what you're told. *A lot*."

Scott laughed.

"How was it for you?"

Scott eyed her.

"Military service, I mean."

Mindful of his interrogation strategy, Scott put down his knife and fork. "I have mixed feelings. I mean, serving my country got me out of a small town. Calabasas, where we're headed now. Taught me some things. Discipline. Clarity and organization. Goal-setting. But it got to the point that I felt that I became all that I could be. I wanted to be something else. So I got my MBA. Turned my attention to more mundane things."

"Like…"

Scott took a drink of coffee. "Business."

"You're a business man?"

"Don't let the leather fool you."

"Don't worry. It didn't."

"Lots of stuff going on up here." He tapped his head.

"I shudder to imagine. What kind of business?"

"I'm a consultant."

"That's why you travel?"

"Somewhat. People pay me to tell them what to do."

"Sounds like that would be absolutely thrilling for you."

"I get goosebumps."

Tolly laughed.

"It's a living," he concluded. "What about yourself? School. Job. Boyfriend?"

"I nearly finished one semester at a community college. It didn't work out."

"Why not? Did you get pregnant?"

Tolly's mouth dropped open. She'd told him last night that she didn't have any children. What was his problem? She kept forgetting that he was rude. Or maybe *he* kept forgetting.

"Well?" he insisted. *Amazing.*

"No." She frowned at him. "My... well... my father died from cancer when I was in junior high. My mother died from diabetes complications the summer after my high school graduation. I handled most of the arrangements. Then... I don't know... I guess things just kind of got to me."

Scott set down his coffee cup with care. "Look, I'm sorry. There's a fine line between comedy and stupidity and I just crossed it."

"It's okay. You didn't know. It was some time ago." Tolly smiled. "Don't you dare ask me how long ago I was in high school. Now *that* would be crossing the line."

"No longer ago than me." Scott indicated his silvery lion's mane.

"I like your hair." He smiled at her compliment.

She smiled back. "It's pretty."

He winced. "Thanks."

"I think I ate some of it on the road."

"What?"

She enjoyed the look of surprise on his face. "The wind kept blowing it back into my face."

He laughed. "And you were hungry, if I remember."

"Very hungry," she acknowledged.

"I wondered what was going on back there. Speaking of that, here." He tossed her the last bit of his pancake. "You keep looking at this. Have a little before we hit the road again. I don't want to go bald."

If only he knew what she really intended for the pancake. Why did she giggle so much around this man?

"Anyway, like I said, things got a little hard for me to handle with all the distractions. Before I dropped out, I told myself that one day I'd re-enroll, but I never did."

"What do you do now?"

"Hitchhike."

"Good one." He inclined his head with a grin. "Speaking of that, it's time to hit the road, isn't it?"

They checked out of the motel to continue the journey down eighty. It didn't escape Tolly's notice that she wrapped her arms and legs around Scott the exact same way he did her that morning.

Even after the brisk, early morning shower, she still remembered his mouth and breath on her neck. She'd felt so safe wrapped inside the tight cocoon of his arms. It had been so long since she'd felt that type of touch. But then, she'd never felt safe with Rafael.

She sat so close to Scott, that she was afraid he might feel her heartbeat and breath quicken. So she pushed those dangerous thoughts away.

Instead she reveled in the scenery. The countryside they sped past made her feel as though she were in a movie.

At one point, Scott jogged the bike around an old tire on the road. Tolly tightened her grip around his waist.

"Hey, wake up!" she screamed into his ear.

Scott laughed. He gunned the bike faster in response.

Tolly screamed again.

He threw his head back to scream with her.

She yanked at a piece of his hair the wind blew into her mouth with her teeth. Again, he gunned the bike.

They surged forward into the brightness of morning.

Riding with Scott felt like flying.

Chapter 13

Wednesday afternoon, Scott stopped the bike in downtown North Platte next to a brick wall. He leaned on it next to Tolly. They both stretched. Scott squeezed her hand.

"That was funny, the bit with the hair. And the screaming," he told her.

"You like that?" she teased.

"I love that." In fact, he loved the way she laughed.

"Just earning my keep."

Scott couldn't look away from her smile and the way her entire face lit up with joy when she did. He decided to change the subject. "Well, I don't know, maybe an unexpected windfall might come your way and you can finish college."

She shrugged. "Things like that only happen in movies."

"Life imitates art."

"Not my life."

Interesting, he thought.

"So," Scott looked around the small business district, "what's in North Platte? Or should I say who?"

"Just a little break from the ordinary."

He raised his eyebrows. "In Nebraska?"

Tolly shrugged.

"So is this really your last stop?"

"I'm trying to make it as far as Patina."

"And you decided that it might be a good idea to ditch me in North Platte, just in case?"

Tolly nodded. "Just in case."

"In case what?"

She shifted her feet. "In case you were a serial killer. What else?"

Scott laughed. "That reminds me, when I get back home, I need to see if my basement locks are still holding."

"There you go." Tolly laughed. "Okay, I figure you're not going to sew a skin jacket out of me."

"Good God, lady, look at me. It would be way too small."

"Right, right." She giggled again.

"Look. The reason why I'm asking is I have a younger sister, Nellie. She's married to an idiot and I need to check on her. So I'm on a direct route to Calabasas. Have to turn off eighty."

"Of course. I understand."

"Why don't you ride with me to Calabasas? Hang out. Let me handle the family thing. And then I can swing you down to Patina."

"Well…"

"Look, Tolly. I didn't tell you before, but my father called while we were at the motel."

Tolly nodded. That explained the quiet conversations he had while she was in the bathroom.

"Said her husband was…" Scott smacked his right fist into his left hand. "You know."

"I see."

He didn't miss Tolly's shiver, as if a cold wind blew past her. Her old boyfriend must have shown her a whole new world. He hated guys like that. Had no respect for them as men, and his sister was married to one of them.

"I'm really worried about her. Otherwise I'd take you to Patina first."

"Well, I've never been to Calabasas. And this is your family."

He watched her eyes to see if she meant it.

"Let's go right now," she said with a decisive tone.

Rather than return to eighty, Scott drove the bike along a confusing route of back roads and switchbacks. Tolly lost track of their location after the first ten minutes, but Scott took the changing surfaces with confidence. She decided to just hold on and enjoy it.

The journey ended when Scott pulled into a bare space in the grass next to a two-story cabin built with pine logs. Tolly unwrapped herself from Scott's body with reluctance.

"Nellie!" he exclaimed to the woman who laughed as she emerged from the front door. "New house!"

Tolly noted right away that Scott's sister shared his features, however, her hair was still black, the front cut into a straight bang over her dark brown, nearly black eyes. After a brief introduction, Scott left Tolly with Nellie so she could change clothes. He would visit with his father for a while, and then when he returned, he and Tolly would eat dinner with Nellie and her husband.

Tolly walked back inside with Nellie who offered Tolly a few extra clothes and toiletries from a cedar chest of drawers. Even though Nellie's arms and legs were shorter than hers, Scott's sister had a build rounded from childbirth, so Tolly knew the knits would fit. She was pretty sure that she and Nellie were close in age, since Scott mentioned she was the youngest of his two siblings.

"Are you Scott's new girl?" Nellie opened up girl talk.

"Just a friend. He's giving me a lift to Patina."

"Oh. So he knows you from Lake City?"

Tolly started. She hadn't realized that she and Scott lived in the same city. He'd never said where he was from. But then again, neither had she. Funny how neither of them asked the other.

While she wouldn't lie to Nellie, she certainly wouldn't advertise the fact that Scott picked her up hitchhiking from a truck stop.

"Something like that," she replied, at last. "How long has it been since Scott lived here?"

"After military service, he stopped here for a little while. Then he headed to Lake City for a job."

"Lake City. Oh, right. Business." Tolly wondered what else she could learn about her driver from his sister.

"A lot of people move away from Calabasas for opportunities elsewhere. Most of them never return."

"That's too bad."

"I mean, I don't blame them for leaving. There are so many problems here—gangs, drugs, not enough healthcare. People look for better opportunities in the cities."

Tolly's mind wandered back to King's brutal behavior and the wrong coldness of his mother's false sympathy. "I wonder if life is better in the city?"

"Well, we've been having problems with suicides. Early deaths. And rape. I don't know how it is in Lake City, but just imagine how would it be to go to the prom and then in ten years, half of the female attendees have been raped and half the males have committed suicide?"

"That would be awful." Tolly shook her head. "But it can get kind of rough in the city too."

"Yeah." Nellie blew out a breath. "I suppose so."

Tolly thought about it. "I guess there's no perfect place, really."

***

Scott dismounted.

A cloud of dust settled around his motorcycle. He clasped James Windrunner in a bear hug and held on to him longer than he meant to.

"Been real busy around here, Scott," his father told him once Scott released him.

"How so, Pop?"

"A bunch of us in the community met with some city guys from Patina to talk about green energy and green building."

"You too?"

His father nodded with a serious expression. "Some of us feel since we missed out on ownership of gas and oil maybe we can make a bid for the sun and wind, if you can imagine that."

"There's a lot of both of that in Calabasas."

"Exactly." James smiled at his eldest son. "So many of us are homeless or overcrowded into homes. And then some of us still don't have running water or electricity."

Scott sighed. "I know, Pop."

"Poor indoor air quality and poor insulation. Many homes are non-electrified."

"I remember how hard it was when I worked with housing development."

"How do you think I got my new home built?"

Scott raised his brows. "They did this?"

"Nellie's too. See what you started? We want to build more."

Scott looked around the log cabin's pine log exterior. "I like what I see here. Someone did a good job."

"Jack helped with mine and Nellie's before he left for Lake City. He remembered what you taught him about housing while you were working on the business degree."

Scott's face heated. He stared at the ground without words. He should have been here to help his father.

James shrugged it all away. "Some things we talk about now and then. Jack," he called over his shoulder, "Show your brother around the inside."

His father stepped away to speak with an old friend who passed by. The friend waved cheerfully at Jack, who emerged from the log cabin's doorway, but directed a more cautious wave towards Scott, who nodded his head, on guard.

Jack lowered his voice. "You still have her with you?"

"She's at Nellie's changing clothes." Scott wondered for a moment how his sister and Tolly were getting along. Nellie had no idea of their real relationship. At least he hoped not. "I'm taking her to Patina."

Jack led him inside. Scott was taken aback by the number of elk and deer skins that hung on the wall and the buffalo and bear furs draped of furniture. He wanted to take time to explore his father's new home, but he needed to keep his thoughts straight.

"There was nothing in her luggage," Jack told him. "So she has to have it on her." Jack looked at Scott with inquiry. "You didn't see anything last night? You know, when…"

Scott's tone was a trifle dry. "I wasn't able to search quite that thoroughly, Jack."

Jack raised his eyebrows.

Scott felt his face heat. "Just her shoulder bag," he continued gruffly. "It wasn't there. I'll keep trying. Look, stay here at Dad's. I don't want her to recognize you from the apartment or the truck stop. She saw you both times so she'll remember what you look like."

"Yeah," Jack shrugged, "I look like you."

"You look like me ten years ago when I still had dark hair. I still can't believe this place." Scott looked around the quiet, regal interior of his father's cabin.

Windrunner   77

"God, you're not that old, Scott."

"Well, she still hasn't made the connection yet."

"Oh." Jack thought a moment. "Then maybe you *are* that old."

Scott met that with a grimace. "Good one."

He walked back to his bike, waved at his father and brother. On the way back to Nellie's, his father's parting words echoed in his head. "Scott, try to maintain an even keel."

Yeah.

Nellie greeted Scott with a smile. Tolly was still in the bathroom. What was it with that woman and bathrooms?

"Your girlfriend's nice, Scott."

"Uh hunh." He gave his little sister another hug.

"It's been so long. You haven't brought anyone home since Laura."

Scott decided to change the subject. "Nellie, can we talk for a minute?"

Nellie closed the downstairs bedroom door on her and Scott's discussion.

Tolly emerged from the bathroom back to the living area. She noticed that even though most of the furnishings emanated the smell of woodsy cedar, she also detected the stale odor of cigarettes crushed in a tray. Comic books, a baseball glove, and a nail polish set partially covered water rings on a couple of end tables. The dark wood floor had been scuffed.

Tolly had just seated herself on Nellie's sofa when she heard a vehicle pull to a stop outside.

"Who the fuck parked in my goddamed space?" The front door of Nellie's house slammed open. "Nellie!" the voice roared.

A man with straight, black hair that fell past his shoulders entered. He was of medium height and build and unshaven. His eyes, though unfocused, still managed to look mean and hard. They scanned the room, trying to adjust to the interior light. It took a few moments for him to register Tolly seated on the sofa.

"Who are you?"

"Tolly. I'm a friend of Scott's." She hesitated then held out a hand.

"Oh yeah." He grabbed her hand into his sweaty palm, then stroked it with his other palm. "So Scott likes hot chocolate these days." He leered at Tolly. "I heard all about girls like you."

"Really?" Tolly commented coolly. She pulled her hand back and then wiped it on her all-purpose khakis. She reminded herself to wash it soon.

"Girls like who?" She had a feeling she already knew the answer.

He laughed, at ease. He moved into the kitchen. "Black girls."

Tolly heard Scott's voice behind her. "Just checking, Sonny. You are still married to my sister, right?"

"Scott," Nellie reprimanded. She closed the bedroom door behind her.

"Oh yeah." Sonny crossed his arms. "Me and Nellie *are* still married. Unlike you and what's her name..." He snapped his fingers together. "Oh right. *Laura.*"

The room tensed.

Sonny shrugged, walked to his refrigerator, opened it, then turned with a can of beer. "That's his ex-wife," he informed Tolly.

Tolly examined the floor, uncomfortable.

Sonny flipped the beer tab open. He leaned against the counter. "She remarried, you know. Rich guy."

He snorted then took a large swallow of beer. "Yep, she upgraded. Don't see her around the community anymore."

He took another long drink. "Me and Nellie are in it for the long haul though. In it to win it, no matter what anyone says." Sonny belched. He'd ended his obnoxious performance art on the perfect note.

"Win what?" Scott smiled. He took a step forward. "Middleweight championship? I hear you've been using Nellie for practice."

Sonny pointed an outraged finger towards Scott. "What the fuck," it took a moment for his thoughts to catch up to his finger, "are you in my house, and in my parking space, trying to imply, man? What the fuck did you tell him, Nellie? Why are you always playing games? Hunh?"

Scott took another step forward.

"How'd she get those marks on her arms, Sonny?" he asked in a quiet voice.

"What marks?"

"The marks hidden under her long sleeves even though its ninety degrees outside. I saw them just now."

Tolly bit her lip. She looked at her own long-sleeve cotton shirt. If he saw the marks on Nellie's arms, then did he also see the marks on hers? She rubbed her arms, self-conscious.

Sonny chuckled, undisturbed. "Tell him how that happened, Nellie."

Nellie remained silent.

"Go ahead. Tell him."

Tolly's stomach lurched.

"Well why don't you just shoot me, Scott? Like you do everyone else?" Sonny laughed in an ugly way. "Oh wait. I'm armed."

He pulled a folded up pocket knife from his pocket then tossed it on the dining table. He kept the beer in his hand though.

"How about now?" Sonny held up both arms and the beer in the universal tough-guy challenge. "That's what you do, isn't it?" He added a sneer to the final insult. *"Hero."*

Scott clenched his jaw. Tolly braced for what would follow.

"Yeah." Sonny steadied himself. "Go for it. Make us all proud."

"Sonny, stop it," Nellie pleaded.

"I'm your goddamed husband, Nellie!" He turned to his wife full of wounded outrage. "Good times and bad times," he slurred.

"Sonny." Nellie shook her head. "Please don't do this."

"For better or for fucking worse!" Sonny roared again with renewed energy.

"Shut up, Sonny." Scott's voice grew even quieter. "Shut up right now."

Sonny turned to Scott. "Excuse me?"

Nellie grew desperate. "Scott, please don't talk to him like that. Not in his own home. This isn't helping anyone."

Sonny's face grew redder. "This is my damn house!"

Scott tried reason this time. "Nellie, you have two children who depend upon you."

"I know that, Scott."

"Well, if you know that then," Scott finally lost control, "at least try to care about them even if you don't care about yourself." And with that, Tolly knew the conversation had no further hope of recovery.

"Fuck you, Scott!" Sonny pointed first at Scott, then at Nellie with indignation. "That's my wife you're talking to."

"She's my sister. I've known her all her life and I'll be damned..."

"She chose to be with me." Sonny thumped his chest with his fist then took another drink.

Scott started to reply, but Sonny interrupted him, too fast on the swallow. "Fuck you, man. You changed. You don't know how it is here. Not anymore. You got out and left everybody else behind."

Once again, Sonny's voice escalated in volume. Another thump of the chest. "I'm the one who stayed! I'm the one who tried to get us all out of this dump. Next thing I know, I'm laid off and everyone's got something to say about that. I've had enough!"

Sonny slammed the front door open and stormed out. "Fuck this family!"

Nellie shouted, "Sonny wait!"

"Bye, Nellie!" Sonny yelled from outside.

Scott's voice was full of disgust, "Let him go, Nellie." He thought better then decided to follow Sonny outside.

"Scott," Tolly called a warning. He ignored her, kept going out the front door.

That left Tolly and Nellie alone in the living area. They didn't look at each other.

Chapter 14

Sadness settled over Tolly. She recognized who stood in front of her. Scott's sister was where she herself used to be... with Rafael. But at least Nellie had a son and a daughter while Tolly remained childless.

Tolly swallowed a large lump down her throat.

Everything she'd tried so hard to forget played back like her own private horror movie. Tears fell from someone's face. Someone begged for love. Someone begged for forgiveness for an endless list of transgressions. Someone covered bruises and scratches with long sleeves and long pants. Then someone tied beautiful scarves and made up her face with pancake and concealer to hide the collage of ugly secrets.

Nellie excused herself to the bathroom. Tolly waited for it.

Sure enough, running water provided the perfect cover for crying. A splash of cold water took the red out of the face. Eye drops returned the whites of the eyes to their normal color.

Five minutes passed before Nellie re-entered the room.

"Nellie." Tolly cleared her throat. "I understand your situation."

"Just, please go. Both of you." Nellie struggled to keep her voice even.

Tolly looked away.

"Now's not a good time for us to... I'm sorry." Nellie indicated the door. "Please."

Tolly, nodded. She didn't wish to add to Nellie's distress. She gathered her shoulder bag then left without a word.

Outside, Scott's large frame leaned against the logs of Nellie's house. She didn't see Sonny anywhere. In a small act of mercy to the entire Calabasas community, he'd left his car parked at a crooked angle across the small lawn.

Scott sighed, "Sorry you had to see that."

Tolly touched his arm. "It's okay. It's not your fault, Scott." But Tolly did wonder how much Scott's military service contributed to his protective streak. "Not entirely, at least."

"Thanks," his tone was wry. Scott shook his head with regret. "Obviously, I cause more problems than I solve. Which has always been the case around here."

He indicated his bike. "Let's go."

Tolly mounted behind him.

"I'm going to have a quick word with Pop again, give him the latest update. Then we'll figure something out." He turned to Tolly with a slight smile. "Okay?"

"Okay." She smiled back at him. They cruised through Calabasas. Scott pointed out the occasional landmark with shouts though his hair whipped her as usual so she didn't see much. Minutes later, he brought the bike to a halt in front of a newly-constructed log cabin similar in style to Nellie's.

He made the introductions. Right away, Tolly noticed that Scott inherited his large build from his father. However, while Scott's hair had silvered, his father's hair remained salt and pepper, mostly pepper. Tolly tilted her head, puzzled.

"James," the older man told Tolly to call him. She nodded and smiled.

"How's Nellie?" James asked his son.

"Pop, I don't even know why I came here. It's the same old story."

Tolly started to walk away to allow Scott and his father their privacy. Scott stayed her with a light hand around the waist. Surprised by the intimate gesture, she stood still. If Scott's family wondered about their relationship, they would wonder no longer. With that subtle move, they would assume she was his girlfriend.

"She needs to know that she has people who care about her, Scott. People she can turn to. Sonny needs to know that too. Your sister tried to marry a man like her eldest brother."

"I am nothing like Sonny, Pop." The hand around Tolly's waist tightened. "He's nothing like me."

James inclined his head. He sat in one of the chairs in the front yard, then gestured for Tolly and Scott to sit near him. Scott finally released his hold. Tolly missed the warmth of Scott's touch. He moved his chair closer to hers.

"He's a punk, Pop. A coward and a bully. We all know he is. Why can't she see that?"

James leaned his head back to examine the stillness of sky. His long curtain of silver-threaded black hair hung down. "Perhaps your sister mistook aggression for courage. But, you are right, son. They are not the same."

Scott leaned back in his own chair. "Well, what's it going to take?" he asked, weary. "This has been going on for years. Short of throwing Sonny off a cliff, I'm out of ideas."

James and Tolly chuckled. A restful quiet settled.

Scott's father cleared his throat. "You know, in marriage, there is a balance. For better. For worse. In your case... with Laura."

Scott shot Tolly a quick glance. This was the second mention of Laura, Scott's ex-wife. Tolly shifted in her chair. James continued either oblivious or uncaring of either her or Scott's discomfort.

"The one time things got worse, Laura forgot all about the other better times."

Out of the corner of her eye, Tolly watched as Scott gazed into the distance.

James proceeded with his consideration of the lives of his children. "In Nellie's case, the few better times she remembers with Sonny make her forget all the worse times. The two children Sonny gave Nellie, whom she loves dearly, whom we all love, cause her to forgive all the bad he's done and maybe will do. Things get out of balance."

"One of these days I'm gonna..." Scott's voice roughened. He clenched his fists.

In that moment, Tolly understood the anger, disgust, and frustration her own relatives felt during Rafael's reign of terror over her life after her mother died. She became less of a person. She refused to take action. Her guilt and her family's judgment widened a gulf that Tolly still had not overcome, not that she'd tried.

James, expert storyteller, cut into her memories. Tolly noted that Scott, like his father, never raised his voice, but each man knew how to make a point heard and understood.

"Sonny lacks compassion. You do not lack compassion, Scott."

Scott relaxed next to her.

"Someday, hopefully soon, Nellie will understand the difference. Nellie has to change her circumstances just as Jack changed his. *Nellie* has to find her own way."

James, content to allow his eldest son to roll those thoughts through his head, turned to smile at Tolly.

"Families are fun, aren't they Miss Tolly?"

"I," Tolly looked down and away, "wouldn't know."

James contemplated the sky. "Scott, I see you've got your lady friend with you. Why don't you and she bunk at the cabin tonight?"

Scott looked at his father's cabin, uncertain. "Okay, if you're sure there's room." He had to figure out what to do about Jack. Now way could he allow Tolly to see the same man she saw on her doorstep and at the truck stop.

"I was thinking it might be a good time to do some weatherization on it."

"Weatherization on the cabin?" Scott repeated. Again, he looked at his father's cabin, this time puzzled. Jack just told him he'd weatherized Pop's cabin before he left for Lake City.

"The cabin down by the lake, the spot where you and Jack used to go fishing. If you have a little time?"

"Oh. *That* cabin. The one down by the lake."

James smiled.

Scott looked at Tolly who nodded. "Course we can," Scott answered. "It shouldn't take too long."

"I'll get the key." James padded into his own cabin.

Scott waited a beat. "Tolly, I have no idea what he's talking about."

She shrugged back at him. "I'm here for the adventure, Scott."

"And then tomorrow, we have the community celebration." James said, returning outside. "Tolly, this is how we keep our people close with stories of battle. We observe the passage of time. What has been, what is now, what will be."

"Ha!" Scott threw his head back with a laugh. "And eat ourselves silly."

James joined in the laughter. "That too." He described dish after dish that would be on the menu that made Tolly's stomach rumble.

Scott gave her a secret smile when he heard it. She flushed.

"And, of course, I am the master of ceremonies. I have so many stories. You're in for a good time, Tolly," James promised.

Scott said something under his breath.

"What was that?" James cupped a hand to his ear. "Your father's an old man now. Can't hear so well."

Scott snorted.

"Still can't hear. Did you just ask me to pull out your baby pictures?"

Scott looked horrified. "You're not serious."

"I think I still remember where the photo album is." James turned a puzzled glance to his front door. "Next to the video tapes we made of your school plays."

"Okay, you win!" Scott shot Tolly an uncomfortable look. "We'll come tomorrow about eleven. How's that?"

"Well," James shrugged, full of innocence. "Only if you really want to."

Tolly laughed at the blatant manipulation. "Sounds like fun, Mr. James."

"Everyone will be glad to see you. You too, Scott."

"Pop, you're pushing it." Exasperated, Scott waved Tolly to the bike. "You're really pushing it. We'll be there, okay?"

She and Scott mounted, their bodies synchronized to each other's routine by now.

"I get his goat every time, Miss Tolly." James smiled at Tolly.

"What?" Scott gunned the motorcycle's engine. "What was that?" The motorcycle roared through Scott's shouts. "Can't hear you, Pop!"

She and Scott pulled out to the road with a spit of dust. Tolly looked back to see James wave with a delighted grin. The origin of Scott's naughty sense of humor became altogether clear.

Scott's hair massaged her face and neck.

Tolly laughed.

Chapter 15

Wednesday evening, from the back of his Harley, Scott reminded himself that he needed to focus. No matter how good Tolly's breasts felt pressed into his back, no matter how velvet soft her cheek moved against him, no matter how her fluffy hair tickled his neck, no matter how her sweet, low voice stroked against his ear, he had a job to do.

He shook his head. Tolly tightened her hold on his waist in response. His breath caught in his throat. She made it so hard for him to keep his hands off her. He found excuses to touch her. He felt delighted whenever she touched him. He had to remind himself over and over that Alexander King had brought them together. He had a paycheck to earn.

Scott wondered just how much Jack, safely stowed inside Pop's cabin told their father about the situation with Tolly. Scott was sure Pop knew something which was why he didn't mention Jack and also why he didn't invite them inside. But that's how conversations with his father had always gone. Things that James Windrunner said often didn't make sense until days, weeks, or years later.

For instance, the cabin where he and Jack used to fish held no reference, because as far as he knew, there was no cabin where he and Jack used to fish, just a tree house. And now he needed a key for that?

Scott made the turn that took them off the road to the lake path. Tolly leaned into the turn with him. Electricity zinged from her hold to the lightning rod below his waist.

He flinched. The bike jerked.

All of a sudden, the pine log cabin, similar in design to Nellie and Pop's two-story structure, only larger, loomed in front of them. He nearly lost control of the bike. He used that surprise to cover his reaction to Tolly's warmth. Her softness wrapped so tight around him made the stumble almost worth it.

They dismounted. Together they looked at the cabin accented by a balcony, porch, and deck, also pine. Here and there, construction debris sprinkled the yard.

"Me and Jack used to always fish here," he pointed towards the small lake. "Pop taught me, and then I taught Jack."

"What about Nellie?"

"Nellie wasn't interested. She was into girl stuff. It was always me and Pop, or me and Jack." Scott sighed. "And then I signed up for military service and everything changed."

She waited.

"Pop got older and got busy with storytelling for the community. I came back for a while, but Jack was busy with computer classes at the community college. I didn't stay around too long."

"Now, here's a cabin."

"It's nice." Tolly looked at the impressive structure. "How long do you think it's been here?"

"Beats me." Scott stood arms akimbo. "Not too long. Let's go inside."

Tolly found tools, equipment, and supplies. And so, at the request of James, Tolly and Scott spent their second night together in a log cabin on the lake. First, they cleared the front yard and the interior of sawdust, bits of wood, and other random pieces.

Already, the new construction looked better for their efforts. Though empty and bare of the essentials that made a house a home, Tolly dusted what cedar furnishings there were. Scott swept the floors. Scott took out the trash. Tolly cleaned the windows.

Then Tolly took charge of weatherization. She argued with Scott that since he did most of the driving, and provided room and board, that was the least she could do. To his amusement, he waited for her instructions. She pointed him towards a drill.

"Aye, aye, captain." He snapped a sharp salute.

Tolly laughed. Even after emotional conflict, Scott's humor never failed to return. She realized that she liked that about him.

She took up a caulking gun and got to work which always calmed her mind.

Scott peeked at her now and then. When Tolly caught him, she explained that she learned how to caulk from her father, a carpenter and electrician. Her mother cleaned houses. They both had higher hopes for her. They dreamed that she would attend college and make their sacrifices worth the effort. Instead, she used her college fund to invest in renovations for her building.

"Between the two of them, I learned how to handle almost every household situation." She aimed the caulking gun and fired. Direct hit. She smiled.

"Tolly, I gotta tell ya. I've never seen another woman handle a tool like that."

"Ah, here we go. Scott 'Double Entendre' strikes again."

Something in Scott's eyes flickered.

Tolly tilted her head. Something she said affected him. But he continued before she could ask about it. "I'm serious. You don't even look afraid."

Tolly winked at him. "Pretty good for a hitchhiker, hunh?"

Scott laughed.

"Come on, Scott. How can you look so amazed? Women served with you overseas, didn't they?"

"Yeah, and they did great." Scott's demeanor grew serious. "I respect their service. Hell, I'm grateful."

"So..."

"But you're a civilian."

"Who's been trained by the very best." Tolly told him, chin up.

"Yeah, I can tell." Scott walked over for a closer inspection. "These air leaks don't stand a chance, do they?"

"Nope. Air leaks never stand a chance when I'm around. Lake City is no joke in the winter time. I can save forty percent off my building's heating bill if I weatherize." Tolly caught her breath.

That was her first admission to Scott of where she lived. But Nellie, a talker, would've told him that, anyway.

"Lake City?"

"Yeah. That's where I'm from." Tolly waited a beat. "She said that you live there too."

"Uh hunh. I do." Scott examined her caulk work as if fascinated. He carried the conversation smoothly past the point of the coincidence of them both being from Lake City, headed west on the same road at the same time.

"I still remember my first encounter with lake-effect snow. All that humidity dumped foot after foot in just two days. I kept waiting and hoping for it to melt or burn off. Six months later, it finally did."

"No altitude. Lake City is flat so the snow just forms layers until spring. Sometimes summer."

"Tell me about it."

"And then we find all manner of scary things on the bottom layer."

"Snow is beautiful when it first comes down. Especially in the mountains. But doesn't last too long around here."

"Because of the altitude?" she asked him.

"Well, the altitude, yeah. But the air is so clear and dry, that a day or so later, it's gone. Unless you're at the highest elevations."

"I guess that makes the skiers happy."

Scott nodded. "They love it. So do the resorts." *Now*, he decided. "So your father and mother taught you all about maintenance?"

Tolly nodded back. "Yeah and I'm grateful. That's how I keep my head above water and save on repairs. Hard work."

"So you make ends meet?"

"I get by."

Scott calculated to himself that it was not quite the end of the month. Therefore, Tolly didn't have her rental payments in yet. She was down to eleven dollars. How did she intend to survive in Patina? He couldn't prevent the ugly answers. *Stolen cash and blackmail.*

Tolly continued, "I may get on permanently with a nonprofit agency back in Lake City. You've heard of Lake City Balance, right?"

Scott thought about it. "Oh yeah. Alternative energy and all that. Doing what?"

"Making renewable a reality," Tolly quoted the non-profit's slogan.

Scott remained quiet.

"Probably communications type work. Education and outreach. Stuff like that."

Again, Scott didn't reply. Tolly picked up her caulking gun and got back to work.

"Mmm." Scott worked a while in silence. "Sounds good. Of course, there's always bingo."

Tolly laughed. "Don't play."

"The lottery."

"Don't play that either."

"Bank robbery."

"Nope. Too high risk."

"Blackmail."

Tolly paused helding the caulking gun in the air. "What's the deal, Scott?"

He shrugged.

She examined him in return. "Are you trying to recruit me for something weird? Feeling me out for something you have in mind because I know how to use tools?"

She set the caulking gun on the floor with care.

"I don't know what kind of *business* you're into, but whatever you're thinking, the answer's no." Tolly picked up the caulking gun again. "You're mistaking me for someone else because I'm not that kind."

She jammed the point of the caulking gun into a crevice. "Ill-gotten gains don't last."

He wondered whether she referred to Rafael, killed in a prison shower, so his research told him.

"There's no such thing as get-rich-quick. Only hard work." She pulled the caulking gun's trigger with force.

"Loud and clear, Boss."

"Two the hard way. That's you and me, Scott," Tolly told him with firmness. She shifted to another wall. "Let's get this done, tonight. Okay?"

Another silence descended.

Never say die, Scott tried another tactic. "Tolly, my father is a wise man. I think he knew that Sonny might create an uncomfortable situation and that we couldn't bunk at Nellie's. Especially after my and Sonny's blowup."

"Think so?"

"He assigned us to this cabin to give us a place to stay and to prevent a meltdown."

"He's a wise man." She grinned at him sidelong. "He certainly gave you a run for the money."

"I'm sorry about that 'families are fun' remark."

"That's okay." Tolly shook her head. "He didn't know. He just met me."

"I think he understands now. It won't be a problem."

"It's okay, really."

"But I was curious, you never mention brothers or sisters."

"Don't have any."

"Cousins? Aunts? Uncles?"

"Yes."

"In Lake City?"

"I think so."

"You think so?" Scott kept his tone casual. "You mean you don't know?"

"All over the Midwest."

"Lost touch?"

"Sort of."

"Circumstances?"

"Well, you know... things happen." Scott noted the blank expression on her face and the closure in her eyes. She clamped her mouth closed. He let another moment pass. Then he walked over to squeeze her hand. "I tell you, Tolly. You caulk like a champ."

"And you drill like a god."

Scott, pleased to see her humor recover, took the bait. "That's what I'm told."

"I knew you were going to say that. It just *never* stops, does it?"

"I'm also told that. Frequently." He drilled a screw home. "And then thanked," he crowed.

"Thank you, Scott!" Tolly shouted, then fell out laughing.

Scott's grin held a bad taste in his mouth. He didn't have the heart to manipulate her any more. He much preferred to make her laugh and smile and sparkle, as she did now. Back to even keel and the air cleared, for the most part, the shimmer of tension eased between them.

Scott reached around Tolly to grab another box of screws. Her laughter stopped. Scott's heart thudded. Tolly was a job he needed to finish so that he could sever ties with Alexander King forever. He had responsibilities to his family and to his own future.

He needed to stay focused... on her mouth.

Instead of a box of screws, his hand cupped her chin. He bent his head closer to hers. He brushed his lips over hers, then once again. And once again.

"You have a lot of appeal, Tolly," he whispered against her lips. "For some reason, I keep picturing you in that white motel towel and nothing else."

She smiled, her eyes unfocused.

He stroked his hand down her arm. She trembled under his touch.

"How did you get those marks on your arms and wrists?"

She stiffened, tried to withdraw from him.

"Whoa, whoa," he told her, then pulled her body tight to his. "I'm sorry." He stroked his chin and cheek over the top of her fluffy twists. "Don't worry, no more questions, he promised.

He picked her up, and then took her upstairs where he found a bed covered with a quilt.

Three times, he insisted that Tolly cry out her acceptance of his apology. Then he held her close to his chest so they could sail away together through clouds, moonbeams, and stardust.

Chapter 16

Thursday morning, Scott stood in front of the lakeside cabin. His back faced the windows. His larger body concealed Jack's smaller frame, also hidden behind the large trunk of tree that supported their decrepit tree house.

"Search her luggage again, Jack. I'm telling you, she doesn't have anything on her."

"Are you absolutely sure?"

"I searched her myself."

"Thoroughly?"

Scott narrowed his eyes. Yes, he'd made a thorough exploration of Tolly's body. He'd rained kisses all over the creamy softness of her skin then begged for forgiveness from her breasts, her stomach, her legs...

"Nevermind." Jack put up his hands in defense. "I'm not even going to ask."

Scott flushed. "She doesn't have it with her, Jack."

"Bruce was thorough in his search of her apartment."

"Bruce left her apartment a complete, unprofessional mess."

"I know."

"But he'll damn well clean it up. Have you heard from him?"

"No. You?"

"No. Nevermind him," Scott replied. "At least he's out of our way."

"All right." Jack tried to reason it out. "So she must have given it to someone between her apartment and the bus station."

"I don't know about that, Jack." Scott ran a hand through his silver mane, but stopped when he remembered how Tolly stroked her fingertips across his scalp. He still felt the tingles.

"We were just steps behind her. She certainly didn't pass it to Lake City Balance. We'd have heard something by now. Or they would have offered her a job or some kind of compensation. She's still got nothing on her. Look, Jack, just one last time with the luggage. Take each side apart, including the wheels and handle. Everything."

"Okay, I'll do it." Jack shrugged. "But all I've seen so far are lady's things. Clothes, little boxes of snacks..."

"Cosmetics?"

"Yeah. Things like that."

"Take those apart too. And the boxes of food."

"Okay."

***

Rather than the full body hug of thick limbs wrapped around her torso, Tolly woke up alone that morning tangled in the bed sheet. She wondered what pulled her from sleep. Not Scott's snores. The quietness woke her. She missed the low, steady rumble that provided the soundtrack of their nights together.

Their first kiss put a stop to further work on the house last night. When he pressed his lips to hers, she quivered, helpless. She assumed Scott had been lost in the moment with her until he asked about the bruises. She didn't answer, but then he'd learned every secret curve and corner and crevice of her body anyway.

He'd made her shake and tremble over and over with the gentle then rough touch of his fingers. She'd lost complete control over herself. She'd cried and pleaded with him for relief, then sprawled across the bed like a limp rag doll when he gave it to her.

The bed they shared still smelled of him—windy, breezy, male.

Tolly paused mid-stretch. She overheard voices that drifted on the breeze of an early morning wind that whistled through the tiny spaces between the logs that remained unsealed on the second floor.

"I'm getting a bad feeling. Something's not square in this. I've been this place before, Jack, and I don't like it."
"I know."
"Those civilians..."
"Don't do that to yourself, Scott."
"Still..."
"You still think Alex is lying?"

Tolly crept closer to the front side of the cabin. She thought she heard something strange. She thought she heard... *Alex.* But she couldn't have. That would be too much coincidence.
But then, everyone knew Alex King, according to his mother.
Tolly listened harder. She still couldn't see the other speaker.

"He's the lying kind, Jack. It's not that far a stretch. But the thing is, we've always been on the same side." Scott paused. "Until now."
"What do you mean, until now?" Jack frowned. "Are we working for him or not?"
Scott folded his arms. "I really thought I could go the distance. At least until the end of his campaign, for the bonus, you know. I'd get a stake and then walk away. That's part of the reason I wanted you in Lake City so you could take things in a different direction, if you wanted to."

Tolly craned her head to an unnatural angle. Through the glass door to the balcony, she saw the top of Scott's silver head of thick hair and his massive back. Her heart quickened. She remembered how she clutched at that broad back and dug in her nails so that he couldn't get away.
Her legs tingled.
The other man looked somewhat familiar. He looked like... a younger Scott. *Jack*, Scott called him. The brother with whom he used to fish.
Tolly felt a sense of dread. *Walk away*, something said. But she couldn't.

"What are you trying to say, Scott?"

"I intended for you to take over Windrunner Security in practice, not just name."

"You're kidding me."

Windrunner Security.

She remembered now. The security car and two men outside her building's front door. The security car and two men at the truck stop... where she first met Scott.

His brother. His company?

Sick to her stomach, she'd heard enough. She slipped away from the window and the urgent whispers carried to her on the wind. Her heart pounded. Scott need never know that she knew about his lies and deceit. She would act normally until she could get away from his grasp.

Below, Scott continued. "I'm losing my edge. I can feel it."

"What're you talking about?"

"My head's not in the game. I can't believe the number of wrong calls I made on this case."

Scott decided not to tell Jack about the bruises on Tolly's arms. He'd upset her so the night before that he spent hours making it up to her. His body heated at the memory of her cries when she finally forgave him. He felt protective over her and her body. He would never discuss the warmth of her skin or how sweet it smelled.

"Tolly's getting to you, isn't she?"

"Not really." How could he possibly explain the way he stared at curves of her back and marveled how they fit perfectly into his hand? How could he share that he brushed the back of his hand over the cottony-soft springs of her curly hair? Never would he reveal the warmth and softness that greeted him between her legs.

"No?"

"Let's talk about it later." Scott was ninety-nine percent sure that he'd been duped by Alex.

Memories of his last mission surfaced again. Orders from his superiors directed him to action. He'd repeated those orders to the men who trusted him.

Scott closed his eyes. "I still remember them, Jack. Their voices. The screams. The shooting. And then the silence."

"Scott, don't. Stop it!" Jack snapped his fingers by Scott's eyes. "That was then. This is now. Don't do that to yourself anymore."

On the way to the shower, Tolly noticed Scott's black leather bag where he set it beside the bed they shared. Perhaps because of his distraction by his and Tolly's late night or, more likely, his early morning meeting to plan her destruction, Scott forgot to lock it.

She didn't have much time.

Tolly unzipped the soft black leather with shaky fingers. She might have misunderstood what she overheard through the cracks in the log wall. But she had to know for sure. She reached in a hand and drew out the Windrunner Security badge. She found a file folder with her name on it. Inside, sheets of paper described her appearance, her acquaintences, her finances, everything. He even had photos of her—still shots from the security cameras at Celara Wind.

"No," Tolly whispered. She dropped her head.

It became hard for her to breathe. Her head felt light and dizzy. She worked to calm herself down.

The front door to the cabin slammed. The sharp sound brought her back to focus. She stepped into the bathroom then twisted the shower knob. She could hear each of his steps on the stairs. As quickly as she could, she returned everything to his black leather bag in the order she found it. She rested the Windrunner Security badge on top. Then she jumped into the shower to scrub his touch off her. As she well knew, running water masked the sound of tears.

Underneath the warm spray, Tolly added their conversations up, including last night's baiting on robbery and blackmail. Scott withheld information her. He misled her. He lied by omission. Even the love he made to her was a lie.

Scott made her sick, but her own gullibility filled her with absolute nausea.

Her and Scott's meeting at the truck stop was neither accidental nor providential. Scott stalked her like a predator stalked prey. He used the kiss and the charm and the true confessions to break down her defenses. She fell for it like she was brand new. And maybe she was. First Rafael. Now Scott. Who could she trust anymore?

A sob escaped her. She couldn't remember which was worse, Scott's underhanded deceptions or Rafael's fists. Tolly made up her mind to flee Scott's custody as soon as she could.

Scott stared at the leather bag on the floor. It appeared unmoved, but still... He listened at the bathroom door. Tolly seemed to take a long time in the shower, even for her. He should have waited to join her. He tested the knob. Locked.

Last night, he knew that he'd made her happy. At the same time, he held back his own physical demands. But this morning, he woke with a raging hard-on. It killed him to leave her side, but he knew he had to meet with Jack before she woke. Under the cover of his own shower, he stroked to achieve the relief that he'd denied himself last night.

Scott exhaled. He returned downstairs to rustle up whatever kind of breakfast he could for her. After he found a few items that would do, he got to work at the stove and reflected on the last moments of his and Jack's conversation.

"I know Alex, somewhat," he told Jack. "He's always guarded against women using him for money, so he's somewhat paranoid. He drove his first wife to alcohol. He and his eldest daughter had some kind of falling out, so she's spending the summer in Paris with his half-sister. Celara's daughter."

Jack shrugged. "Well, that's unfortunate and maybe a bad marriage, but it doesn't make him a monster."

"The mother of his older son, Christopher, communicates with Alex through lawyers. He's allowed only supervised monthly visits. But I think he's been too busy for even that."

"Well, okay, he's a bad father too. But then a lot of men are. Sonny, for instance, right?"

"That fuckup." Scott spat on the ground.

"Now you, me, and Nellie, we lucked out with James Windrunner."

"Thank God."

"Every single day, big brother. Every single day."

Scott shuffled, restless. He'd wanted to get back inside before Tolly woke up. She looked so beautiful while she slept next to him. He wanted to slip back under the covers with her. So soft and warm. So delicious.

"I think Alex improved his efforts with the youngest girl and boy—the twins—but that has more to do with the mayoral campaign and public relations than anything else. I could tell you stories."

"Remind me of why you work for this guy again?"

"I ask myself that more and more."

"And now you want me to take over the company so that *I* can work for him? Come on, Scott."

"I'm still thinking that one over, Jack. There's a way to get through this last, and I do mean very last case for Alex. Tolly's a good person who maybe made some bad choices. I tell you, if I'd paid attention to my gut before, a lot of things would be different now."

"So what do you want to do?"

"We finish this case." Scott walked back to the cabin. "One and done."

"What about Tolly?" Jack called after him.

Scott didn't answer.

***

Tolly's eyes tried to absorb the vivid swirl of movement in the minutes before the grand entry. A multitude of women braided each other's hair and tied on beaded jewelry. Men pulled multi-colored costumes over their jeans and cowboy boots. A drum sounded the universal rhythm of a heartbeat and the ceremonies began.

During that afternoon's color guard, Scott made no move to join the march of the military veterans. He stood expressionless, his hand over his heart. Tolly stood next to him. She and Scott applauded with respect when the ceremony with the staffs and the flags concluded.

She felt Scott's tension, but made no comment on it. Despite their intimacy the previous evening, something changed in the air between them. A wall had gone up. They didn't talk to each other.

Instead, they laughed with James as he reveled in his skills as the humorous master of ceremonies and chief storyteller. He told jokes about his friends and commented on the costumes. Occasionally, he slipped in a profound statement.

"If our ancestors weren't strong, we would have died a long time ago. You can remove a person from a country, but you cannot remove the country from a person."

James called for more participants for the intertribal dance. With a smile, Scott pushed her towards Nellie and her two children, already part of the show. She held back, uncertain.

"Come on, Tolly! Show 'em what you can do! Go!" he pushed her again with a laugh.

Suddenly, she recognized this as her best chance. She'd better take it if she knew what was good for her.

Nellie's daughter skipped and shook the jingles on her dress. Her son bobbed and weaved inside his fancy dress costume. Once Nellie showed her the steps, soon Tolly skipped along with them. She made one circuit, hiding amongst the shawls and feathers and fringes.

Scott nodded at his father and then found a place in the food line, and waited for Tolly to get tired. He should be easy enough for her to spot when the music stopped—the tallest man with the whitest hair.

He scanned the crowd. Then again, he should be easy for him to spot—smooth toffee skin, a mass of curly dark brown hair, beautiful chocolate eyes, and curves that...

"Prophets control the religions of other cultures," his father announced over the music. "But Indians connect directly to the source of life—sun, light, mountains, water, trees. Still, to walk in two worlds, you have to be strong. Strong on the inside."

Scott didn't see Tolly anywhere.

**

Tolly hefted her shoulder bag filled with the toiletries Nellie supplied her the previous afternoon. She found a lift to the main road and then hitchhiked to the Patina bus station. She had five dollars in her pocket, since she gave one of her drivers three. She had food and other necessities in her luggage.

She was finished with Scott and his lies. She wanted to be done with Alexander King and his crazed efforts to control her. She needed to disappear again until after King won the primary. Scott would forget about her once King took her off his shopping list.

**

After Scott got two plates from the food vendor, he found Jack who ate with Nellie and her children. Sonny was off somewhere sulking. No one seemed to miss him. Nellie didn't know where Tolly had gone, she hadn't seen her since the intertribal dance.

"She's not with you?" Nellie asked.

Scott put the plates of food down, then walked around for twenty minutes. When he returned, he pulled his younger brother aside.

"She knows," Scott told him.

"Knows what?"

"Something. Maybe everything. She's not here. I just checked the community bathrooms and back at the cabin. She's running again. She must have seen you this morning. Or she found something in my bag."

"Did she hear us?"

"I don't know. I don't think so. We were quiet. But she's probably on her way to Patina to pick up her luggage. She doesn't have much of anything with her."

"You mean the luggage lying in pieces in the back of your pickup truck?"

"Tell everyone I'm headed out, Jack." Scott put on his sunglasses, his expression grim. "I have to find her. Stay here. I'll call you from Patina."

Chapter 17

"But ma'am, why didn't you pick up your luggage yesterday morning when you arrived?" Late Thursday afternoon, the bus station attendant was sympathetic, but not stupid.

Tolly didn't answer, because she didn't have an answer that made sense.

Ever helpful, the bus station attendant held out his hand. "Do you have your bus ticket and photo identification?"

Tolly looked at his hand. She didn't move.

"We can fill out a claim form to trace it."

Tolly knew for a fact that the name on her bus ticket didn't match the name on her identification.

"Now, I remember. Where's my head?" She smiled. "I left it in the bus locker! I can get it myself. Sorry about that."

"Well, if you're sure," the bus station attendant shrugged, just on the edge of concern.

"I'm sure. I just mixed myself up." Tolly giggled. "Sometimes I do that. All this crazy coming and going. Sorry!"

She walked back towards the bus station's row of lockers. Then she pretended to fiddle with a random lock. She glanced over her shoulder. Another customer stepped up to talk to the bus station attendant.

Tolly walked back to the bus station's front entrance.

Through the glass doors, a motorcycle with a familiar large-sized man with tan skin accentuated by silvery-white hair growled to a stop. She'd spent too much time talking to the bus station attendant.

An electric thrill of recognition ran through her body. She bit her lip. Scott had no right to her physical response, not after his deceitful behavior.

Tolly headed to the women's restroom to figure out her next move. She recalled all the quiet phone calls Scott made during their trip. He claimed that he'd spoken to his father about Nellie, and that may be so. But there was also a call he finished outside their motel room that he didn't want her to overhear. He must have given instructions to Jack to snatch her luggage while she played accidental tourist. Or did he report her whereabouts to Alex King?

She used a stall. Then, she washed her hands.

Tolly regretted her gullibility but she didn't dwell on it. King would not win and neither would his mother, the witchly-bitchly Celara.

Tolly lingered at the sink. She splashed water on her face. She looked at herself in the mirror. She would make it through this somehow. Another bus must have pulled into the station because other women entered the bathroom.

Scott wouldn't win either. If she couldn't outwait him, maybe she could outwit him.

Inside the bus station's lobby, Scott held out the surveillance photo of Tolly captured from Celara Wind's security cameras.

"She was just here a second ago asking about her suitcase. Then she remembered she left it in a locker. I don't see her now though."

"Did you see which way she went?"

The bus station attendant hesitated. Scott slid a twenty across the counter for his perusal.

An older woman, who appeared homeless, sponged herself off two sinks away. Tolly eyed her. She was short, but heavy, approximately two hundred and fifty pounds. Finally, she called it a day at the sink. She approached the hand dryer. On the way, she decided that it was time to notice the older woman.

"That's such a pretty shirt. I've never seen quite that shade of purple before. It's so shiny."

The woman stared at Tolly to see whether Tolly made her the butt of a joke.

"Why," Tolly gushed, "I'd be willing to trade this yellow cardigan that a friend of mine gave me for that shirt. It's not really my style... and... and... the sleeves are too short for me."

She ignored the stab of guilt for trading Nellie's gift. She had to do what she had to do.

The older woman gave her a sly look. "You wanna trade that for this?" She pointed to her shirt.

"Well, why not?" Tolly laughed to cover her desperation. "My friend won't know."

Agreed, they made the deal. The woman waddled away in a hurry, no doubt in case Tolly came to her senses and changed her mind. The large purple shirt smelled of perspiration.

Tolly swallowed.

Another woman, about mid-twenties, with a long tangle of hair, either dark red or bright purple entered the bathroom. She pushed a screaming baby in a stroller.

"Oh, that's lovely hair you have." Tolly pretended to straighten her new shirt that ballooned over her white t-shirt and khaki pants. "What products do you use?"

The woman rolled her eyes. "It's a wig." *Dummy*, she didn't say.

"Oh? I thought it was real." Tolly cleared her throat. "It's so pretty. It would go so well with my shirt, I just know it."

The bus attendant pretended to put the twenty-dollar bill into a drawer. Only Scott, who loomed over the counter saw it go inside the attendant's pocket.

"Why don't you check the women's restroom?" the attendant recommended. Then he got back to work, busily tapping nonsense on the computer's keyboard.

Scott positioned himself inside the bus station's lobby for a good view of the women's restroom.

Five dollars poorer, Tolly noticed a red shawl in the garbage can. It too smelled, not of perspiration, but of other things. She washed the wig, the shirt, and the shawl in the sink with industrial strength anti-bacterial hand soap. She rinsed them in hot water then wrung everything out. She dried the shirt and shawl as well as she could under the hand dryer. They hung in stiff wrinkles.

She held the matted but clean clump of magenta wig hair under the hand dryer. She decided not to comb it. She needed the wig to look messy. Her hair barrette held her long twists flat beneath the wig.

Almost done, she dumped everything from her shoulder bag into an empty plastic grocery bag that she also found in the garbage can. She used large wads of tissue and paper towels to pad her stomach to the size of a basketball underneath the purple shirt. She needed to hide her true build with which Scott had unfortunately become familiar by now. Thoughts about the intimacy of the previous night still caused Tolly pain.

In the lobby, the bus station attendant eyed Scott with unease. Then he shifted his eyes. Scott followed his line of vision to the security guard who shot him a dirty look. Scott realized that he watched the women's restroom with too much intensity.

The only way to leave the bus station besides the front door, was to board a bus. The security guard enforced this rule between the dirty looks that he continued to send Scott's direction. Tolly didn't have enough money to buy passage on another bus. So she would have to use the front door.

Scott elected to watch the front entrance of the bus station from the street. He put on sunglasses, then left for his motorcycle.

The security guard, emboldened by his successful intimidation of Scott, decided to clear the lobby of all the other riff-raff. A group of homeless drunks and crack whores followed him from the bus station's front entrance.

Scott held his breath.

The scruffy group shuffled and cat-called their way to the next destination that would have them. One of the women, extremely pregnant, grabbed a bottle of liquor, with a curse and a deranged laugh.

Scott returned focus to the bus station's front entrance.

Where was she?

***

No emails.
No phone calls.

No credit cards.

Then no way to track her.

Tolly knew if she would make it until next Tuesday, she had to go even further below the radar. She would have to survive the next few days without support, without revealing herself to Scott, and without alerting King. Her new friends shared a few best practices to survive Patina.

Some of the methods were legal.

Tolly sat in the city park. The sun eased closer to the horizon of Patina's skyline and glowed a hazy mauve over the mountains in the distance. A plethora of Patina's tourists and residents romped and strolled through the park.

She saw old married couples and wondered whether they ever rode cross-country on a motorcycle. Some of the older couples walked with adult children and excited grandchildren. She wondered how she or Scott would have behaved toward each other in a normal life—the jokes he would tell, how she would giggle, how he would kiss her.

Horse-drawn carriages and bicycle rickshaws jingled their way past cars, trains and shuttle buses. Skateboarders zigzagged their own trails. Sports fanatics and cowboys hooted and hollered. Ethnic representatives of every nation in the world promenaded through the park on their way to the great western city's downtown.

Tolly got up to follow them. While she was in Patina, she may as well experience all that was to be experienced. On the way, homeless people lay under blankets behind trees and under bushes. Being August, most didn't bother with blankets.

She wandered through full flavors of culture and language that emanated from the bookstores and cafes amid a cacophony of jazz and blues, country and western, and rock and pop music.

Tolly passed a coffee shop's patio. She circled the block. Found the patio again. She dug an empty paper coffee cup out of the trash can. She sat the used cup on the table. Then she sat down in front of it, just another customer. A shadow fell over her.

"Miss, you can stay fifteen minutes, but then you have to move."

Tolly turned to see a security guard with a "don't even try it" expression. He stood with his hand hovered over a canister of pepper spray.

"Move where?" she asked him.

"That bus stop, for instance." He pointed it out to her. "You can stay there all night if you want to. But you can't stay here. Have a good evening, miss." He walked away.

In the darkness, Tolly watched the headlights of city buses come and go past her bench. Again, her disguise worked too well. A police car drove by at a slow roll. She decided to move along before the car circled for a closer look, a call to dispatch, and then an alert by Lake City police.

On her travels through the Patina night, Tolly passed by a bed and breakfast. The outside resembled a wedding cake stretched over the architecture of a castle. Soft light glowed through the downstairs windows. Tolly imagined high ceilings, polished wood floors, expensive fabrics, and Victorian furniture illuminated by candles and multi-colored lamps.

Breakfast.

Tolly's stomach grumbled and growled. She'd been so sickened by what she found in Scott's bag that she fled Calabasas before getting a meal, the meal that James Windrunner described in succulent detail. Big mistake. Her last meal prior to that was the quick breakfast that Scott prepared for them at the cabin.

Scott.

Tolly refused to think of him further. She winced when her stomach growled again. Chainsaw, Scott called it. She erased the smile that formed at the memory. Scott said and did a lot of things he didn't mean.

Tolly swallowed a few times to settle her stomach. She walked around the block to get a feel for the neighborhood and to let the night fall darker.

Scott did not lie to her. But he didn't tell her everything. But then, neither did she tell him everything.

He'd seduced her. She let him because she needed him. And he knew she needed him. So he gave her everything she'd begged of him. Almost. She'd begged for him to fuse his body completely to hers, the final human connection, but he turned her down.

Her face burned. Now she knew why. He wanted her dizzy and breathless while he maintained his control over her. What a business consultant, he was. No, detective. For Alexander King.

Tolly fell asleep on the patio furniture in the back yard of the bed and breakfast, surrounded by flowers and Victorian splendor.

Chapter 18

The city buses of Patina woke Tolly before dawn, Friday morning. By now, she reasoned that the interstate bus station's night shift must have gone home. She wouldn't be recognized by the morning shift. She pulled off her disguise. It attracted the wrong kind of attention. She needed to use the bus station's bathroom before the first buses rolled in.

She sponged herself off, then sat inside the bus station to try to figure out the next plan of action. In order to blend in, she carried on a conversation with a janitor on his way home to family in Los Angeles.

But the bus station's security guard announced, "Anyone without a ticket, please consider yourselves advised to leave."

Tolly left. So did several of her comrades from yesterday evening.

She felt light-headed. She couldn't remember where she wanted to go or from where she'd just come. The others headed to a day shelter for breakfast. Having no other plan, Tolly walked with them.

One of the staff spooned scrambled eggs, stewed tomatoes, and rice on a plate. She got juice from a side counter then took a seat. As was her custom, she faced the window. Through the glass, a news team parked its van outside. A woman with perfectly coiffed hair entered the shelter with a man who carried a camera at his side. She reminded Tolly a little too much of the brittle Celara King. The news team exchanged a few words with the shelter's director who nodded. Her homeless comrades didn't miss a trick.

"Oh, here we go again."

"Get ready for fifteen minutes of fame."

"Get ready for the homeless reality show."

They cackled together about it.

Tolly knew she had to keep off the radar. She didn't want to find out the hard way how far King's reach stretched… again. Been there, done that. Bruises to show for it.

She finished her eggs, rice, and tomatoes as quickly as she could. Then she turned away from the table to pull the rat's nest of a wig back on. It swung forward and covered most of her face.

Her comrades didn't miss that trick either.

"Miss, there's another shelter where cameras aren't allowed."

"Oh?" Tolly shrugged. "Where's that?"

They told her the address.

"It's not popular though."

"She's real strict," another added his two cents.

"Why? Is it religious?"

"No, because you have to work for your meal."

"Well I can do that."

"That's more than some are willing to do," the first man told her. "I hear the food's good."

"Thanks." Tolly nodded to the table. When she left, she made sure to turn her head away from the camera.

Mid-morning, Tolly sat in the park again. She tried to remember how her life got to this point, but nothing made much sense anymore. No one was who they seemed. Not Alexander King. Not Scott Windrunner. Not even Tolly Henry.

She closed her eyes, then snapped them wide open. She didn't want to be told to "move along" for sleeping in public.

She found a street map of Patina in the public library. She also saw a sign that advertised a lecture and "refreshments served." It would start in an hour. Great. She'd be there.

In the meantime, she scanned the latest newspapers for wire stories on the King-Yashuda mayoral rivalry in Lake City. Alex King's game of cat-and-mouse twisted the Yashuda campaign to knots via Lake City media during debates:

We need to make sure that the candidate sent to the general election is actually electable. I am electable. Tina Yashuda is not. She's a fine person and would make a great contribution to any administration in a support capacity. In fact, I would love to have her on my team. However, numbers don't lie and polls as recent as yesterday show that Lake City voters do not have confidence in Tina Yashuda's ability to lead this city forward to a national standing.

The King campaign crushed the upstart primary challenger, considered dead-in-the-water, in multiple interviews:

The next mayor of Lake City must have the ability and the skill and the strength and the confidence to negotiate and form the necessary coalitions to improve infrastructure, to make hard decisions, and to bring jobs. My record shows that I have done that and I will continue to do that.

The Patina Public Library's copy of *Lake City Tribune* predicted an easy victory after he told them:

> I was born here. I live here. Lake City is the greatest city on Earth. There's no place like it. But the voters want to know. Why are we settling for less? Why don't we make Lake City even more world-class than it already is? Why don't we take it to the next level? I believe in that same vision with all my heart...

Tolly bit her lip.

That sinking feeling in her stomach was not hunger. It was guilt and shame. And fear.

She may as well admit it to herself even if she couldn't admit it to anyone else. Alexander King intimidated her. Because of that intimidation, she'd concealed evidence of his unstable, abusive behavior. Years after Rafael finished her conditioning, King picked up the baton.

Tolly shivered. She dropped the newspaper back upon the shelf and walked far away from it.

***

Jack called Scott. "Did you find her?"

"No." Scott didn't elaborate further.

"Well, what happened? Did you go to the bus station?"

"I did." Scott paused. "They remembered her because she asked about her luggage."

"There's nothing in her luggage, Scott. Nothing. Not a thing."

"Right." Scott's voice flattened. "I waited at the front entrance. Then I went back inside. The security guard let me look at the security tape." Hip to Scott's game, the security guard held out for his own twenty-dollar bill.

"And?"

"She wore a disguise. So we're even."

"What do you mean a disguise? How are we even?"

"She walked right past me at the bus station. I didn't even see her."

"How'd that happen?"

"She dressed up like a crack whore."

"A crack what?"

"You heard me."

"Wow." Jack chuckled. "Way to go, Tolly."

"I'm not kidding, Jack. I don't like it. None of it. We did her wrong. We took everything from her. She's penniless. She's hiding. I don't know where to find her now. I couldn't return her belongings even if I could."

"Well, we'll just have to fix it somehow."

"You know, Jack, a few of us vets had moments when we looked at the enemy combatants, our so-called enemies and realized that they looked a lot like us. And we wondered, really wondered. Kind of the way I'm wondering now."

***

Tolly sat inside the library's lecture hall near, but not too near, a table full of little sandwiches, chips, and cookies.

A man spoke about a musical instrument that resembled nothing Tolly had ever seen before. But even the smallest similarity to Scott, the musician had a full head of silver hair, caused Tolly to shudder. Her body would not allow her mind to forget the man who betrayed her. The musician played a few notes then looked with expectation at the small audience of four—Tolly plus three other people who wore library badges.

Tolly tried to think of a relevant question to ask about the music in case the library's security guard told her to "move along." Nothing came to her mind. But none of the guards took notice anyway. The lecture ended.

She walked past the table for another bag of chips. Her eyes lingered over the silver-haired musician. Then she moved herself along to the park to consider her circumstances for a while longer.

She felt sad while she watched the children play. She didn't know if her mood darkened because of the children or because of Scott. Probably both. She missed the man who made her body bubble like sparkling champagne. The man who betrayed her. The man she thought she knew.

***

"Alex King," a familiar voice snapped in his ear.

"What is on Tolly Henry's video?"

"What're you talking about, Scott?"

Scott didn't even want to consider the thought, let alone voice the question aloud, but he needed an answer. "Did Tolly Henry seduce you, Alex? Is the actual seduction on the video?"

Alex remained silent.

The thought of Tolly's hands anywhere on Alex, or worse, his hands on her, sickened him. He determined to keep his voice level. Demon that he was, Alex feasted upon the emotions of others.

"Did she steal cash campaign contributions?"

"I told you..."

Scott cut him off. "How much?"

"How much what?"

"And why were you carrying so much cash on you, in the first place? Why didn't you deposit it or leave it in your office or your car?"

"What's this about Scott?"

"Which documents did she steal?"

"You tell me. You have her with you, don't you? Ask her."

Scott didn't respond.

"Don't tell me, Scott."

"Tell you what?"

"Never did I ever think I'd see the day that you fell for the backstroke." Alex laughed. "Looks like our little Tolly knows how to work what she's got."

"Still waiting on some straight answers."

Alex laughed again. "Not Mister Steel and Brick and Stone himself. By the way, how's things out in Calabasas? Family okay?"

Scott's voice became quieter. "What did you just say?"

"Your father, James Windrunner, still telling those old-timey stories, is he? Nellie and the kids... your brother, Jack, just starting out in life, isn't he?"

Scott squared his jaw.

"You know, for some reason, Bruce didn't like him. Or you. He's thinking... maybe somewhere along the way he got screwed. Because he's certainly not getting paid. Not by me. I told Bruce to collect his fee from you and Jack, and the rest of the Windrunners for *screwing up my fucking deal.*"

"I really wouldn't do that if I were you."

"For all I care."

"You sick fuck."

"Sick fuck." Alex laughed. "That's rich. You calling *me* a sick fuck? *You?* Hey everybody! Scott "Double D" Windrunner's calling me a sick fuck! Classy."

White heat rendered Scott speechless. He should have known before he made the call how the conversation would end.

"Listen close to me, Windrunner. I will *ruin* you. I will destroy you and anyone who looks like you. Anyone who has your name or breathes the same air as you. I hired you when no one would spit on you to wipe the dirt you brought back from the war off you. And you're gonna try to challenge me and my word? Who the fuck do you think you are?"

Scott accepted what he already knew, what he'd always known.

Alex was full of shit.

"I want to know the real reason I'm after this girl."

"You don't even want to know the things I could do to you." Alex continued with a low laugh. "I want that bitch brought back. I want that video. Everything! You will not be allowed to fuck with my thing. And that bonus? Yeah, you'll still get it. Unlike you, I do what I say I'm going to do. I keep my promises and my loyalty."

"And fuck you very much for that, Alex."

"Just bring everything back to me before the primary like you sat here in *my goddamed office and said you would!* Don't worry.

You'll get your money, Scott. And then we're fucking done with each other after that."

**

Tolly walked towards Canela Street, the shelter her new homeless friends told her about. According to the bulletin board, she could make phone calls, use computers, and read newspapers and books. She could stay cool in the summer. She could stay warm in the winter. They would help her to find housing and provide job training.

There weren't too many takers today. Crawfish on the lunch menu scared many away.

Tolly looked around the dining area. She was familiar with crawfish because both of her parents migrated from the South to Lake City before her birth. Until she became too weak, Tolly's mother made the small shellfish a regular part of the Henry menu. Tolly contemplated the large pile of crustaceans boiled to a bright red. Her stomach chainsawed again. Nothing wrong here that she could see. Indeed, it felt good to see a full plate of food.

She held one of what one of the shelter's clients referred to as "bait" and "mudbugs." Then she went to work on it. Astonished that she chewed and swallowed, the others offered her their piles. Tolly calmly waved them over. They clattered their empty plates onto her table then took off.

A nametag identified Valerie, the director who looked about her mother's age. She perked up at Tolly's demolition of several piles of the shellfish.

"You're one of the few people who look happy today."

"These are good." Tolly cracked open a crawfish. "So's the rice."

"The rest of them think we're feeding them bait. Say they look like bugs."

"More like tiny, lobsters."

Valerie laughed then walked away to clear dishes off an empty table. Tolly tracked her movements out of the corner of her eyes. Survival odds had been in her favor until now, but she knew she had to get off the street as soon as possible. She didn't know this city.

The work-exchange deal with Bill Martinez for her building worked for Mr. Martinez and her father for years. Maybe something similar could work for her at least for the next few days.

Tolly finished. She cleaned her place at the table and the places the others abandoned after they gave up on the exotic lunch. Then she sought the shelter's director.

Valerie greeted her from the reception desk. "Need some help, miss?"

Tolly tried a smile. "I was about to ask you the same thing."

"I saw you clean the tables." Valerie eyed her sidelong, then shuffled a few papers on the desktop. "I need to work on a grant application to keep this place going." Valerie wiped her forehead. "But I can't seem to find the time."

She sighed as she looked around the messy dining room. "I don't have enough volunteers, but I still have to keep an eye on the volunteers that I do have. And the supplies. And the cleaning. And the check-ins. All the paperwork to keep track of who comes and goes and what services they use."

Tolly approached closer to the reception desk, but kept a respectful distance. The last thing she wanted to do was get in Valerie's face or on her nerves.

"I used to manage an apartment building."

"Used to?" Valerie looked sympathetic. "Don't tell me. You got laid off too?" She shook her head. "Is that how you wound up at Canela Street?"

"Somewhat." Tolly nodded. "I'm... trying to get my feet under me. Trying to figure out the next move."

She risked another step closer to the director. "You know, I could help you with the rest of it today." She glanced over her shoulder at the dining room. Most of the visitors chose not to clear their places, figuring since they didn't eat lunch, they didn't owe Valerie any chores.

Valerie considered Tolly's proposition the same way Tolly considered her lunch, trying to find something wrong with it. "You got time?" she asked, at last.

"Mostly." Tolly decided to clear another table as a demonstration. "I have to find a place to sleep tonight, but I'll worry about that later."

Trial balloon sent into the air, Tolly got to work.

***

Friday afternoon, Scott called his brother. "Jack, I need you to stay in Calabasas to watch over Nellie and Pops."

"Why? Because of Sonny?"

"No. Not Sonny this time."

"Scott, are you angry about my performance on this investigation?"

"No, Jack. Like I said, I've already made several mistakes myself. Both of us in Patina would make finding Tolly easier, but something's changed." Scott explained to Jack what Alex threatened against the Windrunner family. "While you're in Calabasas, I need you to get on a computer to investigate Alex King's weaknesses and vulnerabilities. I mean you have to deeper than you've ever gone with the past cases I sent you."

"You know I can do it, Scott."

"That's life in the big city, bro," he finished. "I need you to keep watch on the family. I'm going to stay in Patina to find Tolly. She's not safe either."

"Sounds like you care about her."

"We broke into her apartment. We stole her luggage. We chased her cross-country. *I* lied to her. All that based on the word of a man who would sell his own mother if he thought it would be good for business. That is, if she didn't sell him first."

"Someday he'll be president of the United States."

"Not if I can help it. I have to find her, Jack. I'll stay in touch."

Tolly didn't have any money—either hers or Alex's. He didn't know the story about the video other than the interview that Jack recovered from her computer, full of Alex's false modesty. Tolly Henry obviously either had something stashed or she knew something that still posed a direct threat to Alex. He'd never seen Alex this frantic. Not for years, anyway.

Scott started the truck. He had to find her. He needed to protect her. He needed to fold her into his arms and tell her that he would either make it all right or die trying.

This time, he targeted the low-income side of town, desperate to discover any information about Tolly's whereabouts. He paid people on the street, in shelters, and at food banks to identify Tolly's photos with and without her disguise.

Hours later, Scott located the shelter where Tolly ate breakfast that morning. A few dollars more bought him directions to Canela Street, the place to which Tolly's breakfast companions referred her for lunch. He didn't see her in the lobby.

By then, dusk had fallen. Scott decided to drive back to the cabin in Calabasas for an early night. He was exhausted and needed to sleep.

The cabin seemed too quiet without the sound of Tolly's laughter. He took another look at the work they did on the first floor. She was so damn good.

He loved the nights he spent with her, including the first night in the motel. She ignited whenever he so much as drew a breath to speak to her. He relived the second night in the cabin, the moments when she trembled inside the circle of his arms. Then she tucked her head under his chin, satisfied from his loving touch. He'd felt so proud that it was he and no other man who set her off like firecrackers.

He imagined him and her in a boat together with fishing poles. Maybe they'd pick tomatoes for a salad to go with the fish they caught. He'd tell her his corny jokes. Her face would light up with laughter. He'd kiss her and then... he imagined her spitting in his face when she confronted him.

The wind blew in lonely and mournful through the logs of the cabin's second story walls and stirred the sawdust that remained on the floor. His night filled with dread.

The nightmare came to him as he knew it would. Women and children screamed in fear at the sight of him. They cowered away from the destroyer of lives. Their eyes bulged. Their mouths begged for the mercy of a quick death, for an end to the pain.

One of the screaming women had toffee brown skin and chocolate eyes and fluffy red-brown hair.

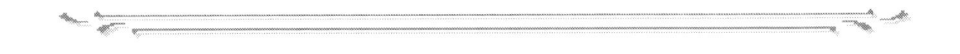

Chapter 19

"I've been to Santa Fe, but Albuquerque is better," Valerie said. Her hands shuffled sheets of colored paper into collated stacks for Tolly to staple.

"Better how?" Tolly asked then pounded the stapler closed.

"Santa Fe's one of the most beautiful places I've ever seen but tourists are more tolerated than welcomed there."

"How do you mean?"

Valerie sighed. "The city bus driver refused to look at my map to help me with directions and then he berated me for asking. Then he passed the bus stop I asked for so I had to walk a long ways back to get to where I needed to go. And it was a hot day, I can tell you."

"What else?" Tolly asked. She tossed the bundle of papers onto a growing pile.

"Well, I stayed at a hotel which was more hostile than hospitable. 'Where are you coming from? Where are you going?' they asked me."

"Why'd they ask you that?"

"Which is what I asked them. They said, 'We don't serve people from Albuquerque here.'"

"I told them, 'Good thing I'm not from Albuquerque.' After they checked the address on my identification, they let me stay." Valerie's hands flew back and forth.

"So other than the bus driver and the hotel, how was the rest of Santa Fe?"

"Hmm." Valerie tapped a pencil. "Got real frosty looks from the locals. A resident told me he admired Santa Fe's arts and the environment, but not the social climate. That the locals were mostly affluent, upper middle class Whites who enjoyed the food, clothing, and culture of other ethnicities, but not the people."

Tolly slammed the stapler closed. "I wonder why."

Valerie shrugged. "I stopped by the public library. I told the librarian that I wasn't a resident, just visiting. She goes, 'Well then we can't help you.' Then she said that she was kidding."

"Interesting."

"Sure. But that's not all. This store owner, I think it was an art gallery, happens to see me. He tells his store employees to lock the doors as they've been having problems with homeless. He looked at me when he said it."

"Wow."

"I went to the office of a weekly newspaper to to ask about a job opening they'd advertised. The editor told me that I was 'aggressive.' I decided to take the next train out of town. I went to the coffee shop in the depot. The barista spilled my drink all over the cup then handed the wet cup to me."

Tolly waited.

"I drank it." She shrugged again. "No big deal, right? But I'm still thirsty. So I waited at the counter to order another drink. The barista looked at me, then kept talking to another customer. She didn't get up until a White couple came through the door. Then she turned to serve the White couple. It was just ridiculous."

"So what did you do?"

"I raised my voice to speak over the man who tried to order past me. He was offended, but so what? I ignored him, the same way he ignored me. Got my drink. Got on the train. Left. Have not been back."

Tolly laughed. "I hear the weather's great there."

"As a matter of fact the weather's wonderful. A guy I met in Albuquerque told me that he likes Albuquerque because of the colleges and universities. I asked him what he thought about Santa Fe. He also noticed the strange behavior. Santa Fe's the capital city, but it's isolated for a reason. So, I'd say, if Patina doesn't work out for you, then Albuquerque might be the best choice. But I happen to like Patina."

Valerie's hands stilled between the stacks of paper. "I guess what I'm trying to say is, there's no perfect place."

Tolly hesitated, then continued to staple. Valerie reminded her too much of her own dear mother—stories that ended in lessons.

"You aren't here for long, are you?" Valerie asked—questions that had no answer.

***

Alex looked as if he'd put in a long day at Celara Wind. His eyes glimmered blue-white. "Scott's gone renegade," he muttered.

"You mean he's gone native, Boss." Bruce laughed.

A smile ghosted Alex's face to acknowledge Bruce's attempt at humor. "My friends down at the police station tell me that Scott's near Patina, probably Calabasas, where he's from."

"How do they know that?"

"He's using his cell phone."

Bruce nodded.

"Bruce, she's turned his head around—the big one and the little one. Where you find one, the other's close. You find him, you find her." Alex paused, his eyes hardened to stones. "What do you say? Ready to give it another try?"

Bruce nodded.

Alex stood up. "You know what to do. Stay in touch." He shuffled a few papers from his desk into his briefcase.

Bruce got up, then walked through the office doorway. To his surprise, Celara King stood just outside. She took his arm in a firm grip.

***

The sun set hours ago. Valerie flipped the blinds over pitch black windows shadowed by trees. Tolly decided she'd better speak up.

"Like I said earlier, I need to find a place to sleep tonight. Unless you need any more help tonight, I'd better make a move."

"Well, we're still backed up on laundry."

"Laundry's no problem for me," Tolly said without hesitation. She flipped the other blind closed. "Whites white. Brights bright."

Then she waited.

"The thing is we have that long waiting list for the beds." Valerie sighed and walked back to the reception desk.

"I know." Tolly followed her.

A light went on in Valerie's eyes. "Tell you what, Tolly. I've got a cot in the back. Sometimes I need a rest during the day, or when I work late." Again, Tolly noted the maternal foundation of Valerie's personality.

Tolly dared not to speak.

"You stay there tonight. I'm going to work on this grant probably until midnight." Valerie walked Tolly back to a small spare room next to the laundry. "See that bathroom? You can use that." A layer of kindness over the motherly base.

"Yes ma'am."

"So get yourself some soap and towels," she said, reminding Tolly of her mother. "And while you're back there, you can check out the laundry situation. See if you're still up for it. I'm locking the outside doors before I go home." A layer of concern.

"Okay."

"If you leave in the night, you lock yourself out for the night. I don't come back to let you in. Stay inside." Valerie sat with a long sigh in her office chair.

"Deal."

Valerie eyed Tolly. "You gonna be all right?"

"Yes ma'am."

"No trouble out of you?" A layer of stern.

"No ma'am."

Frosted over by a layer of sweetness. "If things are all right in the morning, we can do it again."

"Yes ma'am." Tolly could have cried but she didn't want to make Valerie nervous.

Negotiations concluded to her satisfaction, Valerie flicked on her desk light and positioned her laptop for more work.

Tolly figured out the laundry routine. She filled the washer and dryer. She reserved beds at the shelter from the waiting list, checked in clients, handed out towels and toiletries, and cleaned rooms. Then she rotated the laundry loads, and folded the linen into neat stacks.

She took a break in Valerie's small room. Then she went back into the kitchen to chop vegetables and to prepare the dining area for tomorrow's breakfast and lunch the way she remembered the set-up from earlier that day. Just before midnight, Tolly switched the last laundry loads. She washed then retwisted her hair. She flopped herself into the little bed and waited for sleep to take her away from it all.

But other than the distant rumble of the dryer, the room seemed too quiet. Despite her best efforts, a sob escaped her before she could smother it in the back of her throat.

She'd done it again. She'd bent down and allowed Scott Windrunner to step onto her back in order to stand on a pedestal the same way she had for Rafael. From that pedestal, he kicked her square in the face.

She must have imagined the closeness and intimacy they shared. All of it lies. Why did he betray her? Didn't he feel anything?

***

Scott looked out of the second floor window of the log cabin, nerves taut. His mouth thinned to a line.

Days like this, he felt like an oversized, Frankenstein's monster, dead pieces of a man sewn together with silence and denial.

He wouldn't sleep tonight.
He couldn't sleep tonight.

***

Cock of the walk, Bruce whistled as he strutted to Scott's security car with renewed confidence. He was a man with a purpose. He was a man people counted on to get the job done right.

Bruce knew how to handle things provided he had the proper tools and proper information as well as sufficient motivation. Now he had all three.

A man with a pocketful of cash and free reign to wreak vengeance and havoc across the Southwest would have no problem finding two homeboys for a cross-country field trip filled with adventure.

They would hit the road at first light.

Chapter 20

Saturday morning, Tolly woke to the smell of bacon and coffee. She dressed in the small bathroom. She folded the bedding on the cot then put her tiny stack of belongings inside her plastic shopping bag.

She followed her nose to the kitchen to find Valerie already hard at work. Tolly helped her serve.

Recovered from the menu of the previous day, breakfast diners filled nearly every seat in the shelter. Tolly rushed through the dining area setting platters of eggs, bacon, hash browns, and toast in front of those in need. She approached a table where a large man sat by himself, his back to the room. He wore a brown knit shirt, ragged jeans, and a red scarf over silver hair. Again, her heart leapt. Why couldn't she forget Scott?

"Here you go, sir. Don't want you to be left out."

The man turned his head, closed his hand over hers, then took the plate.

Tolly gasped.

Scott Windrunner's dark eyes crawled over her.

"Thank you, ma'am," he replied, his voice low and grave. He began to eat.

He scooped up a large spoonful of hashbrowns. He shoved them into his face and chewed.

"Scott..." She didn't know what to say.

"Wait." Scott held up one hand. He tried the bacon with the other. "Mmm. Not done yet."

"What are... how did..."

"Mmm," he groaned again.

It wasn't possible. She took such care. No one followed her. She knew that. So how did he keep finding her?

Valerie must have noticed Tolly's preoccupation. She walked over with a concerned expression.

"Tolly, how's everything over here?"

Tolly and Scott eyed each other, then looked at Valerie.

"We're old friends." Tolly decided to get her story out first. There was no telling what Scott would say.

Scott leaned back in his chair to watch the show.

Face aflame, Tolly admitted, "We knew each other, back in the day." *Back in yesterday.*

Valerie looked from Tolly to Scott, then back to Tolly. "You don't say."

"Right," Tolly answered.

Scott took another unconcerned bite of bacon.

Valerie sensed something strange, but probably realized she wouldn't get the full story from either of them. "Tell you what," she said. "You take a break, Tolly. You've been working hard this morning. I'm going to bring you a plate."

Scott shoved the chair next to him from under the table with a large foot, an invitation for Tolly to sit next to him. She complied with reluctance. Then she and Scott exchanged glares for a full silent minute. Valerie's return with Tolly's breakfast plate forced them into a jolly exchange that ceased the second Valerie walked out of earshot.

Again, Tolly took the initiative. "You lousy, lying motherfucker."

"Thanks for saying good-bye, Tolly."

"You've got a lot of explaining to do, Scott Windrunner of Windrunner Security Company."

"So you do know about that."

"I know everything!"

"Then there's nothing for me to explain."

Tolly pointed a finger at him in accusation. "I found it all, Scott. I found your badge. I found the file on me. You've been hunting me down, lying to me, deceiving me, trying to seduce me."

"Tolly..."

"I heard everything yesterday!"

"What exactly did you hear?"

"Everything!"

"Everything?"

"I heard enough to know that you work for Alex King. You and your brother, Jack."

"What else?"

"Wasn't that enough, you lying jerk?" Tolly stabbed his chest with her finger. "Don't you dare try to deny it, Scott. Not to my face."

"You might notice that I haven't denied a single thing."

Valerie walked back over, still puzzled by their fierce whispers. She asked Tolly and Scott to help with the dishes once they finished eating. Silence descended. Neither of them took another bite of food. Then Tolly led Scott back to the kitchen.

This time, Scott took the lead. "Tolly, we talked before about my military service."

"What's that got to do with anything at all?"

"I was dishonorably discharged."

"Oh," she answered.

"Yeah. *Oh*. That's the usual reaction. Then people wonder what caused it. Then they decide they don't want to know."

Tolly nodded. Fellow diners clattered their plates into the bins next to the sink. She started hot water.

"Whatever," Scott continued. "Having that mark on my record made traditional employment difficult, if not impossible. An employer sees that double d then looks at me with the same repulsion as someone with a felony conviction."

Tolly dropped the plate she intended for the soapy water. Scott, quick as ever, caught it and then handed it back to her.

"I used my business background and military training to open Windrunner Security Company. But that double d never leaves you."

"Double..."

"It stands for dishonorable discharge."

Tolly nodded. She started the water again. That was why Scott flinched when she called him Double Entendre. He thought she was about to say something else.

"Anyway, I'm not proud of this... episode. How could I be? I made a deal with the devil."

"King?" Tolly guessed.

Scott waited for someone to finish scraping a plate. "He contracted Windrunner Security for few simple jobs. I completed them. Suddenly, Windrunner Security was the go-to for just about everything Alex needed. I didn't notice until it was too late that the jobs had gone too far past strange."

"He hired you to track me down?"

Scott nodded, then picked up a towel to dry the dishes.

"Then why are you still working for him, Scott? You know what he is, don't you?"

"Yes, Tolly. I do know what he is. Now more than ever. I also know what I've done for him. But more than that, I also know what I am and what I'm not."

Tolly gave him a quick look. "Does that mean you'll turn me loose?"

Scott set down a plate with care. "Been thinking about this case. You." Scott exhaled, started to run a hand through his hair. Instead, he tugged off the scarf. "I'm planning to retire."

Tolly's eyes widened.

He took a deep breath. "The other night with you, when we were together, I..." He hesitated.

"Yes?" Her voice sounded breathless, excited. Last night, she nearly passed out from the intense pleasure of Scott's touch. In fact, the quivers started again at the mere memory.

His cell phone rang. He pulled it from his pocket to check the caller.

He looked at her with apology, "Excuse me. I have to take this."

Her mouth dropped open. "You're kidding me."

"It's my brother." Scott flipped open his cell phone. "What's up, Jack?"

"Jack?" Tolly's voice raised in volume. "Otherwise known as the man who broke into my apartment, followed my bus from Lake City, and stole my luggage?"

Scott tried to cover the cell phone's receiver, to no avail.

"That brother Jack?" she shrilled.

Jack overhead. "So... I take it you found her again."

Scott turned away from Tolly and lowered his voice. "What's going on now?"

Tolly threw more dishes into the sink, hard enough to splash his back. She slashed at them with a scrub brush as if she wished they were his face.

"Pop just told me that Nellie has a gun."

"How'd she get it?"

"Who knows?"

"You mean you don't?"

"Scott, it wasn't me. Someone else either gave it to her or sold it to her. Anyway, she's fed up. And with what Alex implied he'd try to do to us, she might need it. I'm frankly glad that she has it."

"I'd be glad if she were trained to use it."

"Well..."

"This is not good."

"You want me to try to get it from her?"

"Well for God's sake, Jack. She's got two kids in the house. One of them could find it and shoot the other. She could hit herself or one of them trying to load it. Even if she does manage to hit the right target, they could charge her with first degree."

"All right. Um, so that's the bad news."

Scott shot Tolly a quick look. "Give me the good news. I could use some right about now." She gave him the evil eye in return.

"I have a full report on Alex," Jack told him.

"You got it from Clark?"

"Yeah."

"How bad is it?"

"Bad. Meaning bad for Alex, good for us. Clark's information plus what I found adds up to a real naughty one."

"An understatement. I'll pick it up from you in Calabasas."

"I could drive it down to Patina."

"No. Stay with Nellie. Keep an eye on Pop. We're almost at the end of things, Jack, but it's not over yet. God, I can't wait to finish this and retire."

Tolly tensed next to him.

"How'd I do, Boss?"

"Did great. See you soon."

Scott snapped his phone shut. He looked at her.

"Tolly..."

"I know. You have to go."

Windrunner

"My sister... Nellie. Everything's just..."

"I know."

"Look." Scott stumbled for words, then paused. "We're not done here. You know in your heart that we're not."

Tolly washed more dishes. "Not by a long shot."

"We still have to talk about..."

"Just go," she interrupted. "You have a job to do, don't you? Alexander King is waiting in Lake City, isn't he? And so's your retirement money."

"Tolly, it's not like that anymore."

She had to bite her lip to keep from screaming and bursting into tears. "You've got people to take care of. Things you want to accomplish. I understand that." She heard the crack in her voice. The detritus of dirty dishwater covered her hands. She was sick of Scott kicking her heart around.

"Just... please, Tolly. Wait for me here. Please trust me just this once."

She decided his request didn't even deserve a response.

"I'm not going to hurt you anymore. I mean it."

Tolly stared at the counter top she just cleaned. Rafael used to say those same words to her every day. Then every night, he hit her, among other unspeakable acts. Scott had his secret shame. She had hers. They were quite the pair.

"Please wait for me here, Tolly. I'm sorry for my part in this. Okay? You don't have to be afraid anymore." Scott took her chin between his thumb and finger. "I'm going to take care of you."

He lowered his face closer to look into her eyes. "I'm not going to let anyone hurt you again."

She couldn't look away from the intense beauty of his face. Her body, as always, quaked at his touch.

"Okay Scott." She smiled for him but inside, she felt like the walking dead. "I'll wait here for you."

Scott looked at her with regret, still uncertain. He took her soap covered hands in his. "Tolly, we can work it out. Just... wait for me here. Please. I'll come back for you."

She nodded. Of course he would come back for her. How else would he get his last check from King for a job well done?

Scott kissed her mouth too quick for her to turn her head away. He'd kissed her hard with possession, as if to stake a claim. Her insides liquified. Every time she heard his voice, smelled his skin, or felt his touch, she quivered like a leaf in the wind.

He strode outside to his bike. She watched him mount in a smooth movement through the plate glass window. He rode away. She took an uncertain step toward the front door.

She wondered why he didn't ask her to come with him. Then she wondered why she wanted to go. She longed to run after him, to hold him close once more. She wanted to chase dreams into the sunset and beyond. But dreams were all she and Scott had together.

Hit me with the good news, he said. But face it. Anyone involved with Alexander King brought their own bad news. Tolly finished the kitchen chores. She had to leave. She would make sure that he couldn't find her. No, he always found her. So this time, she would make sure that he wouldn't *need* to find her.

Ever.

She walked into the small back room to gather her belongings. She loved Scott Windrunner. She loved everything about him, except the deceit. Deception, she could not accept from anyone anymore.

In the bathroom mirror, she watched herself unsnap the flash drive from its hiding place inside her hair clip.

She would provide him the means to finish at least part of King's job, get paid enough to retire, and protect the family that needed him.

She would get Scott off her trail and out of her life. He had his priorities. She had hers. It would take her years, but she would have to forget him.

***

Scott couldn't ignore the conflicted emotions on Tolly's face—mistrust and something else. Something similar to what he saw the magic night they shared in the cabin, the night he manipulated her with acts of love.

Scott clenched his hands. The bike surged faster.

She and he were not done with each other. He had to get back to her. He had to explain things better than he did. Tolly deserved no less than complete honesty.

He flipped out his cell phone.

"Jack, I can't deal with Nellie's situation and Tolly at the same time. But I still need to have Alex's information. Get in the pickup. Meet me halfway to Patina. You know where."

Chapter 21

Far away from the traffic, the grind, the grime, and the crime of Patina and Lake City, Tolly stood on the side of the road. Midday Saturday, the occasional *whoosh* of a vehicle racing towards the end of a long day of errands or the start of a fantastic Saturday night interrupted the quiet.

Tolly looked at the sky's wide open expanse. Cerulean blue streaked to gold, then melted into a warm peach haze on the western horizon. She smelled clean air. She felt the open space and freedom. Birds screamed and called overhead.

A brown sedan pulled over to the shoulder in front of her. "Can I pick up a friend of mine from work then take you to Colorado Springs?" The middle-aged Latino man asked her.

"Probably not a good idea. But you can let me out here, please."

"Here?" The man looked at the emptiness around them. Patina city limits on twenty-five. "Sure?"

"Thank you. Here's just fine." Tolly got out.

***

Saturday afternoon, Scott returned to the shelter. He didn't see Tolly anywhere.

The more he knew about Tolly, the more he cared for her. The more he cared for her, the worse he felt about how he'd treated her. Filled with dread, he waited his turn in a long line at the reception desk.

***

Scott featured foremost in her thoughts, their time together, the laughter, the intimacy. The first night in the motel, he held her so close that she could feel each beat of his heart. The second night in the cabin he made her whole body shake with the lightest touch. When he kissed her at Canela Street, she wanted to throw herself into his arms and beg him to carry her away from everything. But before she could move, he'd walked away. Before she could run after him, he'd zoomed off on the bike.

What had he intended to tell her about the night in the cabin when he showed her the sweetest bliss? She might not ever know because by now, he knew that she'd skipped out on him again.

A pang of regret shot through her. It seemed as if the wind itself fought against her walking away from him. Huge gusts of hot air pushed her arm back from the road. Tolly crooked her thumb, determined to catch a ride away from more mistakes.

***

Valerie dispensed services and advice behind the desk with clockwork precision. Like the other clients, Scott leaned in close to make his own discreet request for help. Valerie waved a volunteer over to take her place at the desk. Then she gestured Scott towards her office. She closed the door shut behind them.

***

A middle-aged White woman and her mother gave Tolly a lift from Patina city limits to Castle Pines. Tolly helped them to unload several gallons of iced tea for tomorrow's church event.

"I'll pray for your safety and that God blesses your journey," the younger of the two women told her.

"Thank you, ma'am," Tolly replied. She shut their door with care. Nice people.

Despite it all, she loved Scott. She wouldn't cry on the road, though. Tears would bring out the worst in the next driver. Tolly blinked her eyes. She would cry alone.

**

"Who are you, really?" Valerie faced him with no expression. "You are neither homeless nor poor. Even though you dress the part, that shiny new bike I just saw you park outside says different. What are you, her probation officer?"

"No."

Valerie reassessed. "Husband or boyfriend."

Scott hesitated. "Not exactly."

Valerie scowled. "You been beating on that girl?"

"No!"

"Then, mister, why does she keep running from you?" Valerie cocked her head to the side, bullshit detector activated.

Scott ran a hand through silvery hair. "It's a long story," he admitted.

"Mm hm." Valerie looked skeptical. "It usually is."

"Look, Miss Valerie. I'm very, very sorry that I came to your establishment under these circumstances. I sincerely apologize to you for that."

She narrowed her eyes. "Under what circumstances exactly *are* you here?" She crossed her arms. "What do you want?"

Scott spotted it in her hand. "That flash drive you're holding, for instance."

"This?" She shook the small file at Scott. "What about it? You want this?"

"Yes."

"Okay." She held it out to him. Surprised that it was that easy, he took it from her.

Valerie took a piece of paper out of her pocket. She handed that over to Scott as well. "She wrote that she left this file for you so I haven't looked at it. Maybe I should."

Scott read the note. It didn't say much other than what Valerie already told him. No clue as to her destination. "Maybe you should," Scott agreed.

They sized each other up in silence.

"Valerie, I have a feeling if we look at this file together, everything will be explained."

"Okay." She shrugged.

"And then, after you understand more, would you please consider telling me anything you might know of where Tolly might have gone? She's in big trouble." He ran a hand through his silver mane. "I think you'll see for yourself."

Scott retrieved his laptop.

***

A Black Cuban man stopped. He gave Tolly a ride from Castle Pines to Castle Rock. He owned his own construction company. He had children, he told her.

***

"You've been referred to as the Bill Gates and Andrew Carnegie, Henry Firestone, and, let's see here..." Tolly referred to her notes, *"and Henry Ford of green industry and manufacturing. Some of these men have legacies that are viewed both positively and negatively."*

Alex nodded with a sober expression.

"What do you think of that?" she asked him over the sound of quiet whimpers. "Do you agree?"

This time, he smiled with a full-on electrical brilliance

"You know, Tolly, as long as they call me the man who did everything in his power to do the very best for the people of Lake City, that's okay by me."

***

A Latina in a yellow sports car, who reassured Tolly that she didn't speak a word of Spanish, gave Tolly a ride from Castle Rock to Colorado Springs.

"I work at a seafood restaurant. It's on the way. I just couldn't leave a woman on the side of the road," she said. For some reason, Tolly's driver couldn't handle two things at once. She looked at Tolly instead of the road while she spoke.

Tolly decided if the woman couldn't or wouldn't watch the road from the driver's seat, then Tolly would have to watch the road from the passenger seat. She'd shout a warning if she needed to.

But she just did not understand where her life was going anymore. She didn't understand anything except that she loved a man who revealed layer upon layer of secrets and hidden agendas.

Her preoccupation with Scott distracted her vigilance.

Sure enough, her driver overshot the destination, making her turn-off to the seafood restaurant from habit. Tolly thanked her then walked back to the road at Colorado Springs.

***

Scott's mouth thinned to a line.

Valerie shook her head and said, "For shame."

Alex lied to Scott about Tolly each time he opened his mouth. No documents. No cash. No seduction. Only Alexander King who assaulted two women, followed by Celara King's guest performance.

***

The sun moved closer to the horizon, an electric tangerine ball that blazed heat across the road. Though still summer, the sun would set long before she managed to get to Albuquerque unless she stopped someone on a long haul.

She didn't know what kind of wildlife roamed the mountain ranges of southern Colorado.

Coyotes? Wolves? Cougars? Rattlesnakes?

She couldn't spend the night out here in the midst of wilderness that surrounded the highway on both sides. So much for adventure. The patio of a bed and breakfast in Patina was one thing. Closing her eyes while all of God's creatures great and small (like scorpions), crawled over her was quite another.

With renewed energy, she stuck out her thumb.

***

Valerie whistled. "I heard Lake City's mayoral race was getting kind of crazy. I just didn't know how crazy."

"Well, as you can see, one of the candidates will likely bark at the moon tonight."

"Let me guess. Not the Asian lady."

"No, the other one."

"Tolly filmed him?"

Scott nodded. "She did."

"And this, Alexander King, doesn't want her to show it to anyone? That's why he's after her?"

"It would finish him in the primary, Valerie. He'd never make it to the general election. He'd never be mayor or even dog catcher if that became public. That's why he wants the file. And her."

"So what are you going to do?"

"With your help, I'm going to find Tolly before he or his men do."

"They're after her?"

Scott nodded.

"She was here trying to lay low."

"I think that was the idea."

"But you found her."

Scott looked away.

"You love her, don't you?"

"Please help me, Valerie. I need to find her before Alexander King does."

Valerie waited a beat. She scanned his expression.

"I talked to Tolly about Albuquerque." Again, Valerie watched his face. "I told her if things didn't work out in Patina, then Albuquerque was the place to be."

Scott hugged the older woman then ran to his bike.

***

A Mexican American family outfitted with boots and cowboy hats stopped. Groceries filled their pickup's truck bed. They'd stocked up for the week or maybe just for Sunday dinner. They agreed to take her from Colorado Springs to Trinidad.

She slung her plastic grocery bag into the back of the pickup. Then she hurried to sling herself amongst the boxes of detergent, soda, and cornflakes. She didn't want to lose whatever meager possessions she still owned. As Scott pointed out in their motel room a lifetime ago, she didn't have a lot.

The pickup truck moved uphill. Tolly's stomach swam the opposite direction. She drove a pickup herself, until it died on her. But she'd never ridden in the truck bed along a twisting mountain road with no separation from the road pavement and the red rocky expanse but crystal clear air, wind, and sunshine.

She discovered an unknown fear of altitude, never addressed in pancake-flat Lake City despite its many skyscrapers. She'd never been inside one, not even for a school trip. In fact, there were a lot of things she hadn't done. For instance, this unguided tour of the Southwest. She smiled at her own joke. Her parents had driven her West when she was a toddler. The photos opposite her desk at home proved that. But it was so long ago she couldn't remember anything about the experience.

She took deep breaths.

***

He flipped open his cell phone to call Jack. "She's walking either twenty-five or two-eighty-five. She's got about two hours lead." Scott gave Jack further instructions. "I need your help, Jack."

"I'm on it. Think you'll find her?"

"I know her."

"You love her, Scott. Don't you?"

Scott sighed. All week long, he'd taken it on the chin. Everyone and everything connected to Tolly burrowed deep under his skin.

"I'm going to find her."

***

Tolly tried not to crush the groceries of the people nice enough to pick up a complete stranger. If she vomited on their food, they would surely order her out of the truck. Then where would she be? Back on the side of the road. She needed to pull it together, control her terror, and get her breathing back under control.

After a few minutes, Tolly adjusted to the pull and tug of the road that dipped, inclined, and curved through the red-orange-yellow landscape. Just before the exit to Trinidad, the white pickup truck pulled over. Her drivers had more shopping to finish at the outlet mall. They waved and wished her luck. Tolly waved back. The family drove off.

Closer to the Colorado-New Mexico border, she no longer feared the jagged red rocks. But the going remained slow. Day descended to dusk.

Again, she stuck out her thumb.

***

Bruce hated Kansas.

Nothing but straight road ahead interrupted the vast flatland that stretched to the horizon. Either a drought or a prairie fire shriveled the grass to an ugly yellow with smudges of deadened brown.

He mooed at a cow just to keep himself awake. Irritated, he woke up the men. He needed extra eyes.

Something about their location rendered the car's global positioning system useless. They used the car's interior light to consult a map. After some discussion, the men plotted a complicated route that required vigilant attention to multiple road signs.

Bruce sped forward on a trajectory to intercept his quarry.

Chapter 22

The rocks that soared with such majesty to the sun and sky by day towered over and smothered Tolly at dusk. The jagged edges bit across the sky like teeth that might seize her any minute.

She needed to get off this road before nightfall. She didn't know the terrain. She had no idea what lay behind the mountains that bore down over the road.

Determined, Tolly stuck her out her thumb. A large rig tried to pull over to the shoulder but a sport utility vehicle veered into the right lane. The rig shifted through gears, passed her, then picked up speed.

Tolly sighed.

She stuck out her thumb again. When she got to Albuquerque, she would make a collect call to Bill Martinez. See if any rent checks came in. See if he could make the deposits to her bank and then have them wire her the money...

Tolly shook her head. No phone calls. She didn't know for sure how far Alex King's reach stretched. She didn't know whether he'd use his police friends to monitor her cell phone or the landlines of her building's residents. Would he think to access her bank account? Could he? Could Celara King? If so, they would trace the wire transfer to Albuquerque. Scott would be on her faster than she could fold the cash and put it in her pocket.

None of her plans made sense. She was tired and hungry and couldn't think. If she could just hold out a few more days... But then, that didn't make sense either.

She knew Alexander King had an unstable temperament that rendered him unfit for office. He knew she knew it. He would never forgive and he would never forget.

Not in a few days. Not in a few months. Not in a few years. He'd marked her as a threat. She knew that too.

A big rig zoomed the other direction on the opposite side of the road. She recognized the sign on the side as the same sign on the rig that tried to stop before. The driver waved to her. She stared back, uncertain. The rig exited the road then circled the overpass behind her.

She turned to watch its progress, a tiny toy truck in the distance, decorated with multiple lights. She didn't quite remember the names of all the horror movies that involved a hitchhiker and an eighteen-wheeler. The rig got bigger as it drew closer. Then its headlights blazed over her when it slowed to a stop a few yards behind her. The headlights blinked.

Tolly walked back.

A man, the dark rich color of teak or mahogany and a salt and pepper mustache and beard looked at her from the driver's seat.

"Where you headed?" he asked her.

Tolly looked at the sky. Full night, lit by a bright moon pressed down upon her.

"Albuquerque."

"I'm going that way. Come on."

Tolly hauled herself into the cab. Her driver shifted gears to accelerate, then pulled the rig back on the road.

Tolly eyed the security badge that swung from his rear view mirror. "Frank Griffin," it said, next to his picture.

She decided that she would work day labor in Albuquerque for the next few days. She would formulate a well-thought-out plan that involved food to eat and a place to sleep.

The man stuck out a hand. "I'm Frank. You?"

"Tolly." Then she would buy a bus or train ticket back to Lake City.

"Tolly, eh?"

"Yes." She would figure something out once she got home. "Rhymes with Molly."

"Yes it does." Tolly wondered too late if she should have made up a name. Too busy planning, she forgot to think.

Frank must have noticed her unease because he restarted the conversation. "Well, I tell ya. I'm making a delivery. I pick up oil in Albuquerque. Drop it in Patina. Pick up water in Patina. Bring it to Albuquerque. Then back again, jiggity-jog." He gestured back and forth to illustrate his transportation network. "That's what I do."

Tolly made her own effort at conversation. "You must know this road like the back of your hand."

That pleased him. "Roads. People. Water. Oil. I see it all. But you know, my wife tells me all the time, I should write a book with all the stories I tell her about what I see."

"You going to tell her about me?" Tolly asked.

"I don't know yet." Frank grinned at her. "Have to see how it ends."

**

North of Trinidad, Scott revved his motorcycle.

He pushed through the wind as fast as he dared. He didn't want to attract police attention. While he had no problem negotiating a ticket (or paying one), he couldn't afford to lose more time than he already had.

Jack could take care of the folks in Calabasas.

But Tolly was alone.

**

"Me and my wife—that was her that called just now—we've been together for seventeen years. Married for ten. It's a good thing. Once you find a good thing, you don't let it go. Know what I mean?" Frank waited for a response.

"No," Tolly answered, surprised at her forthrightness. But that was the intimacy that developed between strangers. She doubted that she would ever see Frank again.

"You know, we love each other," he continued. "We respect each other. Her parents. My parents. We all get together. We have three children. Another on the way right now. Not for a few more months, but it's on the way. I always dreamed about a family. Being a father. Watched my own father growing up. I learned from him. People wouldn't let him work. They wouldn't hire him. He didn't let that stop him. You know what he did?"

Tolly shook her head. She settled back for the rest of Frank's story.

"We-e-ell, he'd wait where trucks unloaded. Trucks like these. Same time, same place every day. This was in Houston. He'd jump in there and help unload the truck. He said people tried to call him lazy, but he wasn't. No matter what names they called him, he'd get right in there and outwork everybody. Bring whatever money they paid him home to my mother. He knew we had to eat so he made sure we ate."

Frank took a swig out of an aluminum can. Tolly tensed. She had not forgotten Sonny's wild behavior in Calabasas. Neither had she forgotten Rafael's temper that worsened whenever he slugged back alcohol. The last thing she needed was a drunk driver. But neither did she need to wander the unknown roadside in the dark.

"You want to know the secret?" Frank asked her.

Tolly didn't answer. Frank cleared his throat. Tolly realized she'd focused so hard to form yet another escape plan that she threw off the rhythm of the conversation.

Frank took another drink. "I'll tell you the secret. The secret to marrying the right person is to watch how that person treats his or her parents."

"My parents are deceased."

"Sorry to hear that, Tolly. That's too bad. What about the rest of your family?"

Well, why not, Tolly thought. He probably wouldn't remember the conversation anyway.

"I had this boyfriend... He had problems. Well... actually... I allowed my boyfriend's problems to push the rest of my family away."

"Mm," Frank shook his head. "Why'd he do that?"

Tolly didn't answer.

Frank persisted. "Why'd he do that?"

Frank and Tolly had a duel of silence which Tolly lost.

"It's too late now, anyway," she said in a low voice.

"It's never too late," Frank responded with utmost confidence.

"I lost touch with everyone. I missed weddings, birthday parties, graduations, funerals... holiday functions. They invited me, but I kept turning them down. Then they stopped calling. Years go by. Phone numbers and addresses change." She shrugged. "You know."

"They'll always be your family." Frank paused. "But there's only one reason a boyfriend or husband will push the rest of the family away."

Tolly remained silent. She couldn't voice the thought aloud. She couldn't face what she'd tried to avoid for so long. Right after her mother passed away, Rafael rode in on a white horse to save her. At least, that's how it seemed in the beginning. Towards the end, Tolly walked on eggshells inside her own home.

"Control," Frank supplied the answered Tolly wouldn't.

Tolly still didn't respond. Only Rafael's temper surpassed his good looks. And only his ego surpassed his temper. Get-togethers with her extended family, plain-spoken people, resulted in awkward moments that offended Rafael each time. Afterward, Rafael punished her with his fists, sometimes his feet. Sometimes other ways so the marks didn't show. She'd never met his parents. He'd told her his parents wouldn't like her.

"That why I picked you up on the side of the road? Someone trying to control you?"

"I'm not running from my boyfriend."

"But you are running."

Tolly focused her gaze on the blackness of night beyond the rig's windshield.

***

Armed with new information on Scott's location via his police friends, Alex called Bruce to redirect him on a collision course with Scott in the New Mexican countryside north of Las Vegas.

"Punch the accelerator Bruce. I want the headlights of his own car to put him in a trance."

Alex disconnected.

Bruce punched the accelerator. The powerful engine of the Windrunner Security car surged the group of men across Oklahoma. They left torrent a of dust behind them. Dried prairie grass gave way to rocky scrub. A few miles took them across the tip of northwestern Texas where road signs pleaded with them to visit Amarillo. They ignored those signs, the mesquite, and the cacti that lined the roadside.

They had eyes only for Scott, the traitor.

***

Tolly didn't deny it. Besides, it wouldn't do any good. Frank had already made up his mind.

"From something else, yes," Tolly admitted. Pain inside her sharpened to a stiletto near her heart.

Tolly considered Scott and his father. The respect. The love. The quiet humor. Neither raised their voice in anger. They made important points with jokes and stories. Now that she thought about it, her own father had the same style. Maybe that's what drew her to Scott. His quiet confidence. His belief in her. How he made her feel like liquid silk wherever he touched her.

She loved him.

"They say with alcoholism, the person has to hit absolute rock bottom before they can come back up. It has to get worse before it gets any better."

"They say that, do they?" Tolly eyed the empty aluminum can next to his seat.

"That's what they say." Frank chuckled. Tolly wondered what was so funny about driving a large rig drunk across the Southwest. She needed to say something before Frank jack-knifed them off the road.

"That's what they said to me when I hit rock bottom," Frank said.

"Really?" Tolly gave Frank a quick look.

He lifted the aluminum can so she could see the label—an energy drink. He needed to stay awake. That explained why he talked so much.

Tolly laughed and rallied. "I guess it got better?"

"It's getting better all the time. I'm never going back there to that bottle again. I love my wife and children too much." Frank signaled to pass a slower-moving vehicle. "So how will this story end, Tolly? What am I gonna tell my wife?"

"Tell her that it got worse."

"It got worse." Frank repeated.

"Then it got better."

He looked at Tolly as if she were crazy. "You on the side of the road, by yourself, out in the middle of nowhere, in the dark is better?"

"Well, then he got gone." As in shanked in a prison shower. But Frank didn't need to know all that. "I've come a pretty long way. I won't go back there either."

"Well thank God for forgiveness of ourselves and others. Otherwise, how could any of us possibly want to wake up the next morning?"

Tolly nodded her agreement in silence.

"I mean, there was this guy I knew back in the day." Frank settled back for another story. Tolly listened, half asleep. Frank's voice blended into the creaks of the truck, the scrape of gears, the rush of wind against windshield, and the grind of eighteen wheels against road pavement.

Apparently, a friend of his signed up for military service because of the opportunities for honor and education. This friend became a courageous leader whom everyone trusted.

"He was a hero," Frank whispered in near reverence. The story continued, how the friend returned back to active duty after an education break, but fell to dishonor.

The back of Tolly's neck buzzed. Through Frank's hypnotic voice, she barely formed the words.

"What was his name?" She held her breath.

For the first time, Frank didn't answer.

"Frank. Please tell me." Tolly bit her lip. She whispered each word with distinction. "What was the name of your friend?"

"Windrunner."

Tolly exhaled. She sagged against the passenger seat, whipped. She felt his hair against her skin every time the wind blew. His smile and his laughter occupied her thoughts and daydreams. The crush of his arms around her made her feel so safe. She would never forget him.

"Tell me everything," she said.

Frank admitted that he served under Scott's first command. But he knew about Scott's second command only through rumors and half-truths. These, he refused to pass along, he said.

"Windrunner never talked about it, but he was never the same after the second time. I mean, he's likely the same person overall, but when his own people turned on him and made him a pariah, it got to him."

"How so?"

"He used to laugh all the time. Always had a joke. But when that connection to his community got cut off, something died in him, I think."

Tolly frowned. That didn't sound like the Scott she knew, the man who teased and joked without mercy.

"When's the last time you saw him, Frank?"

"Too long, as a matter of fact." Frank shook his head with regret. "Been years. He left Colorado. Didn't hear too much from him after that."

Tolly narrowed her eyes. "Until now? Until he called you to pick me up and trick me? Was that really your wife on the phone?"

"He didn't call me, Tolly," Frank clarified. "And I didn't trick you. Yes, that was my wife on the phone." But he didn't look at her.

Tolly stared at Frank's profile. A quick study of his technique, she didn't say a word. Frank readjusted his seatbelt.

"It was Jack," he admitted. "Windrunner's brother called earlier today and told a bunch of us to look out for you."

"A bunch of..." Tolly's voice trailed off. She rubbed her temples. She was too weary to run anymore. She had nowhere to go, apparently, where Scott couldn't find her.

***

Bruce patted the large wad of money in his pocket. The infusion of cash meant they could criss-cross the entire United States four times over and still have money left for a wild night in Las Vegas. The *real* Las Vegas, not this New Mexican bullshit.

"You know what I like," Bruce told his two homeboys that he brought along for the thrill of it, "I like putting hundreds of miles of wear and tear on the asshole's car."

He patted the dashboard. Then he punched it with his middleweight fist. That hurt his hand. So he scratched at the dashboard with his ring.

The men laughed.

Bruce pressed the accelerator closer to the floor.

The men cheered.

He left long black streaks of rubber on the pavement when he turned south. The security car began to eat through twenty-five.

***

"By the way, Windrunner's behind us on the road."

A lick of excitement shot through Tolly. "What?"

She looked into the rig's side mirror for headlights. "Where?" She didn't see anyone.

"Further back. He knows you're with me. Jack already told him." Frank tightened his grip on the steering wheel. "He's following, Tolly."

"Of couse he is." Tolly laughed, helpless.

"That's why I need to know right now if he's the reason why you're running."

"What?" Tolly started to shake her head, then stopped, confused. "No, I..."

Who was she running from? Scott? King? Rafael? Herself?

"Is he? Is he the one that sent you to rock bottom?"

"No." Tolly's voice choked. "No!"

"Sure?" Frank's voice grew quieter, firmer. "Let me tell you something. You see that sign?" He pointed out the window as a sign *whooshed* past. "I can take this truck off the main road easy. Drive you straight to my wife to wait while I make my delivery. Get you safe. You don't have to wake up to a fist in your face ever again."

"No Frank. No!"

Frank ignored that. "See there?" He pointed again. "That's Santa Fe coming up in about twenty minutes. I can get you to forty no problem. That'll take you west to Los Angeles. Ten will get you east to Houston. Twenty takes you to Dallas. You hear what I'm saying?"

Tolly shook her head.

"I'm telling you, Tolly, you can disappear into the crowd and he'll never find you again."

The thought of never seeing Scott again sent tears down her face.

Frank saw them. "Tolly?" he asked her for a decision.

Chapter 23

She closed her eyes. "It wasn't him, Frank."
"Not who? Windrunner?"
"No. Not Scott. Someone else. Someone I knew before him." This week had been an education. Life lessons learned the hard way that she would never forget.

One in a million, Scott was. She didn't see it in time. But she knew now. The Kings, the Rafaels, the Sonnys, the men who delighted in the pain of others didn't dwell in the same species as Scott.

Frank nodded.

"Years before I met Scott," Tolly emphasized.

***

"We're almost on him!" Bruce said. "Look for him on the bike!"

The men strained. They trained their eyes down the dark road. Bruce switched the headlights to bright. At this point, he didn't care about anyone or anything else except double the money.

"There he is!" one of the men shouted.

And there Scott was.

***

"Scott never raised a hand to me, Frank. He wouldn't do that. He's not that type."

He might get frustrated or angry or disappointed with her, but never violent. Still, she wondered about the secret of his dishonorable discharge.

"Okay." Frank relaxed. "Then it makes sense. I was gonna say that wasn't the guy I knew, Tolly. Windrunner is a friend of mine. I never turned on him, even after his service ended, though we did lose touch. My own family and driving this rig takes most of my time these days. Still, if his family ever needs me, I come running. I don't know what happened during the last war. I decided not to ask. But Windrunner was always decent to us guys in his unit. We followed him through smoke and fire. Came out on the other side all right, mostly intact. He was a hero. We all were. He did his thing with school and then signed up for more action. God bless him. Me? I stayed stateside. Had the wife and kids. Had enough of guns and shooting."

Tolly sighed. Tears of relief washed over her. "Thanks for that, Frank."

***

Scott came to groggy and disoriented. He wasn't sure how much time had passed. His head and torso ached. He remembered bright lights and tires that screeched.

He looked left and right from where he lay in the dirt. His motorcycle canted on its side a few feet away, still running. He had an accident?

A moment passed. No. Someone ran him off the road. He felt in his pockets for his cell phone, made a call.

"Where are you, Scott?" Jack's calm voice belied urgency only an older brother would recognize.

"I'm... not sure. I haven't reached Santa Fe yet." Scott struggled to clear his head.

"What do you see around you?"

Scott described the mountainscape as well as he could in the moonlight.

"I'm already on my way. Calabasas is fine. I'm almost at the New Mexico border."

"Jack, they're looking for Tolly. Call Frank back. Tell him to get her off the road right now."

"I'm on it."

***

Frank's cell phone rang. He answered it with a look of apology to Tolly.

"We're just about to reach Santa Fe. We're on the outskirts right now." Frank peered at the sprinkle of lights in the distance.

"Is that Scott?" Tolly demanded. "Scott! Scott! I'm sorry. I love you!" she shouted.

"Get off the road?" Frank was incredulous. "What are you talking about?"

Tolly's skin chilled.

"For what?" Frank paused. "Well, where's Scott meeting us? I thought it was Santa Fe?"

Tolly stared at Frank's profile. So it wasn't Scott on the phone.

"What happened, Jack?" Frank asked. "Where is he?"

Something happened to Scott. Tolly rested her head in her hands.

"Las Vegas? On the north side?"

"Frank, what is it?" she asked with a sharp tone.

"Shit!" Frank snapped his cell phone closed. He took a moment to think.

"Frank, what is it? What happened to Scott?"

"Jack said... some men caught up to him."

"Oh my God." *King.*

"He wants us off the road."

"But where's Scott? Where is he, Frank? Did Jack say?"

"Just north of Las Vegas," Frank replied.

"We have to go back. We have to find him."

Frank shook his head. "Negative."

"Negative?" Tolly repeated. "What do you mean, negative? This isn't some military operation. We have to help Scott, Frank. We can't just leave him there."

"No go, Tolly." He looked at her. "Jack said they have guns."

"Frank, you just said Scott Windrunner was your friend. He's my friend too. Please!" Tolly was desperate. "Whatever happened to never leave a man behind?"

He looked uncertain. She knew that she could wear him down. But each mile Frank drove, each second he took to decide, put them further away from Scott. He could bleed to death while he waited for help.

"Frank! Stop this rig and let me out. I'm going back for him myself!"

Frank flicked the turn signal. "Okay, Tolly, we're gonna do it. Never leave a man behind." He shook his head, then doubled back on the road.

Tolly closed her eyes, relieved. She tried to reason out the latest development. King sent men after Scott. That must mean Scott turned against King and tried to protect her.

"What else did Jack say?"

"He said..." Frank trailed off.

"What, Frank? Tell me!"

"They left him laying on the side of the road."

"No!" Tolly gasped. "Is he..."

"He's okay. He's awake. Jack's coming from the north. Between us, we'll find him, Tolly."

"My God." Tolly felt sick inside. She wiped the tears from her face. "What about the men who jumped him? Where are they?"

"Heading straight for us on twenty-five." Frank glanced at her. "Jack said they're looking for you."

"Looking for me?" Tolly clenched her teeth. "Oh really? I'm looking for *them* for what they did to Scott!"

Frank laughed. "My wife will think I made this up."

"The story's not over, Frank." No more! After years of fear, shame, and victimization, tonight, Tolly would turn the tables.

"I think know what one of them looks like."

***

On the road between Las Vegas and Santa Fe, Bruce felt a sense of satisfaction. The headlight hadn't broken, but the security car's bumper had a nice Scott-sized dent in it.

"You sure you're headed the right way?" one of the men asked him.

"How the fuck should I know?" Adrenaline and testosterone made Bruce snarl his response. "He was riding this way on that bike like a bat out of torment. Probably wants to get what she has for himself, greedy bastard."

Bruce checked the gas gauge. "Fuck!" He hit the steering wheel with his fist.

***

Tolly kept watch on the opposite side of the road. She spotted the Windrunner Security car at a gas station illuminated by neon and moonlight. She could see the driver— the same jerk who broke into her apartment with Jack, the day the madness began.

"I see him!" Yes. The same man who waited for her with crossed arms at the truck stop in Omaha.

"Frank, that's them!"

Frank looked as they passed, then took his foot off the accelerator. His phone rang. This time, he muttered low enough so Tolly couldn't hear. Then he snapped the phone closed.

"Jack found him, Tolly."

"Is he okay?"

Frank nodded.

Tolly leaned back in relief.

But Frank had more to add. "Jack said they're coming this way to pick you up."

The gas station grew smaller in the distance behind them.

"But we have to stop them." Tolly clenched her hands. "They hurt Scott and now they want to hurt me. They're getting away!"

"Well what do you want me to do? Scott said to get off the road. Jack was pretty clear on that."

"We can disable their car. We can immobilize them so they can't get away and then come after us again."

"What?" he looked at her, incredulous. "How? What about what..."

"Scott said for us to get off the road." she pointed to the exit ramp. "We can get off the road here, then circle back to where we saw them at the gas station."

"That's what you're going to tell Scott when he..." Frank just looked at her.

"They'll come after all of us anyway, Frank. You can run them off the road with this thing, can't you?"

Frank sighed. "Windrunner's going to kill me."

"Technically, we're doing exactly what they told us to do, Frank. See? We're getting off the road right now."

Frank shook his head at her tortured logic, but he did it. A few more turns and the eighteen-wheeler approached the gas station. The security car re-entered the road a mile ahead of them.

Frank accelerated the rig. The large mass crept closer to the sedan.

"Hold on!" Frank shouted.

The rig pounded into the smaller sedan. He twisted the steering wheel. The security car's tires screeched then rumbled off the road into a cloud of dust. Frank pushed the car further away from the roadside into the rocks and scrubby grass of Indian country.

Three men swarmed out of the car, guns drawn.

"Tolly, wait!"

Before Frank could stop her, Tolly threw the rig's passenger door open. She jumped to the ground. "What did you do to Scott?" she screamed.

The dark-skinned man she recognized from her doorstep in Lake City met her halfway. Two others followed, one fat and one skinny.

"What did you do to him?" she demanded.

He ignored her, looked past her. In fact, all of the men pointed their guns not at her, but behind her. Tolly looked over her shoulder. Frank lowered a shotgun to the ground. Outnumbered, he raised his hands.

"Get him," the leader ordered. He turned his gun barrel towards Tolly. The two men overwhelmed her new friend. She gasped to hear the sounds their fists made against his body. Frank sagged to the ground with a groan. He didn't move.

Tolly screamed. She reached past the leader's gun to claw at his face, the last thing he expected. The years of abuse she suffered finally had their release. She shrieked and kicked. She fought the brave fight that surprised the other men.

"Crazy bitch!" The leader struck her in the face with his meaty fist.

Tolly hit the dirt conscious, but disoriented.

The other men laughed, in near admiration. "Bitch has kick," the skinny one said.

The leader touched his face. Red lines slashed by Tolly's fingernails tic-tac-toed his skin. He examined his hand covered with blood, then swore. The laughter stopped.

"Get her in the trunk. She's gonna pay for this."

Tolly's tormentor bent over her still form. "You hear that? You're gonna make daddy feel real good tonight. Then after I wipe myself off on you, I'll pass you around like a dirty rag." He wiped his bloody hand on Tolly shirt. The other men looked at him, then at Tolly, unsure.

"Get her in the trunk!" The leader shouted. "Move!"

Never let them transfer you to another location, her safety instructor always told her.

Tolly groaned in protest when they lifted her by the arms and legs. Someone popped open the car's trunk. The black hole of her destiny yawned wide to receive her into its depths. Tolly knew that once she went into the trunk, her life, what she had left of it, would be destroyed beyond repair—a type of destruction that Rafael attempted, but did not complete.

Fight to the death because they will kill you anyway, her instructor, a retired police officer, always said.

"No! No!" Tolly came to with demented shrieks. She twisted every limb. She bit at the arms and hands that held her. "No!" She clawed at eyes. She kicked soft body parts.

Someone dropped her legs. As if possessed, Tolly kicked every direction her range of motion allowed.

"Goddamn it, hold her!" The leader shouted at them. "Get her in there!"

Chapter 24

The pickup's headlights swept over fresh black tire marks that looped then ran off the road amid a trail of broken glass, smoky clouds of dust, and bits of metal bumper. From the passenger seat, Scott directed Jack to follow the trail of chaos.

Far into the scrub, Frank's big rig sat at an angle. The mangled security car sat beside it, as if thrown by the hand of God. Near the trunk of the car, a small knot of men struggled with a woman.

Tolly.

Cold rage speared through Scott. It tasted metallic and bitter in his mouth. He would use that sword to destroy them all.

"Jack, get ready." Scott unfastened his seatbelt. He opened the passenger door.

"I'm ready." Jack held the wheel steady. The pickup bounced over the rough terrain.

"Gunman, Jack!" Scott shouted. "Run him down!"

Jack drove the pickup into Bruce.

With a roar that would have frightened a lion, Scott launched himself through the passenger door. He tackled Bruce's men like a bowling ball knocked down pins.

Tolly fell to the ground like a sack of potatoes. She didn't make a sound. She didn't move.

Jack yanked the truck to a stop in order to join the fight. But Scott had already used his fists to put down the other men. Then he kicked their guns further into the scrub. But he and Jack turned to Bruce a split second too late.

Still in pain from the monster truck's body blow, Bruce trained his gun on both Windrunners. Scott and Jack raised their hands.

A few yards away, Frank Griffin groaned then stirred back to life. However, he was too far away from his shotgun to take care of Bruce.

Scott called over, "Hey, Griffin, it's been a while."

His old friend groaned again with a laugh. "Seems like old times, Windrunner." He got to his hands and knees.

"It does seem like old times. Except now we're just as old as those times."

Frank rose to his feet.

Bruce sneered. "Ah, by the way, guys, I do have a gun."

"So we see," Scott answered.

"Scott Windrunner," Bruce clicked the safety. "You're a dumb motherfucker to come back for more."

The other men recovered somewhat from Scott's brutal fist assault. They circled in the grass to find their weapons.

"And what's with this hobo getup?" Bruce indicated Scott's ragged jeans and brown shirt smudged with dust. He shook his head in disgust. "Fuck you for not carrying a piece."

Scott stalled. "Bruce, do you honestly expect to collect a dime from Alex?"

"Still playing catch up, Windrunner." Bruce threw his head back to laugh. "*Alex* isn't the one you have to worry about." He aimed the gun square at Scott's chest.

In the car lights, Tolly saw Scott's eyes narrow at Bruce's braggadocio.

"Not only am I gonna collect from you for screwing me over," Bruce told him, "But I'm also gonna collect from *her*." Still holding the gun on Scott, he nudged Tolly's still form with his foot.

Scott started forward.

"Oh no you don't." Bruce waved the gun in Scott's face with a provocative smile. "But tell me this. Does the carpet match the drapes? Because with a Black girl," he nudged Tolly a few more times as if to prove to everyone that he could, "you can never be sure."

From the ground, Tolly grabbed Bruce's foot. She yanked it as hard as she could. The gun in his hand fired. She rolled.

Bruce hit the ground beside her. Scott fell upon him in a blur of arms, legs, and fists.

Tolly rolled again. She threw a fistful of sand and dust into the eyes of the fat gunman who cursed and howled.

"Jack!" she shouted, then crawled towards Frank.

Jack sprang forward.

"Stop!" The skinny gunman fired into the air before Jack could reach him.

Everyone froze.

"Back off, little brother," The gunman ordered Jack.

Jack took a step back. Then he joined Tolly and Frank.

The skinny gunman pointed his weapon to the dust-covered heap of Scott and Bruce.

"Get up," he muttered to Scott.

Scott uncoiled. He rose to his feet, pulling Bruce up with him by a fistful of the man's tattered shirt.

"Let him go," the gunman ordered.

Scott released Bruce, who found his gun again, then moved to stand with his men.

Scott held his hand out. "Tolly, come here," he said in a quiet voice.

Tolly ached all over but managed to stumble towards him. "Scott," she breathed never so glad to be back inside the cocoon of his huge arms again.

"You can't kill all of us," Scott told Bruce.

Bruce smiled. "I don't have to kill all of you."

He aimed with care. "Just her."

Scott's arm tightened around Tolly's waist.

"I saw the way you looked at her. You've been protecting her all along, haven't you? Fuck the rest of us trying to earn a living."

Scott didn't respond.

"I thought so," Bruce answered for him. "You shouldn't have let me see that. You really wanna risk it?" he invited.

Scott remained quiet. In a fair fight, she knew he could whip all three men by himself, but they had the advantage. Neither she nor Frank was in any shape to help Scott and Jack overpower three men with guns. Even with Jack's help, Scott wouldn't risk a bullet striking his friends. After all they went through together, King still won in the end.

Checkmate.

Bruce looked Tolly over from head-to-toe. "Bitch, get back over here. You think you're in pain now, wait until I..."

A roar of souped-up engines announced the caravan of pickup trucks and sports utility vehicles that caught and held the combatants in headlights. From the scrub, several men on horseback galloped closer.

Jack answered Scott's look of amazement with a slight nod.

Headlights criss-crossed and reflected off all manner of weaponry—crossbows, rifles, shotguns, baseball bats—pointed towards Bruce and his men in a promise of unfortunate events to come. Twenty men, all dark-haired, all with year-round tans surrounded the smaller group. Outnumbered, outgunned, and outdone, King's thugs calculated the odds, dropped their guns, and then raised their hands.

Scott saw something else in the multiple headlights. He pointed to the red mark on Tolly's face. "Which one of you did that to her?"

The fat man and the skinny man looked towards Bruce.

"They're lying!" Bruce shouted

Tolly pointed in Bruce's direction.

"She's lying!" Bruce's voice rose to a shriek.

"Everyone's lying, Bruce?" Scott shifted Tolly behind him towards Frank.

"Everyone?" He took a step closer to Bruce.

"He did it, Scott," Frank confirmed, taking Tolly's arm.

"So the middleweight champ hit an unarmed woman, did he?" Scott poked Bruce in the chest. Then he shoved Bruce's shoulder. "Big mistake, little man." He balled the front of Bruce's shirt into his fist.

"She kicked me in the nuts!" Bruce was indignant. "And fuck you too, Double D. Don't act like you're new to this. I know all about you in the military. Alex told me everything."

Sheer anger distorted Scott's face. It took five men, including Jack, to pull Scott off Bruce who skipped several steps backward. But he had no escape. Several of the latecomers to the party pushed Bruce back from the periphery.

"Jack! Let me go!" Scott glared at his younger brother who locked Scott's arm in his. Frank braced his feet against the ground to hold Scott's other arm. "Let me go, Griffin. Now!"

Scott swore. Tension bunched the muscles in his arms to the size of small tree trunks. Tolly wondered if she were in a movie. The look on Scott's face promised death.

All the loud voices, the violence, and the curses reminded her too much of the past. Her heart pounded. Cold sweat coated her arms.

Jack whispered urgently in Scott's ear. He kept his hold on Scott's arm, but looked around. Then he gestured with his head for a man with a baseball bat to come over. The man held a brief consultation with Jack. Then he nodded and stepped back with a large grin.

"Where do you want me to hit him, Scott?" he asked in a loud voice.

Scott stared in silence with a confused expression. But the tension in his arms relaxed.

"Take your best shot," he growled.

Several men stepped up. Each gripped Bruce and his two henchmen with tight holds. They waited. In no hurry, the man with the baseball bat tapped the business end of the bat in the palm of his hand.

Then, with dignified pride, he wound up to take his best shot— a baseball bat to the abdomen of Bruce, then the fat henchman, and then the skinny henchman.

Amid coughs from Bruce and his men, the batter swelled his chest. "How's that, Scott?" he asked.

Scott seemed to have regained control of his faculties. He remained calm, but watchful. He nodded his approval, a solemn expression on his face. Then the batter switched places with another of the men who held Bruce.

"You can't do this to me, you red motherfucking savage!" Bruce yelled.

"Look around you, Bruce." Though Scott remained calm, the grim smile didn't reach his eyes. "You're in Indian Country now, city boy."

One by one, the men consulted Scott for his recommendation. One by one, Scott gave them the same answer. They delivered their favorite shots then rotated. Bruce and his men didn't look so good. But they received no rest. The men held them in place for each blow.

Frank took a turn and so did Jack. Scott supervised the bizarre ceremony's conclusion, arms crossed.

"Good job, Jack," he said.

But it wasn't over. Tolly didn't ask Scott's opinion because she already knew what to do.

"This is for me," she announced.

Then she delivered her best shot, scissor kick, straight to Bruce's chin. The men released Bruce, not expecting Tolly's legs to fly out of nowhere.

Bruce staggered back.

Tolly whirled to regain her balance then set up her push kick to his solar plexus.

Bruce fell backward.

"That's for Scott," she told him where he lay on the ground.

He didn't get up.

Chapter 25

Somehow, Scott managed to hide the astonishment on his face. Never a dull moment with his Tolly. *His Tolly.* He liked the sound of that.

She didn't bother with the others. The fat man and the skinny man sat on the ground next to Bruce, the fight already whipped out of them. Someone already collected their weapons.

Scott burst into laughter. "I'm in fucking love," he announced. He meant for it to sound sarcastic, but it didn't. He didn't risk a look at Tolly to see how she responded to the declaration.

She moved back into the circle of his arms. Where she belonged, he thought.

"Scott, I'm sorry," she whispered.

"Shh." He held her as close as he dared in light of their mutual injuries. "It's okay now, Tolly." He stroked her hair. "I told you I wouldn't let anyone hurt you, and I meant it."

"I know that now."

The multitude of men filled the awkward pause with laughter.

"If I wasn't already married with three-and-a-half children, I'd be in love too." Frank chuckled.

"Back off, Griffin."

"So it's like that, Scott?" Frank asked with a sly smile.

Scott rumbled low in his throat. Frank laughed.

"Okay, okay." Thankful that Tolly couldn't see his heated face, he kissed her then snuggled his cheek in her fluffy hair. "Wait for me in the pickup. I'm gonna talk to Jack and the boys a quick minute."

For once in his life, she complied without a word, exhausted.

Frank clapped Scott hard on the back. Scott gave him the one-arm man hug.

The other men surrounded Scott to do the same. One of the men supplied rope to tie Alex's henchmen up where they sat defeated in the dust.

After a few more words, most of the rescue caravan either rode away in vehicles or galloped for home on horseback. Their headlights bounced and hooves jounced over the uneven terrain.

Scott told Tolly that Jack would drive the Windrunner Security car, somehow still operational after the hits from Frank's eighteen wheeler, north to Calabasas. Three of Scott and Jack's friends hopped into the back of the security car for a lift north.

Frank announced that he would finish his delivery with a whopper of a story to tell his wife. The remainder of the men returned home after another round of back slaps and jokes.

Scott loaded his motorcycle into the back of the pickup for the ride back to Calabasas with Tolly. She had no idea what he intended for Bruce and the other two men and she didn't much care.

Scott started the pickup truck. "Wait a minute." He looked at Tolly, then got out of the pickup. He walked towards Bruce, who lay, arms bound, on his side.

"Scott, wait!" she called. He ignored her.

What would he do now that everyone, including Jack, had driven away? She didn't have the strength to help him bury bodies.

Scott bent over Bruce. He reached his arms out towards the prone man. Darkness hid what happened next. Scott's body was too large to see around. After a long moment, he straightened. He walked back to the pickup truck, got in, and then drove back to the road with a grim look on his face.

Tolly was almost afraid to ask, but she had to. "Scott, what did you do to him?" If they had to flee to Mexico or Brazil, she needed time to wrap her head around the concept.

Scott looked at her. "What are you talking about?"

"Is he... is he..." Tolly swallowed. "Did you leave him alive?" she whispered.

Scott looked at her as if she'd lost her mind. He laughed so hard that they almost went off the road again. Tolly decided that if he'd gone crazy, then she would take the lead on their getaway strategy.

Scott took gasps of air to calm himself. "He's fine, Tolly."

"He's alive?"

"Yes, he's alive. Still talking shit too."

"They're all alive?"

That set Scott off on another laugh bender. Tolly waited until he sobered up again.

"They're all fine, I promise. Bruce took the flash drive from me earlier." Scott shook his head with disgust. "I can't believe I didn't make a copy of that file as soon as I got it from Valerie. But I was in such a hurry to find you."

"Did you... watch it?"

Scott's mouth thinned into a line. "I watched it." His hands tightened on the steering wheel.

"So now you know."

For a moment, she didn't think he would answer. "I do know, Tolly," he answered quietly. So quiet, she barely heard him. "I should have known the moment we met. I'm sorry," he told her. "I'm sorry for everything."

She squeezed his hand. "I'm not."

He looked at her, then back at the road.

"Did you get it back from him?" she asked, at last.

Scott sighed. "It's destroyed beyond all recovery. The baseball bat, I think."

This time, Tolly laughed longer than Scott. "God, what a day."

"I know." Scott replied, frustrated. "You trusted me with the evidence, Tolly, and I blew it."

"You won't get paid now, will you?"

Scott stared at the dark road ahead of them. Disappointment speared through him, but then, he deserved her mistrust. What must she think of him after he'd deceived her?

"Tolly, that video was undeniable proof of Alex's violent nature. It would have provided leverage to protect you. It would have finished his political career once and for all. As it is, Alex can still use his connections to try to discredit... and destroy both you and me and anyone else who threatens his power. If he becomes mayor, he'll be harder for me to reach," Scott predicted.

"Us," Tolly corrected. "Us to reach."

Scott shook his head, still preoccupied. "I lost the evidence. Twice."

"What's this *I* and *me* stuff, Scott?" she asked. "We're in this together. Two the hard way," she reminded in a firm tone. "I told you."

"You mean like we're a team?" He teased.

Tolly sucked in her breath. The familiar thrill coursed through her. She would always be there for him... if he wanted her on his team.

"There's one more copy of the video," she told him.

"Seriously?" He looked at her with hope. "Where? Did you store it online?"

"No," she shook her head. "I was too afraid to do that. Back when I made the copies, I thought it might get distributed by accident and that it would be traced to me. But I don't care at this point. Not after everything we've been through."

"So where's the copy?"

"At the post office in Patina."

It took a second for that to register. Comprehension dawned. The mailbox just steps away from her building. Then the coffee shop. Then the bus station. He looked at her in admiration.

"We have to wait until Monday to pick it up," she cautioned.

Scott frowned. "That's cutting pretty close to Tuesday's primary vote."

"I know, but it's our best shot. We have to go with what we have."

"Okay." Scott nodded. He squeezed his Tolly's hand. They caught up to Jack, who chugged the road ahead of them in the damaged security car. The sedan would have to undergo serious realignment among other maintenance imperatives. But it would make it to Calabasas.

"That's some escort we have," Tolly commented.

"All the way home," Scott said. "Tolly, there's just one last errand we need to run before we hit the post office Monday morning."

"Anything, Scott." He saw her smile in the dim light of the moon.

"Anything?" Back to good spirits, he didn't hide the suggestion in his voice. He felt greedy for her, all of a sudden.

Tolly didn't answer. Her heart had filled with an unexplainable longing when he said the word home.

She couldn't trust her voice to reply. Instead, she watched the road, definitely in love with Scott Windrunner.

They rode in silence the rest of the way back to Calabasas.

Chapter 26

So late Saturday evening that it would become Sunday morning in minutes, Jack parked the battered Windrunner Security car in front of Nellie's log home. Scott pulled the pickup to a stop behind his brother.

"Tolly, wait here," Scott ordered. He brooked no argument from her. He joined his younger brother and the three other men who rode up with him from New Mexico at Nellie's front door. For a while, no one answered.

Tolly imagined Sonny on a late Saturday night, toppled into bed, disheveled, yelling for the racket to cease. He would stumble into walls and around furniture to the front door. He would scream to find out who created the ruckus and what the hell they wanted. Jack, or one of the other men, would initiate the conversation with Sonny because Scott remained number one on Sonny's bad list, the rest of the world came in second.

Tolly watched the confrontation unfold through the windshield. Sonny stood in the doorway. Scott and Jack grabbed him from either side. The other men hustled him around the back of the house. After that, Tolly couldn't see.

Nellie came to the doorway. Tolly waved her to the truck. She got inside.

"Nellie, where are the kids?" Tolly asked her.

"At my father's."

"Where did they take Sonny?"

Nellie stared through the windshield. "Out of my gun range."

Tolly had no reply to that. Instead, she listened. Somewhere in the dark, she heard multiple voices and rough scuffles. Serene about the whole thing, Nellie seemed to be in a mood to talk, unlike Tolly's last visit.

"My son told me that he wanted to get away from Sonny so he wouldn't see what Sonny did to me—the beating and the choking. Sometimes, Sonny pulled knives on me. I could see the disrespect in my son's eyes and hear it in his voice that I allowed it to happen. And that I made him and my daughter witnesses. Does a real head job on a kid, you know?" Nellie paused.

"It took me a long time to see, but I knew that I had to stop it. It was about my children, not just me."

"Why didn't you leave him, Nellie?"

"Why didn't you?"

Tolly flinched, shocked.

Nellie looked into Tolly's eyes. "I'm right about you, aren't I?"

Tolly looked away. "Scott told you?"

"No." Nellie shook her head. "He wouldn't do that. I don't know if you realize it, but Scott really cares about you. I can tell."

"Then how did you know?"

"You told me when you were here."

Tolly frowned.

"I saw the look on your face when I was dealing with Sonny. Like you could see all the way through me. Like you knew how it felt to be treated like that and it shamed you too."

Tolly studied the pickup's state-of-the-art dashboard. She knew how to street fight. Every girl who grew up in Lake City's Central District either learned how to handle situations or stayed home. But her education lacked in that her parents, good-hearted people who cherished one another and Tolly too, both died before it occurred to either to teach Tolly harder lessons about the real world.

"I couldn't bear that look," Nellie continued. "I felt so ashamed that someone could see so far inside my head."

"No." Tolly shook her head. "No, Nellie."

After her parents died, she latched on to Rafael who made her feel special. However, once she became dependent upon that type of attention, Rafael diminished her self-esteem, her pride, and her dignity a little more each day. He refilled her with shame and fear to the point she had no tools left with which to counter the abuse.

"I'm sorry I asked you and Scott to leave. That was so…"

"No. You're right, Nellie. I do understand. Trust me, I do."

By the time Tolly surfaced from the murk, she realized to what extent Rafael had isolated her to his control. She'd lost touch with everyone who might have helped her. But even after his prison sentence and subsequent death, residual shame lingered.

"I guess the guys are helping a little," Nellie acknowledged in a quiet voice.

"Once you showed them you were ready." Tolly smiled. "I guess that's what family and community are for." The words echoed inside her ears.

"To restore balance," she concluded.

But, to this day, Tolly still had not reached out to those she knew years ago. She didn't know if they would recognize or accept the woman she'd become. As she told Frank, too much time had passed.

"We needed to allow you the time and space to work things out and you did," she finished. The words rang false. She felt like a hypocrite.

"Now you sound like my father."

"Where do you think I got that from?" She laughed with Nellie, a gallows type of humor.

After Rafael, Tolly vowed to never let another person dominate, humiliate, or degrade her. Years later, she combined self-defense with assertiveness training at the local gym. Thanks to the retired Lake City police officer, her head began to unravel the tangle of knots that constricted her ability to think straight. That was the woman still under repair that King assaulted at Celara Wind. But that was not the woman who defended herself on the road to Santa Fe.

Jack and Scott and the men returned. Nellie and Tolly got out of the pickup truck. Scott bent to kiss her. Then he held on to his younger sister for a long moment without words.

None of the men looked the worst for wear, so maybe Sonny accepted the new domestic situation without too much damage. Nellie certainly had.

Scott turned to her, "Tolly, I'll meet you and Jack at Pop's, okay?"

Tolly nodded. Scott drove off into the darkness with the other men in the pickup truck.

"Where are they going?"

"Visiting with family and friends. It's been a while."

"Scott too?"

"Yeah. Well. They're with him for right now. But they'll bunk with me and Pop tonight, then catch a ride south tomorrow. Or whenever." Jack gave her a sidelong glance. "Scott'll probably stay somewhere else, with someone else tonight."

Jack, Tolly, and Nellie got into the crippled security car and set out for the log cabin home of James Windrunner. This time, Jack let them inside with his key since their father wasn't home.

"Probably chewing the fat," Jack guessed.

Nellie wanted to talk with her son and daughter, who spent the night with their grandfather in anticipation of Sonny's confrontation. "They will never have to feel afraid in their own home again," Nellie declared on the way upstairs.

Tolly faced the smirk on Jack's face. Before he could speak, she asked him to identify the multitude of skins, furs, staffs, and musical instruments that filled James Windrunner's museum-like abode. Jack agreeably pointed out family photos, maps, and the construction designs of the cabin by the lake. It turned out that James used that cabin as a design model for prospective entrants into the housing program.

Tolly ohed and ahed over that as long as she could, but Jack waited her out.

"So... Tolly."

She braced for it.

"You love Scott."

"You heard that, did you?"

"I did hear that."

Tolly's face heated.

"How very interesting," Jack said.

Though she'd exhausted the inventory of their father's home, Tolly decided to head further commentary off at the pass. "Why did Scott leave here, Jack?"

Jack became guarded. "He enlisted."

"After he returned from military service the last time, I mean. He did come home, right?"

"He did," Jack acknowledged with a nod.

"Then he left a few weeks after."

"He did."

Tolly waited. She wanted to give Frank's trick a try.

Jack cleared his throat.

Tolly still didn't speak.

Jack looked past her then seemed to come to a decision. "There was a rumor after Scott's service that he would be considered for a leadership role here in the community—*the* leadership role of our community should the time come that it proved necessary. Scott was respected as a veteran of an elite branch."

"Was?" Tolly asked.

Jack fell silent.

Still Tolly didn't speak.

Jack continued with reluctance. "Scott was tough. *Is* tough. He's a fighter. He would lay down his life to protect people who can't protect themselves. He doesn't back down. *You* should know that, Tolly."

"I do know that." That was only one of about a million things she loved about him. Tolly looked away. If only he could love her in return.

"Scott respects history and would have worked with other Indian communities."

"What changed? What caused him to leave?"

Jack indicated for her to sit on the sofa. He took a chair.

"Scott left Calabasas to save the Windrunners, all of us, but especially our father from... embarrassment. We couldn't convince him not to leave and we certainly couldn't stop him. He made up his own mind. But me, Nellie, and of course our father never stopped believing in Scott or loving him. That's part of the reason why I joined him in Lake City."

Tolly nodded. "I'm sure he appreciates that."

"That's all I'm going to give you, Tolly." Jack smiled at her. "A man has the right to tell his own story his own way."

"Why thank you, Jack," the voice came from the doorway. Tolly gasped. For such a large man, Scott moved quieter than a cat.

"Does he always do that?" she asked James who walked in behind Scott.

Scott's father grinned at her. "Who do you think taught him how?"

172   Windrunner

Tolly laughed, then used her hands to pull fourteen inches of a wavy halo of hair into her clip. She brushed at the stubborn, red dust that streaked her khakis and white shirt.

Scott joined her on the sofa. James took another chair next to Jack. Again, Tolly marveled at the strong resemblance between th three men. However, Scott's solid build and snowy length of hair caused him to stand out. His guarded, road-weary demeanor and stillness contrasted with Jack's youthful vitality.

Even James, a full generation older seemed younger at heart. The elder Windrunner settled back with a sigh. "Speaking of stories, there's nothing I like better than a good story myself. But usually, I'm the one who has to tell it."

Scott said, "Pop, everybody knows no one does it like you do."

James stared into space. "I have to remember who said what to whom. How much time passed. And then remember to put the punch line in the right place to make people laugh. Otherwise, it doesn't work. Storytelling is not as easy as it looks."

For a minute, Tolly wondered if the older man were tired. "I think tonight, I'd like to hear a story," he said.

"No kidding, Pop?" Jack asked. "The storyteller wants to hear a story?"

"No kidding." This time, Tolly saw the twinkle in James's eyes. "I'd like to hear the story of how Scott met Tolly."

Tolly, Scott, and Jack looked at each other. The brothers shrugged. For the next half hour, Tolly helped to fill in the blind spots of her and Scott's meeting. When Scott talked of how he listened to whispers on the wind to track her down, Tolly rolled her eyes. Jack spoke on his endless phone calls across Indian Country to find help. Scott and Jack concluded with Sonny's comeuppance in the darkness behind Nellie's house.

James enjoyed the tale. He laughed in spots, commented in spots, even high-fived his sons a few times. But quicker than quick, he angled the conversation one hundred and eighty degrees to Scott's military service.

"By the time Scott entered military service, our family already had members who had served in World War 1, World War 2, Korea, and Vietnam. Then the numbers got smaller for the Gulf War and Bosnia. By the second Gulf War, it was just you, Scott."

"I guess that makes me the lucky one," Scott deadpanned.

Tolly wondered if that explained Scott's stillness... and maybe his white hair? He must have seen the unimaginable, the unexplainable. Still, the sparkle in his eyes indicated an undefeated spirit.

"You know, Tolly, we use the conqueror's institutions for Native needs as a sort of proving ground." James mesmerized with his resonant voice.

While Tolly thought that over, James asked, "I wondered if I might speak to my eldest son alone?"

She and Jack wandered outside to sit down. They could still hear the conversation in the log cabin's living area, but Scott and his father had some semblance of privacy.

***

James remained quiet a full minute. Scott knew better than to rush him.

"Son, military service doesn't always win respect from outsiders. It doesn't change bigoted minds either. What outsiders *might* respect, maybe, is the uniform and the institution. Just not always the person inside the uniform or his culture or his people. You know this."

The conversation he'd avoided for years had come, at last. Scott sighed. "I know, Pop."

"Police, fire, rescue, and healthcare professions offer a somewhat similar experience to the combat zone. Maybe it's time we thought of them as deserving the same honor as veterans. Maybe we should push our young people to become paramedics, and nurses, and emergency workers."

"First responders do tend to mature quickly," Scott agreed.

"Maybe they should join our veterans as part of the honor guards at powwows."

"It's a thought. But I don't know how many others are thinking it."

"Well, activism is also another honor tradition."

"Activism? What kind of activism?"

"Community development and safety. Building projects. Health centers. Safety. Police."

"What are you trying to say, Pop?" Scott looked at his father. "You think I should find a new profession?"

***

Nellie joined Tolly and Jack outside. Tolly figured her children had gone back to sleep. Hopefully, that would give Nellie a few more hours to put her house to rights after Sonny's expulsion.

"Cards on the table." Tolly turned to Nellie, sure to talk. "Who's Laura?"

Nellie sighed. "Laura was Scott's first wife." She scowled and shook her head. "She left Scott after…"

Jack made a sudden movement which Nellie and Tolly both caught, but ignored.

Nellie continued. "After Scott left the military, the way he did, they divorced."

"Any children?"

"No children. Well, Laura has a son with her current husband."

"What about after his divorce?" Tolly asked slowly. "Did he ever…"

This time, Nellie cut Jack a sidelong glance. "No one serious."

Jack cleared his throat, but once started, Nellie wasn't about to stop.

"Scott was very hurt by Laura. It made him cautious about long-term relationships. No… clingers or anything. But anyone Scott's ever had a relationship with would describe him as a decent kind of guy.

"Quiet, kind of reserved. But decent," Jack put in.

"Over-protective," Nellie suggested.

"Nellie."

"Well he is!"

"And thank God for that. Especially today. Right, Tolly?"

"Yes," Tolly answered. After all, she did know the worst that could happen.

"See there?" Jack shifted, uncomfortable with all the girl talk. "I'll let you biddies continue to cluck." Jack re-entered the log cabin, then continued upstairs to visit his niece and nephew.

"I'll explain it to you." Nellie moved her chair closer. "What happened with Scott drew us all, the immediate family closer. But it pushed friends, extended family, and tribal community away. It also caused bent, ignorant, cowards to seek to hurt him. And some of them, including Laura, were successful."

"Scott is a good person," Tolly decided.

"Yes, he is," Nellie agreed. "And I don't say that just because he's my brother. He has no regrets but I know that he does feel sad and angry from time to time. He never says it aloud. But I can tell.

He never could stand how the strong and powerful victimized and exploited the weak and vulnerable. Even when we were all little. He was always willing to stand up and defend people who couldn't defend themselves."

"How's he doing since he's been back to Calabasas?"

"I think for the first time in years, Scott feels at home."

***

"Scott, you are a grown man."

"Unfortunately," Scott answered.

James laughed.

"I have something to say. I would ask that you allow me to finish. It won't take long."

"Okay, Pop."

"You have grown into the man you were always meant to be. I have always been proud of you. Even when you came home from school with torn clothes smeared with dirt and grass hanging from your hair from fighting…"

"You knew about that?"

"You'd be surprised at the things I know."

Scott snorted, "Only a fool would be surprised at the things you know."

For instance, Scott knew that he, Tolly, and Jack must have looked a sight after tonight's knock-down, drag-out in the desert. But his father said not a word about their appearance.

James smiled, let a pause go by. "You never allowed anyone to do a wrong to Nellie and Jack and get away with it."

"Those were the days."

"Those were the days." James agreed. He let another moment pass. "But these are new days, son. It's time for you to live your own life."

Scott gazed at the floor, covered in rugs of Native design. Despite his best efforts, his eyes watered.

"It is time now for you to allow Jack and Nellie to stand up for themselves so that they can grow into the people they are meant to be."

"I thought I was doing that when I moved to Lake City," Scott replied, his voice gruff.

"You were doing something else when you moved to Lake City. Something that had nothing to do with Nellie or Jack."

Scott stilled.

"No one in the community was harder on you than you." His father's quiet voice dominated the silence.

Scott flinched, but James Windrunner proved relentless.

"The people who still maintain the common sense granted to them love and respect you. That is why they came to help you when they knew you needed them. Now they are another step closer to being the people *they* were meant to be. Sometimes it's good to allow people to help you, Scott. Especially when you need the help. It makes people feel important."

Scott gave the barest nod of his head.

James stood up, his signal that the story ended. The twinkle returned to his solemn eyes.

"Now, how about you hand an old man his slippers so he'll finally go to bed and stop talking so much? You'll see how good that makes *you* feel."

Scott laughed. Then he embraced James Windrunner in a hug so long that it erased miles of distance and years of silence.

Somehow, the past few days had turned his world upside down. He was pretty sure he knew why.

Chapter 27

In the darkest moments before Sunday's dawn, Scott and Tolly returned to the cabin by the lake. Now that Tolly knew more about its purpose, to encourage more building, the pine log construction seemed even more majestic, though still bare and relatively empty.

"Home sweet home." Scott threw their bags to the floor.

Tolly laughed at him. "How sweet it is."

"Sweets for the sweet." He wagged his dark brows over eyes that snapped and flashed.

Response surged through Tolly. She turned away. "This place is wonderful, Scott. It's so restful."

"It's a nice place to watch the sun come up. Watch the wind blow. Forget about it all and let the world go by."

"It's gonna be hard so hard to go back to Lake City," she sighed.

She and Scott looked at each other with exhaustion. They peeled off their road clothes and stuffed them into the washer. Tolly felt a trifle shy because she remembered the intimacy of their last time together in the cabin. She knew he must remember too.

By mutual agreement, they swallowed aspirins then took turns in the shower. The hot water worked out the wear and tear of the road. Then they collapsed into each other's arms for the sleep of the dead.

Bright and early, Scott put their clothes into the dryer and made breakfast for them in his underwear. She ate it wearing the quilt from the bed. They decided to continue the work from Thursday, fixing up the cabin—sunny and airy—by the light of day. They figured out the off-grid features that fed hot water and electricity into the now-cozier home.

Dressed again, they hauled tools and supplies around, and tried to work out a strategy for Alex King.

"It's so tempting to let sleeping dogs lie," Tolly said while she sanded the caulk smooth to the log cabin's walls.

"You mean turn our backs on the whole affair and never return to Lake City," Scott stated, his tone neutral.

"Well, the problem with that is 'every closed eye ain't sleep.' That's what my father used to say."

Scott smiled. "My father says something similar."

"And every goodbye ain't gone."

He laughed. "That too, which is why we always say, 'see you later.'"

"We could mail the DVD next-day service to the *Lake City Tribune*."

Scott shook his head. "It might not get there Tuesday morning. It could get lost. Besides, we don't know for sure that the newspaper would go public with it. There's always the Lake City Police Department," he suggested.

Tolly shuddered. She had not forgotten her experiences with hostile Lake City police during Rafael's sentencing. She also remembered Celara's sly assurances. "I don't think that's going to work. According to Celara King, Lake City police are friends of the King campaign."

"She's right, for the most part." Scott confirmed. "Besides, the primary vote is all day Tuesday. We don't have that much time to get this figured out."

They worked in silence for a minute.

"There's the other option, Tolly."

"What?"

"Well, like you said. We don't have to go back to Lake City." Scott stopped sanding. "We *could* just let it ride."

"No. You were right the first time. We can't leave it like this."

He nodded at her with *that's my girl* approval. "Look, we're both tired and worn out from working all day. Let's sleep on it tonight and try to get it figured out in the morning."

He walked across the room, took her sandpaper away. "Come here." He drew her into his lap.

Her heart fluttered. "Scott?" Tolly leaned her head on his shoulder.

"Yeah?"

"I'm so glad that I met you."

"In spite of it all?"

"Because of it all."

Tolly turned her face to his. She ran her hand through his silver waves.

"Let's go to bed," she whispered.

He groaned. "Best idea you've had all day, Tolly."

"I have a few more."

His eyes widened, but he followed her upstairs.

In the master bedroom, he faced her. Tolly tensed. Sometimes, Rafael smacked her when she didn't perform up to his expectations. But this was Scott, she reminded herself. Not Rafael.

Scott who lit her body up like a slot machine. Scott who made her fall to pieces with the lightest touch. Scott with the soft fall of silver hair that swept back-and-forth over her. Scott with the massive chest that rose and fell above her. Scott who shouted her name.

Scott.

He was all over her, everywhere. The room disappeared within the tangle of their arms and legs. She drowned in the pleasure of Scott Windrunner. In the midst of madness, she clutched at him to save her, desperate to hold onto her sanity. She cried out for rescue. He held her closer than close, then doubled-down to throw her a lifeline. Giving, giving, giving until she fell back, sated and full.

They lay in each other's arms for a long time without words. She felt the rise and fall of his chest under her cheek. She felt safe. She felt home.

"What do you want out of life, Tolly?" he asked her.

"I want to make up for past mistakes. I want to live a wonderful life."

"That's not asking for a whole lot."

"It would mean a lot to me. It would mean everything. I want to experience the same devotion I remember my parents having. I want to feel safe. And..." *I want you to love me.*

"And?"

"I want to explore the world beyond Lake City," she said instead.

"Well, we can scratch a few items off the list."

Tolly laughed. "Las Vegas, New Mexico is great this time of year."

"Plenty of sun and sand."

"And road pavement." Tolly giggled, but inside, she still couldn't stop the smallest smidgen of fear. She worried about wrong choices. One wrong move would subjugate her to violent domination. She couldn't go through that again. The next time, she may not survive. Maybe that's why her confrontation with Alex King sent her on a run halfway across the country.

Despite the training at the gym, she'd failed to protect herself. Her experience at the receiving end of Rafael's fists meant that she still didn't quite trust her own judgment.

Scott felt Tolly's tension. "Your turn," he told her.

"My turn what? To be on top?" she asked.

Scott laughed "Good Lord, not just yet, Tolly. I'm gonna need a little rest. But soon," he promised then squeezed her tighter to his side. "It's still your turn to let it all hang out."

"What do you mean? I just did."

"I know you must have heard the conversation with my father."

"Most of it," Tolly admitted. "But then Nellie came outside to talk to me and Jack."

"About me?"

Tolly laughed. "I'm afraid so."

"I knew it." Scott shook his head. "Those two..."

"I'm afraid so," Tolly repeated.

"Well, you're here in bed with me. It must not have been that bad."

"They care about you, Scott. They want you to be happy."

"So do I." He squeezed her. "But I meant, now it's your turn to even the equation. Tell me some other things about yourself."

Tolly moved to lay her head on Scott's shoulder. She would tell him. But she couldn't look at him while she did.

Windrunner 181

"Sometimes, I have trouble breathing. When I'm... reminded of something bad, my heart pounds really fast. I feel as though I can't catch my breath. And then... and then my muscles tense up and I feel like I need to run away. And then I'm stressed to the point that I can't sleep. Sometimes, I feel as though something that's not even there will jump out at me."

Tolly closed her eyes. "I look under the bed just to make sure."

Scott was quiet a long time. Tolly's heart sank. He thought she was crazy.

"I don't know if you realize it, Tolly, but that sounds a lot like post-traumatic stress syndrome."

"Am I crazy?" she whispered.

"No more than a lot of people I know."

"People in wars?"

Scott hesitated, then nodded. Tolly opened her mouth to ask him the next question.

In a swift move, he closed his lips over hers. "Now it's your turn," he whispered.

With another one of his swift moves, he rolled Tolly on top.

Chapter 28

Eight o'clock, Monday morning, Scott parked his pickup in front of the main post office in Patina. They read the sign from the street.

"The post office doesn't open for another hour." Scott seemed especially anxious to get the show on the road.

"What about that errand you mentioned, Scott? I thought we were going to do that first anyway."

"We don't have a lot of time to get back to Lake City."

"No, we don't, but we may as well do something."

Scott thought a moment. "We have to hurry."

He drove a familiar path through Patina. The trip ended in front of Canela Street, Valerie's shelter.

"She's not going to be too happy to see me. Not after the way I ran out on her."

"You'd be surprised, Tolly." Scott opened her door. "She already saw the video."

"You showed her?"

He grinned. "How else do you think I was able to find you?"

"For heaven's sake, you told your father that you heard whispers on the wind." Tolly burst into laughter.

Scott kissed her, hard. "I would have said and done whatever it took to find you," he told her.

Her heart flipped. A wave of warmth poured through her.

Scott led her inside. At the reception desk, he thrust a thick roll of cash under Valerie's nose.

Tolly's mouth dropped open. So did Valerie's

Valerie led them into her office. She shut the door behind them, then crossed her arms. "Mister, I run an honest business."

"Valerie, in addition to the grant you have in the works, my client would like to donate this money to Canela Street. The client would prefer to remain anonymous."

Valerie looked at Tolly who shrugged.

"Please do not try to return it or refuse it, because then it would just go to a bad cause."

The Canela Street director raised an eyebrow. "How bad?"

"Bad."

Valerie gave Scott the eye. "I take it you don't want a receipt?"

"God no."

He held the thick roll of greenbacks out to Valerie again. This time, she accepted. She unlocked a desk drawer with a key, buried the wad in deep, then shut and locked it.

"You two are quite the pair." Valerie smiled. "I actually liked having the night off for once. You did good work here, Tolly. Ran it like a clock." She leaned in closer. She looked into Tolly's eyes, her own worried.

"Did it work out the way it was supposed to?"

Tolly smiled. "You did everything right, Valerie. I'm very grateful to you."

"What a relief." Valerie smiled. "Everyone comes in here with a story, but not quite like the one you two told me. I'm pretty sure there's a lot I don't know and more than that I don't want to know."

"That would make you the lucky one," Scott threw his favorite line at her.

Valerie laughed. "Still, it would be great to have someone here to help out from time to time. I'm a little short-handed."

After a quick glance at Scott, Tolly made her pitch.

"She's a great person and won't let you down," Tolly finished.

Scott squeezed her hand.

"How soon can your sister start?" Valerie asked him.

A few minutes later, Scott and Tolly took their leave of Canela Street to return to the post office. Scott walked around the truck to the passenger side in order to open her door. Tolly felt she could really get used to the attention of an alpha male—a man with nothing to prove, and complete confidence in his identity.

"Scott, where did that money come from?" she asked him.

He smiled, but didn't reply.

"Are you the client? Did you donate the money?"

He started the truck. "No, it wasn't my money, Tolly."

"Then who?"

"Bruce."

"Bruce? The man who just tried to kill us Bruce?"

"That's the one," he confirmed with cheer. He said nothing more until they reached the post office.

"Time's wasting." Scott looked through the plate glass window. "Damn, there's already a line in there." He nudged her forward. "Make it fast."

Scott made calls on his cell phone. Twenty minutes later, Tolly emerged with the DVD. They viewed it on Scott's laptop.

"Do you anticipate that you'll be called Mayor Alexander King?"

No sound from the children any more. They must have fallen asleep.

"Well, the people will decide that with the primary vote next Tuesday and then the general next month. But really Tolly, just call me the next guy in line who wants to make the world a better place."

The video arrived to Alex's assault on Tolly. Still angry about it, Scott balled his hands into fists around the laptop. He muttered under his breath. The camera even picked up the audio of Celara King's delicate threats.

"What a couple of pieces of work," Scott commented. "Just in case." He copied the entire video to his laptop's hard drive.

Tolly remained quiet.

"Is it hard to watch?" he asked her.

"It's hard to watch anyone be hurt like that, including me," she responded.

"You know what set him off, don't you?" Scott asked her.

Windrunner 185

"What?"

"The children, the crying in the background."

Tolly looked at him, eyebrows raised. "That's why he hit her and me?"

"Besides the fact that he's nuts, yes." He watched her think that over.

"When I saw Nellie's situation. I told myself there but for the grace of God. But I'm not afraid of King anymore. I feel only contempt. What he did to me was not right and I know that I didn't deserve it."

Tolly's hands shook in her lap. Scott didn't like that so he took her hands in his, then he pulled her across the seat into his arms.

Tears streaked down her face.

"Tolly, Tolly," he whispered and stroked her hair. "It's over now." He kissed her tears away.

Tolly closed her eyes and sighed. She would tell him now. He might be the one person on Earth who wouldn't judge her.

"Scott, there's something else."

He stilled underneath her cheek.

"I... became pregnant while I was with Rafael."

He waited for the rest.

Tolly swallowed. "One night, he..." A sob escaped her. Scott tried to pull her into another hug, but this time Tolly resisted. "He was crazy. Something I said or did set him off. I can't remember what it was."

"Doesn't matter," Scott interjected.

"He slapped me to the floor. Then he kicked me in the stomach." Tolly tried to wipe the tears away, but they fell from her eyes in a stream.

Scott closed his eyes. "Oh my God."

"I... I lost the baby." Tolly looked away. She didn't want to see loathing and horror fill the face of the man she loved. "I miscarried at seven months. It's still the worse day of my entire life."

She shook her head. "Anyone else, someone with sense would have left him before it got to that point, but..." She choked up. "I just felt so stupid that I let him kill my baby."

Scott reached for his glove box. He handed her a tissue. She turned her face away from the hard lines of his grim expression.

"I can't believe I let it happen."

"Tolly, you didn't let Rafael kill your baby any more than you let Alexander King assault you. You were overpowered."

"I know. I just... felt so responsible for staying with him. After it happened, I couldn't face my family because they knew. I've been frozen, paralyzed by the guilt ever since. Living only half a life."

Scott squeezed her hard. "You still have the rest of your life ahead of you, Tolly." He kissed her again then started the pickup. "But we've got to hit the road now." They cruised east back to Lake City.

"Was that the turning point?" Scott asked her.

"Where?" Tolly looked around to see if they missed a turn.

"No, I mean was that what ended the relationship?"

"With me and Rafael?" Tolly didn't miss the way Scott's jaw tightened or how his lips turned down at her mention of Rafael's name. "Not exactly. He was killed in prison. I... never left him, which I regret."

"Don't," Scott said. "Don't do that anymore."

"He left me. Lake City police arrested him for drug possession then took him away."

Scott nodded.

"So, I didn't solve the problem. Someone else solved it for me. I didn't rejoice in Rafael's death. By then, I'd lost everything—self-confidence, self-respect, connection to my extended family. My own life was so far off the rails that I didn't even feel like a human being anymore. That's how deep I fell. Lake City police wanted to escalate Rafael's charges to increase his sentence. They tried to intimidate me into turning on him. I refused. I didn't know anything anyway. Rafael always concealed his activities. Or, maybe I was too passive to ask. They dropped the investigation after he died. After they had no further use for me, that's when they left me alone. I've been alone ever since."

She'd come completely clean. Scott already knew about Tolly's involvement from her background check. But dry facts did nothing to illustrate the pain and anguish of a real life harmed by thoughtless, selfish, criminal behavior.

Scott felt the irrational urge to dig Rafael out of his grave in order to choke the second life out of him.

A long silence passed.

"We need a plan." Scott decided it was time to change the subject back to the present. Rafael was out of reach, but Alexander King still walked the Earth.

She nodded.

"We have three choices: Tina Yashuda, *Lake City Tribune*. Or Lake City Police Department."

"Alex King has hurt so many people."

"The list is long." Scott tightened his hands on the steering wheel. Bad things would happen to Alexander King. Very bad things.

"Like any other bully, he will continue to hurt people until he is stopped," Tolly continued.

"Yes, he will," Scott confirmed. "It's your DVD, Tolly, so that makes it your call."

"*Lake City Tribune* and Lake City police haven't done much in the past to hold the King of the City accountable for anything he's ever done."

"No, they have not," he agreed.

Tolly looked at Scott, her mind made up. "Yashuda."

"That's my girl." Scott smiled. He liked that idea more the more he thought about it.

Chapter 29

They switched at North Platte city limits. Tolly drove eighty while Scott prepared to make his calls. She watched their first trip west in unfold in reverse.

"Do you miss the motorcycle?" she asked. He'd tied his bike, damaged from Bruce's hit-and-run, to the truck bed.

"Do you?" he asked her in return with a dangerous grin.

She blushed, then cleared her throat. "Well, your truck handles like it's riding on air. It's so smooth."

"I needed something reliable that could handle the highways and byways in case I needed to go off road."

"Good looking ahead, especially lately," Tolly laughed. "My truck's more like those old-fashioned types you see on classic television shows and movies."

"Well don't knock it. How do you keep it going?"

"With duct tape, safety pins, and wishes. It was my father's. I couldn't bear to let it go."

"I'd be surprised if you couldn't fix it. You can fix just about everything else."

Tolly grinned. "I took it as far as I could. Now it's in the shop. They've been holding it hostage for two months. I really miss it.

Everytime I drove it, it reminded me of my father and how I used to be his little helper." Tolly smiled a little and blinked the mist from her eyes. "I miss my folks too." Scott squeezed her shoulder.

Just past Kearney, Tolly honked at their favorite cheap motel and diner. Scott waved. Then he got back to business.

He called Tina Yashuda's campaign manager. Tolly listened while he tried to arrange a meeting. From what she heard, the campaign manager didn't take the bait.

They switched places on the side of the road. Scott drove through Omaha where they honked and waved at their favorite truck stop.

"Wait! Stop!" Tolly shouted.

Scott maneuvered the pickup into the truck stop's parking lot. While he filled the gas tank, Tolly went inside. He frowned at the plate glass window. She wouldn't skip out the back again, would she?

Not at this point.

Surely not. Surely she would not make him run her down again.

Tolly skipped out the back. Then she re-emerged from the rear of the truck stop's parking lot.

"What were you doing back there?" he asked her.

"I had to get my cell phone." She checked the battery. Dead, of course. "I hid it in the exhaust pipe of an old rusted bus."

"Of course you did," Scott said with a laugh.

"Let's switch again, Tolly. I'm going to try something."

Tolly drove through Des Moines towards Iowa City. They were running out of road and time.

Scott got back on his cell phone.

"Jack, track the ip address of Yashuda's communications manager. I'm going to send you a photo."

He paused. "I just sent it to you now. Install it on his hard drive." Another pause. "Can you do it?"

Scott disconnected then turned the laptop so that Tolly could see the screenshot. King stood over his wife with his hand drawn back. An ugly expression twisted his features to a Halloween mask. His wife's terrified body language was heartbreaking. Tolly shivered.

Scott's cell phone rang. "Okay Jack, send all the information you copied for me as an electronic file."

He waited. "Wherever, whenever you can get the documents scanned, but I need it tonight."

Another pause. "No, you have time. I'm not going to send it to Yashuda yet. Let's see if they find the image you installed first."

Fifteen minutes passed. Yashuda's campaign manager returned Scott's phone call. Scott set up the meeting. When Tolly heard the time they scheduled, she glanced at the truck's clock and then pressed the accelerator closer to the floor. The truck surged forward. The sun glowed warm and hazy behind them.

They reached Iowa City's outskirts, just as Scott disconnected another call. He took the wheel and then gave Tolly the highlights.

"Until Alex formed the Midwest Consortium, Clark Harlan was Celara's legal counsel. We worked together on a lot of projects for Alex.

"What kinds of projects?"

Scott eyed her. "Similar to yours."

"Ah," she responded with a smile.

"Actually, me, Clark, and Evan Lewis—Alex's former assistant—worked together."

"Former assistant? Where is he now? Are you going to call him too?"

"He's dead."

Tolly turned to Scott with wide eyes.

"The story is he drunk-drove Alex's car over the channel bridge a couple of years ago while the roads were icy."

"The story? You mean... the official story?"

Scott nodded.

"So what really happened?"

"The real truth behind that may never be proven." Scott gripped the steering wheel. "But Evan was not alone in the car."

"Who else was there?"

Tolly frowned when Scott skipped over her question. "Anyway, the three of us—Evan, Clark, and me—investigated all of Celara's employees, including a woman who had an affair with Alex. Alex, being Alex, the affair went south. But she gave birth to his son."

Tolly waited.

"Clark fell in love with her. Then they both broke away from Alex."

"How'd he take that?"

"About like you could imagine."

"Imagine? I've seen it live and up close. It's hideous."

"They'd already protected themselves from him. Alex mostly stays away. For him, they no longer exist. He doesn't see his son. He doesn't talk to or about Martina, ever."

"Martina?" Tolly asked, her voice sharp.

"Yeah, you know her?"

Tolly didn't answer.

Scott eyed her. "She looks like you."

"Martina does?" Her eyebrows rose. That explained King's behavior at Celara Wind—the initial attraction, followed by the volcanic anger.

He nodded.

But, "I see," was all she had to say.

Scott frowned, puzzled. "Anyway, only through lawyers. Clark sees to that."

"Good for him. And her." For Tolly, the stakes in the game had just become higher.

"I needed to give Clark a heads up to brace himself for what may happen in Lake City once we get there."

"What do you think will happen?"

"I don't know, Tolly. I really don't. I've got quite a lot here from Jack. I'll have to see how Yashuda reacts to everything tonight when I see her."

"I?" Tolly asked. "What do you mean *I*? Why do you keep saying that? We're going together."

"Tolly, remember what I just told you about Evan Lewis." Scott didn't meet her eyes.

"That's exactly the reason why we should go together." Now, more than ever, Tolly had committed to the end game.

"Let me think about it," Scott sighed.

"You mean let you think of a reason why I shouldn't go?"

He responded with the same grim smile from when she spoke of Rafael. He turned up the radio to get the latest news on the primary.

The sky shimmered blood red behind them.

Scott drove the last leg. At dusk, the skyscrapers that defined Lake City's vibrant downtown rose against the lakeshore, a cold contrast to the warmth of the Rocky Mountains. Scott looked Tolly over where she slept on the passenger side.

His life before they met seemed so blank and so far away.

He still felt amazed at their nights together.

The way she made him cry out in wonder.

How his heart melted each time she smiled, or each time she laughed.

He loved this woman with her chocolate brown eyes, toffee skin, and cinnamon hair. His own personal campfire who protected him from cold nights and lonely winds and the screams that only he could hear. He would do whatever it took to protect her.

He'd promised her that he wouldn't hurt her anymore. He decided then and there that he would leave her out of the negotiations.

While he didn't have a clear idea of where Alex buried all the bodies or how many they totaled, he had a pretty good idea. After all, he'd provided the information that Alex used to wreck the lives of others. Scott had to redeem himself and all of his own ghosts from wars past and present.

Chapter 30

Monday evening, Tolly woke when Scott brought the truck to a stop in front of his condominium. They'd pushed so hard to get back to Lake City, they hadn't stopped for anything to eat. Scott led her to the kitchen where they scarfed down several of the microwaveable meals that filled his freezer.

"You remember in Las Vegas how I said I didn't think I could ever get enough of that?"

"Yes," Tolly smiled, shy all of a sudden.

"It was all very exciting, very thrilling. But I've decided that I was wrong."

"What do you mean?" Surprised, Tolly looked up from a platter of macaroni and cheese.

"That was enough of that on the road to Santa Fe. Like I said, I'll handle Yashuda, Tolly. Then I'll handle Alex. Alone. I mean it."

She knew he meant it because he put a lot of bass in his voice when he issued the order as though he spoke to a new military recruit. She lifted her chin.

"Scott, you know I can take care of myself. You've seen it."

Scott reflected on the high and low points of Tolly's rundown, including the most frightening when Bruce and his men tried to shove her into the trunk of his own security car. He still couldn't process the memory clearly because the same cold, metallic rage interfered with his thoughts. It made him sick to his stomach to imagine what might have happened to her if Jack hadn't gotten him there in time to stop them. He knew to tread with care because Tolly looked ready for another fight.

"Yes, I do know. But now you don't have to take it all on yourself since I'm here." Scott hugged her. "I won't leave you, Tolly. And I won't let you down."

His best girl blinked backed tears. Good, he'd gotten through to her. She lifted her chin again. He sighed to himself.

"No you don't, Scott Leroy Windrunner."

"Who the hell's Leroy?"

"I don't know your middle name so I made one up just so you'd know I was serious."

"Oh Tolly." Scott laughed and crushed her back to his chest. Her soft brown hair tickled his neck. "It's so hard to be away from you even for a moment."

"Then don't." She looked up to meet his gaze. "Take me with you. I know that I can help."

"You aren't alone anymore. I'm here for you always."

"And I'm here for you."

Scott moved about the kitchen, restless. He stopped at the sink and looked through the window into the dark Lake City night. No choice. He had to tell her so she understood the magnitude of the situation.

"Tolly, you asked me about Evan Lewis."

"What about him?"

"Like I said, he wasn't alone in the car when it went over the bridge."

Tolly stiffened. "Who was with him?" She whispered. She held her breath, a look of dread on her face.

After a long pause, Scott answered, "Alex."

She exhaled and sagged back in her chair.

He left the kitchen to allow her time to think that over.

In fact, Tolly exhaled a sigh of relief. For a terrified moment, she thought Scott would admit to *his* participation in the death of King's assistant. She followed him to the main bedroom. The other bedroom belonged to Jack.

Scott set his black leather bag down next to the bed. "Tolly, stay here. Catch your breath." He took his usual thirty second shower. "I mean it," he reminded her when he emerged.

Back in his black t-shirt and jeans uniform, he glanced over his shoulder on the way out of the door.

"I love you." The words rushed out of her mouth before she could stop them.

Scott froze, his back a solid wall of silence.

"Get some rest," he suggested, at last. Then he pulled on his black leather jacket and left.

***

Tolly took a hot shower that eased the ache in her limbs. For once, she tried to be quick about it.

"Stupid, stupid," she muttered. She could have kicked herself for her outburst. She'd declared her love to a man who didn't love her in return.

He couldn't even look at her. Instead, he turned his back and walked away.

She blinked back tears. Well, she couldn't undo what she'd already done. But maybe she could solve another problem.

Between whimpers, she managed to pull on a gray t-shirt that she borrowed from Scott's dresser. She buttoned her white cotton shirt over that and the khakis. The stiffness from the fight with Bruce remained, compounded by the long trip north to Calabasas, then back east to Lake City.

***

The skyscrapers polluted the night sky with their cold, unnatural light. But the stars shone above the eastern shore of the lake.

Tolly loved him. Scott knew that for sure now because she came right out and told him so. Tonight... he would slay dragons for her. He would give Tolly the world. But first things, first.

With a vague feeling of things left undone at the back of his mind, Scott hunted for a parking space outside Tina Yashuda's office in the congested heart of the city.

***

Half an hour later, Tolly arrived to King's campaign headquarters, also in downtown Lake City.

The mayoral candidate's actions hit closer to home than she realized. He had to be stopped.

Hands in pockets under the bulky t-shirt, she squared her shoulders to enter the belly of the beast.

She watched the frenetic activity for a moment. Men and women buzzed back and forth. Phones rang. One wall held a bank of televisions that blared breaking news about the primary race.

Tolly curled her lips to hear the repeated sound bites, copied and pasted from her interview with King at Celara Wind a week ago.

King's reign of terror would end tonight.

***

Scott sat across from almond eyes, sleek dark hair, and ivory skin. Ever cool and calm, Tina Yashuda's demeanor remained unchanged throughout their negotiation.

"So that's it," Scott told her. We're clear on this?" He stood to leave.

Those words reminded him of what he'd left undone. By now, he understood that Tolly's cooperation didn't come easy. And she'd never agreed to his order for her to stay at the condominium while he settled their affairs.

Scott worked to keep those uneasy thoughts off his face. He would go home to the woman who loved him. He would present himself as her humble hero. He hoped she knew what she was getting herself into because once he loved her, he would never stop.

Yashuda nodded her agreement to the terms. She extended a confident hand for him to shake.

***

Alexander King lifted his hands to still the swarm of activity in his hive. "Everyone, we have a long night ahead of us. We'll be here until midnight, am I right?"

Yeah! His volunteers and staff competed to confirm their dedication with energetic shouts and whistles.

"We're down to the win!" The leader bestowed a smile of benevolence upon his followers. "But I'm calling a mandatory dinner break for everyone. We need you at the highest energy to make the final sprint to the finish line."

What? Did he say dinner? Did someone say food? buzzed throughout the headquarters. With great fanfare and hustle and bustle, his staff and volunteers accepted several hundred dollars of petty cash to spend an hour elsewhere.

King stared at Tolly through the departing crowd with ugly promise in his eyes.

***

Scott was almost to the exit when Yashuda's phone rang.

"Mr. Windrunner," she called without inflection. Then she held up her cell phone's display for Scott to see.

She'd received a text message from Scott's cell phone... not in Scott's possession.

Tolly.

When Yashuda let him read the message, she confirmed Scott's worst nightmare.

Scott left her office at a run. He didn't stop for his pickup.

***

King's team chattered and laughed on their way out the door. Tolly caught a few speculative smirks from the men who misunderstood King's intense focus on her.

***

Though forty-six-years old, Scott ran like the wind.

He might have to yell at her.

He might have to handcuff her to his wrist for the rest of their lives.

But first, he had to save her.

***

Celara King emerged from the inner office to stand behind her son. She directed a look of distaste towards Tolly who found herself the focus of two sets of blue-white lasers.

"Mother, go ahead and catch up with the rest of them," King told her. "I'll handle this."

Tolly waited. Celara got her coat and purse.

King waved Tolly into his office. He sat behind his desk. She stood in the doorway. He didn't bother to offer her a seat.

Tolly decided to set the tone. "I understand you've wanted to talk to me for a while now, *Mr. King*. I seem to have something you consider worth fighting for."

"*Ms. Henry*," he responded. "You know what I want." He pointed to the surface of the desk. "Put it right here. Right now."

"I know what you want. Something worth lying for."

He remained undisturbed. "I want all copies."

"Worth killing for."

King leaned back in his chair, a smile of challenge on his face. "Now, you're just being melodramatic. Save it, Ms. Henry. I don't have time for another one of your hysterical displays."

"Or what?"

"What do you mean what?"

"I'm waiting for the threat." Tolly took a step forward into his office. "What happens if I don't give you the film?"

"You live a very uncomfortable life."

"That's it?" She raised her eyebrows, surprised. "But I've already done that. Got anything else?"

"You have no idea." The cold light in his eyes crystallized.

"I have some idea." To her surprise, she didn't waver.

"Oh?" He opened a desk drawer. He threw a check book onto the desk. "How much do you want, Ms. Henry? What's it going to take?"

"You're a bad man, Alexander King," Tolly told him. "A very bad, bad man."

King shrugged as if to say, *tell me something I don't know.* "I told Bruce to finish this in New Mexico." He stood up. "I should have known I'd have to do it myself like I do everything else."

The King of the City moved from behind his desk. His pale eyes glittered like shards of broken glass. "One way or another, it's gonna end tonight, little bitch."

Tolly backed away. Perception on a genius level brought King to the position of power he enjoyed. However, she could tell that he relied upon his original memory from her visit to Celara Wind last week. He expected her to retreat.

King advanced closer.

He expected her run.

Then closer still. He didn't know all that happened to her on the road.

He reached for her arm.

He didn't know *her*.

Because Tolly was tired of running.

The stretch forward shifted his balance.

Perfect.

Tolly delivered a scissor kick to his chin, her best shot. King fell back across his desk and fumbled around.

She turned to leave but froze when she heard the metallic scrape of a gun safety. Over her shoulder, Alexander King rose to his feet. He narrowed his brilliant eyes, then bared his mouth into a predator's grin of triumph.

He looked... demonic.

Tolly shook her head in disbelief. He wouldn't. Not in his own campaign office. He'd never get away with it. Or *would* he?

Scott roared into the room. The wind from his mad rush blew Tolly's fluffy hair across her face.

"Scott!" She froze at the unexpected shift in the tableau before her.

Scott's large frame slammed into King's mid-sized form. He banged King's arm against the edge of the desk over and over until King had to choose between the gun or a broken wrist. The gun flew in a trajectory behind Tolly.

Too late, she whirled to find it.

"Get off of him you gorilla!" an indignant voice ordered.

Both she and Scott looked up. Celara King held the gun.

But she pointed it towards Tolly.

200 Windrunner

Chapter 31

"Stay back!" Celara angled for a strategic position away from from Tolly's long legs and Scott's long arms.

"You'll never get away with it, Celara," Scott told her. "Alex is done."

"People tell us that, but we're still here." She used the gun to point Scott closer to Tolly.

He complied. "What exactly do you think you're going to do with that?"

Celara raised an eyebrow. "What do you think?"

"Bruce didn't have the heart," Scott told her.

"Clearly," Celara said with disgust. "But that didn't stop him from taking the money."

"King's payment to retrieve me?" Tolly asked.

"You *are* a little idiot, aren't you?" Celara spat back at her.

Alex groaned before Tolly could think of a clever response. He rolled off the desk onto the floor. He didn't move again.

"No, Tolly." Scott said in a quiet voice. "Alex never pays before the job is done. Does he, Celara?"

"Then..." Tolly looked at Celara who smiled like the cat who ate the canary.

"*You* sent him?" Tolly whispered.

Celara's eyes glittered with expectation.

Scott didn't disappoint her. "You added a little rider to Bruce's contract with Alex, didn't you Celara?"

Celara nodded. "Stupid man."

"Agreed," Scott said. "Stupid enough to believe you when you told him he would have a place in Alex's administration."

This time, King's mother shrugged.

"Told him you'd need a new security director once Alex got elected because I wouldn't be around anymore. I'm right, aren't I?"

Celara waited, eager for confirmation of her magnificent abilities to manipulate.

"He said that you had a lot more to offer him if he made sure neither me nor Tolly ever returned to Lake City. That's what he told me, Celara."

"What else, Windrunner?" Celara asked, breathless from the excitement of herself.

"That you would double the money when he killed us." Scott looked her up and down. "Did Alex know about that bit of side action?"

"Grow up." Satisfied, Celara held his gaze, not a bit ashamed. Tolly wanted to smack her.

"Deny it," Scott challenged.

Celara didn't bother. Instead she went on the attack. "We know all about you, Windrunner," she insinuated. "Oh yes! Didn't you know? You can be sure we investigated our investigator. We know your history. So don't think you can just come in here and attack the next mayor of this city and not pay the price."

She turned her focus to Tolly, "And *you*, you twisted bitch. We know all about your involvement with Rafael's drug operation and how you hired someone to kill him in prison."

Tolly gasped. "That's not true!"

"By the time I'm done talking, it will be true," Celara said with a gentle smile. "You had Rafael killed in retaliation for all the times he smacked you around, which you probably deserved. In fact, your Windrunner gave us that bit of information. Thank you, Scott," she finished in a sugar-sweet voice.

Scott narrowed his eyes. "Not true, Celara."

Tolly knew better than to take her eyes off King's mother. "You and King told Scott lies about me, Celara. Lies to cover your son's criminal behavior. How do you plan to keep those secrets if he becomes a public figure? It won't work. Not anymore"

King stirred on the floor.

"Don't worry, Alex." Celara circled closer to where her son lay. She motioned with the gun for Scott and Tolly to move further back. "I'm going to call the police chief on these two lowlifes and have them put away once and for all."

She shot them a triumphant glance. "The chief is our very good friend, you see." Her eyes began to water. "He'll take good care of you two and your threats against me." Her voice cracked. She broke into a dramatic sob, as if to practice for her telephone call.

Outraged at Celara's performance, Tolly spoke up. "I never threatened you, Celara. Not even once."

"Neither have I," Scott said. "Never."

Celara snuffled. "I happen to be in fear of my life from a couple of *killers* who broke into our office and tried…"

"Tried what?" Tolly demanded. "The only thing we ever tried is to get to the truth. Like either you or your son even know what that means."

"In fear of your life, Celara?" Scott laughed. "You're the one holding the gun!"

"I happen to be defending myself and my injured son from *terrorists*, holding us hostage. You'll never get away with it!" Celara seemed ready to commit to that storyline.

"You're the one who made all the threats against me and Tolly. Both you *and* your son."

Celara's smile turned cynical. "Who do you think they'll believe?"

Tolly stared at Celara, fascinated. The woman really was from another dimension. "Never in my life did I think it possible for a barracuda to give birth to a shark."

"Uh, Tolly…" Scott warned.

"You uppity Black bitch!" Celara screamed. "Who do you think you are?" She lowered the muzzle to Tolly's chest.

"No, Celara!" Scott shouted.

"I'm the one holding the phone," Tolly responded with no inflection.

Celara smiled and shook her head. "I'm the one holding the gun. Have you lost the rest of your little mind?"

"Have you lost the primary?" Tolly retorted, even calmer.

Silence fell upon the room. From her pocket, Tolly revealed the open phone receiver in her hand—Scott's phone—the phone she knew by now picked up the slightest noise in the receiver's vicinity. Comprehension dawned on Scott's face.

Tolly used the pause to disconnect, then redial. "Ms. Yashuda, would you play back that voice mail?"

Celara gasped.

Time stood still.

"You two… just don't get it." Tears trickled down Celara's smooth pale face. "I was away from him for… so long in Paris while he grew up. But we've reconnected. This campaign is Alex's dream. It brought us together, at last. I didn't have a chance when he was younger, but I do now. Don't you see?"

Tolly didn't respond.

"Tolly, we talked about this, don't you remember? It's as if you still don't understand what he is underneath it all."

"Is this the best time for you to condescend, Celara?" Tolly asked.

Celara ignored that. "He supports his daughter's ballet programs and her dreams. He supports his sister's doctoral program. And even though there may be a cultural difference between him and his wife, he loves her too and their children. Everyone wants so much. There's just been so much pressure."

"You forgot Christian Butler," Scott corrected. "Remember him? Your grandson?"

Celara stared at Scott, irritated by the interruption.

The phone in Tolly's hand rang again.

"Don't you answer that," Celara ordered.

Tolly clicked the speaker. The entire room listened to a replay of King's foul language, plus Celara's distortions and death threats. The gun wavered in Celara's hand.

"It's not admissible in court," King whispered from the floor. They'd forgotten about him, so had Celara's dramatic soliloquy mesmerized everyone. She steadied the gun.

"But it is admissible online," Tolly responded.

"And on the radio and television," Scott added.

"Over and over again," Tolly concluded with cheer.

Scott's tone was final. "And it is over, Alex."

After a pause, King asked, "What do you want, Windrunner?"

"First of all, tell her to put the gun down." Tolly knew Scott wouldn't move a muscle until he was sure she was safe.

"Mother. Do it."

"No!" Celara protested.

"Mother, please." Alex got up to his knees. Then he hauled himself into his office chair. "Just do it. Please."

Celara lowered the gun, uncertain. Scott snatched it from her, emptied the bullets, clicked the safety, then tucked the weapon into his waistband.

Tolly and Celara glared at each other but the men remained all business.

"What do you want, Windrunner?" Alex asked again.

Scott interrupted Tolly and Celara's staredown. "Tolly, would you get my laptop from the doorway?"

She found it where Scott threw it before he charged into the room. He unlocked the briefcase, then pulled out his laptop and some papers.

"So this is the Windrunner Security Company invoice with expenses attached. Payment in full for Tolly Henry's rundown since I did return her and the video to Lake City." He displayed the same screenshot of Alex King's hand drawn back in anger.

Celara hissed in a breath. King's face turned red. He swore hard enough to peel the paint from the walls.

"Write the check now," Scott ordered.

"Doesn't matter," King said. He filled in an amount that raised Tolly's eyebrows. "I own Windrunner Security's future. You're still under contract to me, but you'll never work in this town again. I'll see to that."

"About that," in a smooth move, Scott extracted another paper from his briefcase. He traded it for the check. "This is a release of all future contractual and legal obligations between Windrunner Security Company and your various enterprises. Fill it in."

"I don't believe I will." King threw down the pen. He sat back in his chair. "If you won't play fetch like a good dog, then your little brother, the true and legal owner of Windrunner Security Company, certainly will. He'd better."

"Hmm." Scott considered that a moment. Tolly held her breath. She had no clue how the brinkmanship would end but she trusted Scott.

King shot his mother a smile of triumph. The barracuda displayed the top row of her teeth.

"You know? You're right." Scott appeared to make up his mind. "If my brother will be working for you," Scott continued, "then I guess it's fair that you have a sample of his work."

This time, Scott removed a thick portfolio full of papers. "Hmm." Scott peered at the label. "

Yes," he determined. "This is, indeed, an investigative package assembled by my brother, Jack Windrunner... on... why, I do believe, an Alexander King of Lake City."

He dropped everything in front of King with a *thud*.

Alex King's face rainbowed from purple to red to white in just thirty seconds.

Scott went through a few salacious details in the file with King.

"So," Scott picked up the pen. He held it out to King.

"Fuck you, Double D!" Alex shouted. "Fuck you!"

Tolly winced when she heard Scott's hated nickname, a reminder of the worst period of his life. She could have scratched King's face off for that.

"I thought you might say that." Scott inclined his head. He held out his hand to her.

"Tolly? My phone please." He gave her hand a hard squeeze before he took the phone from her.

Scott punched the redial. "Tina, I have just made Alexander King aware of the same information that you have saved to your hard drive."

King closed his eyes.

"Just a second, Tina," Scott said. "I'll let you talk that over with him. I'm sure you have a lot to say."

King turned his back to everyone in the room. He muttered into the phone receiver.

"He should have killed you in New Mexico," Celara whispered with malevolence. "He took the money."

"Careful, Celara," Tolly warned. "You never know who's listening. Don't you think you've said enough already?"

"For instance," Scott raised his voice before Celara's rage had time to reignite, "is Alex aware that the real reason he no longer shares custody of Christian Alexander Butler is that you were overheard using racial epithets towards him and his mother?"

Celara King choked back a combination of hatred and despair that cracked the porcelain of her face. King's mother, unmasked, was too much malice for the human eye to bear. Tolly had to look away.

King's conversation with Yashuda broke. He'd overheard Scott's last statement. He snapped Scott's cell phone closed, then sat behind his desk. For the first time, Tolly noted the dark dye that coated his hair, the pancake makeup embedded in the wrinkles at the corners of his eyes and mouth, and the teeth that appeared too white and too even. In a matter of minutes, King aged ten years.

"Give me the release," he said.

Celara also sensed the change in her son's demeanor. "Alex," she whimpered.

Scott slid the paper towards him. King signed it, then shoved it back at his former security officer.

"Alex, Alex," Celara whined. "It's not true." Her son didn't look at her.

The front door of the headquarters banged open. Excited voices filled the main office. Recharged from free dinner and liquor, the true believers prepared to work through the night to send King to the mountaintop.

Amid his mother's cries, King pointed to the door of his office. "Get out."

The staff and volunteers began their work, ignorant of the reversal of fortune. It would be a long night, indeed, for both the King campaign and the King family.

Their own work done, Tolly and Scott left.

On the way back to the pickup, Scott drew in a deep breath to launch the full-minute, deep-throated yelling he'd saved up for Tolly's reckless behavior. But she burst into tears before he could add the vocals.

Relieved, because he really didn't have the heart to lecture her, Scott drew Tolly under his massive arm and leaned them both against the truck.

"Shhh. Yashuda owns Alexander King's future now, Tolly." He stroked her hair.

"Is it over?" she asked.

"We did our part. It's out of our hands." He kissed her. "We'll have to see what Lake City decides tomorrow."

Chapter 32

Scott drove through the streets of Lake City. His truck's headlights picked out signs for the King campaign. They far outnumbered those of Yashuda's.

Tolly laid her head on his shoulder, which he liked.

"I was wrong about Celara," she mused. "I said she was a barracuda who somehow gave birth to a shark. But I had it wrong. *She* was the shark."

Scott allowed a slight smile to ghost across his face. "Alex just realized the same thing. You saw him, Tolly. He had no clue."

"Or maybe he's always known." She exhaled. "And here I thought when Bruce said it wasn't King we had to worry about, it was just trash talk."

"He meant Celara." Scott chuckled. "I didn't mention what else Bruce told me about her. I thought Alex might break down crying and I didn't want to see that. Celara was more than enough."

"Now I *have* to know."

"He said after he met with Alex, Celara got close to him."

Tolly frowned. "How close?"

Scott hesitated. "Let's just say that she gave him that special touch that tends to turn most men's minds to mush."

"No!"

"Yes. He told me that Celara reached into the front of her shirt which got his initial attention. Then she shoved that wad of cash so deep into his front pocket that he couldn't refuse her even if he wanted to. He said he was with her all night."

"Ew, gross! The same money you gave Valerie?"

Scott laughed. "I saw hand sanitizer on Valerie's desk. She'll be all right."

Tolly decided to change the subject.

"Scott, I just wanted you to know that I understand why you contracted with Alex."

He exhaled a breath. "Tolly, war does strange things to a man. There is honor, service, and patriotism. But then there is also the violence and the carnage."

Tolly didn't answer.

"When you talked to me about your miscarriage," here Tolly flinched, but Scott continued, "I recognized your symptoms as post-traumatic stress."

"Right," Tolly responded with a stiff voice. "You said you recognized... what I was going through because a lot of people you knew suffered from PTSD."

"Yeah," Scott said. He ran a hand through his hair. "A lot of people I know."

She couldn't see his expression in the dark. But she knew. "You too?" she asked.

"Me too." Scott parked the truck and walked her inside. They flopped together on the sofa in the living area. He held her in his arms then rested his cheek on her fluffy hair. Then he told her the horrible story.

Bad intelligence to the point of unintelligence. Flash bombs. Twisted, mangled bodies of women and children. Ribbons of flesh. The begging for the mercy of death.

"No one took responsibility. 'Mistakes were made,' was the official stance. Anyone not on the bus, went under the bus."

"You?"

He nodded.

"I couldn't do it anymore. All that numbing, all that blocking out and pushing down... it changes you. You start to avoid certain activities, and places. You try not to think of all the trauma and destruction, or remember how it felt to be a witness. Or a perpetrator. You try to forget."

"Have you forgotten?" Tolly asked. His arm tightened around her.

"I'll never forget," he responded in a soft voice. "Especially at night. Sometimes, I get nightmares. After Laura left me, I relocated to Lake City because I needed to get away from who I used to be. I gathered information for Alex. I provided security. I fixed his problems, most of which he caused. It was something I knew how to do because of my past training and the fact that I had what many called, intuition."

Tolly smiled.

"I was good. I got results. I finished every job. I even managed to enjoy the work sometimes, but I always felt aware of the limits that the dishonorable discharge put on my life. I knew what Alex was and I knew why he hired me. I even considered drinking to make it easier. Some people do, you know."

"What stopped you?"

"I didn't feel like I deserved any escape from it." Scott tightened his arms about her. "After I met you, I just couldn't go on pretending. I couldn't detach from it anymore. You didn't deserve what happened and I knew that too."

Tolly waited.

"I started thinking about the future and where I wanted to go in life and who I wanted to be. I started to think about my home and my family."

"They're great people, Scott."

He kissed her cheek.

"I didn't realize how much I missed everyone until Jack joined me in Lake City. Then when we stopped in Calabasas, it felt... right."

"I heard a little of what your father said."

"I would consider another line of work given the opportunity or something that inspired me."

After a pause, Tolly asked, "Has something inspired you?"

"I want to go home."

Since they sat inside Scott's condominium, Tolly knew he meant Calabasas.

"I want to retire to a few quiet acres where I can have peace of mind, live comfortably, but still have financial stability."

Tolly worked to keep her voice steady. "It sounds like it would be a wonderful life, Scott." He would leave Lake City. He would leave *her*.

"Does it?" he asked her.

"Sure," she responded in a dead voice.

It didn't escape her notice that he didn't include her in his plans. Nor did he request her to come with him. She wanted to cry.

"Tolly, you know what?" Scott interrupted her grim thoughts. "My worst fear in life has always been failing to protect the people who counted on me."

"Um hm," she murmured, distracted. They would see how Tina Yashuda handled Alex King. Then Scott would leave her for the beautiful log cabin by the lake.

"But you know what? The best moment I had in all of this was seeing you defend yourself from Bruce and from Alex and Celara. You gave it to them good, honey. I like that."

"I guess so." Tolly frowned though Scott couldn't see her expression since her back was to him. She'd even told him that she loved him. He'd yet to acknowledge that.

"I had to do something," she continued. Soon, her life would return to normal—everything the way it used to be before she knew Scott Windrunner.

"You handled yourself. I admire that."

Did that mean he was relieved she didn't need him and wouldn't be "a clinger," as Nellie called it? Was this his pep talk for her to live a life of independence, without him? And shouldn't she want that?

Tolly felt agonized. She wanted to shout, and to beg, and to plead, *I do need you, Scott. I love you. I'll always love you.*

But that wasn't what he wanted to hear.

"Let's see how Tuesday plays out." Scott pushed her up. He led her to his bedroom.

She still had no pride when it came to him. Her body would accept whatever he offered her from his. She would take everything he gave her and savor each moment fate allowed them to share.

Scott rushed over her like an ocean wave washed the shore. He pulled and pushed against her in perpetual motion. Warm and gentle, he surrounded her and filled her. She drank Scott Windrunner into her body, then drowned in the dizzy pleasure he gave her.

When he left her to fulfill his dreams, she wouldn't embarrass him or herself with a play for pity. She would say goodbye with dignity.

She waited until after he slept to cry.

Chapter 33

Tuesday morning, Scott finally allowed Tolly out of bed to discover that Tina Yashuda had unleashed a firestorm that exploded across Lake City media and beyond.

While he checked his phone messages. Tolly turned the television to early morning news.

The Yashuda campaign reacted to the Alexander King video, released anonymously to Internet, wire services, television, and radio with a carefully crafted mixture of surprise, sorrow, disgust, and determination.

Tina Yashuda stood in front of her campaign headquarters. A sign that read YASHUDA FOR MAYOR, filled the screen, exactly center behind her. She spoke into multiple microphones.

"The video and audio have both been authenticated as true by objective, neutral experts."

Tolly flipped from station to station. "Scott," she called through the bathroom door. "You're gonna want to see this."

"The true origin of the video cannot be determined," a spokesman for Yashuda's campaign intoned.

The newscaster asked a question that Tolly missed.

"The video speaks for itself," the glee in the spokesman's eyes belied his serious expression. "The abusive behavior is pretty clear, and most unfortunate."

***

Scott finished a quick shower. He hoped the cool spray would clear his head and help him to understand Tolly's strange mood from the night before.

He loved that woman. He slew her dragons… and his. But when he told her that he admired her spirit and bravery, she closed down. They shared another wonderful night together, but something upset her. Likely him, but he didn't know what he did.

Maybe the horrific story he'd behind the dishonorable discharge repulsed her the same way it repulsed everyone else. He'd lifted the stone that covered his past. His history crawled out and slithered beneath her nose.

He did another quick check of phone messages and gathered that rather than accept the subordinate position on Yashuda's team, King overplayed his hand. Her campaign released the video after Alexander King threatened Tina Yashuda.

Hoping to cheer her up, he reported the same to Tolly when he emerged from the shower. "Anyone who knew Alex would already know that he considers himself second to no one," he mused. "It never would have worked."

"But after that brutal primary campaign, Yashuda would have known that," Tolly answered.

"Exactly," Scott agreed.

"You mean…"

"Yashuda wanted to give the appearance of an honorable offer, knowing that Alex would never accept it. Now, she's off the hook." Scott flipped to another news station.

"Notice," Scott pointed out, "she focused on Alex's emotional instability rather than his misogyny as the reason for his unsuitability for office. Lake City might tolerate race discrimination, bigotry, or even sexual harassment, but the powers that be won't stand for someone who can't control their emotions or handle their campaigns."

"Or their mothers."

Scott smiled. "Yashuda always kept a cool head. She stared down a lion, then walked away."

"She's good, Scott."

"That's why she's going to be the next mayor of Lake City."

"You think the fact that Alex's wife is also Asian had something to do with Yashuda taking him down?"

"She'll never say. She knows better than that. But it's fun to watch, isn't it?"

"For a while." Tolly clicked off the television.

Scott nodded. "Look, Tolly. I've got a few calls to make. Why don't you get dressed? I'll take you home, and then I'm going to start packing up around here."

A dagger shot through Tolly's heart. Scott didn't want her. He wanted to be rid of her. Her lips trembled to the point she couldn't answer him.

After all they'd been through he would walk away from her as if from another bad memory he wished to forget. Tolly nodded just the same. She had no claim on him.

She surveyed herself in the bathroom mirror. After a week on the road, she looked a mess. And what did she have to offer him anyway? Anything?

Of course Scott didn't want to drag her around after him. She could barely make ends meet trying to survive a tough economy like everyone else. She was tired. Not just from the road adventure, but tired of the struggle. The time she put into Lake City Balance made her feel overworked and underpaid. Scratch that. She wasn't paid at all. Look how that turned out.

Tolly sniffled under the cover of running water. Then she used her freshly-charged cell phone to make a call.

Mid-morning, she and Scott watched Alexander King withdraw his mayoral bid for family reasons. He told reporters that he wanted to focus on renewable energy and green job creation in the private sector. News analysts had a field day speculating other reasons—alcoholism, bankruptcy, lunacy.

"Lake City scuttlebutt from people I know is that Bruce turned on Alex."

"How did he get back?"

"I didn't take all his money. However, the good advice I gave him as a business consultant *was* pretty expensive."

"Well played, by the way," Tolly told him with a smile.

"Bruce knows who the real enemy is. That's why Alexander King's campaign and his private businesses will come under multiple investigations. It's an information seller's market, and Bruce has plenty of inventory spread out on the table. He'll be all right."

"What about you?"

"I'm done with the whole matter. So's Celara, by the way."

"What do you mean?"

"That *barracuda*, as you called her, got on the first thing smoking to Paris. She won't be back."

"Well, I won't miss her."

Scott laughed. "Tolly, what am I going to do with you?"

Tolly could think of many things. The more she had of Scott, the more she wanted. A little bit of him would never be enough. How could she ever let him go? In a desperate move, she grasped at straws. She would see to it that Scott forgot to take her home tonight, at least.

They didn't have much longer together. Certainly, not at the rate Scott packed. He still had the military precision and efficiency to get the job done in as little time as possible.

Later in the day, King's companies moved to distance themselves from their founder. Celara Sun, Celara Wind, Celara Green Supply, and the Midwest Consortium released statements that expressed their surprise and regret regarding King's actions.

Early voting swung towards Alexander King. But by Tuesday evening, the conflagration that Yashuda ignited burned through his lead.

"She won the primary fair and square," the female news reader announced with cheer. "Back to you, Jim!"

Late Tuesday evening, Scott still didn't understand what had affected Tolly's mood. She'd been a wild woman in bed, as if the world were about to end. He regretted the chaos that he'd introduced into her life. His dubious past and his association with Alex remained, but Tolly told him that she understood.

She smiled at him and he thought she'd never looked more beautiful. It broke his heart to imagine that she might smile like that for another man after he left. He couldn't bear the thought.

"We did it, Scott!" she said.

Scott didn't smile back at her. He sat up against the headboard. "Tolly, there's something I didn't tell you."

"What?" She sat up beside him. He took her hand in his.

"Turns out that my father used the money that I sent him from service to establish college funds for Nellie's children. They're going to be all right without Sonny. Also, that crazy old man saved up enough to buy quite a bit of land in Calabasas."

"The cabin?"

"The cabin and beyond."

"Wow. Gotta love James Windrunner." Tolly cleared her throat. "So, you're going back home?"

Scott studied his hands. "You ever hear back from Lake City Balance?"

"About the job?"

"Yeah, you worked so hard to earn it. Did you get an offer?" He didn't know what she thought about life outside the bright lights and fast pace of Lake City or life with a man with a tainted past.

Tolly didn't look at him. "I called them while you were in the shower."

"What did they say?" He felt hollow inside. That explained her strange mood. She was trying to think of a way to ease him from her life. Maybe she was afraid that he'd stalk her. He knew he wouldn't ever forget her.

He told himself to be happy for her. She deserved nothing but the best life had to offer. If she didn't want him, then he would respect her wishes and step aside.

"They didn't say anything. I told George, the director, that I didn't want the job."

A long pause hung in the air. He didn't know what to make of that. He cleared his throat. "That sort of leaves you at loose ends, doesn't it?"

"I suppose." Tolly swallowed. She reminded herself to wait until Scott left to shed any tears. "Somewhat."

"You know... I could use someone good at weatherizing. The second floor of the cabin still lets in wind."

Tolly twisted to check Scott's face to see whether this was yet another of his tricky word plays. He looked uncomfortable, as though he regretted the offer as soon as he made it.

Still, pathetic hope beat in Tolly's heart. "I'm... I'm pretty good." She waited.

Scott couldn't believe how lame he'd sounded. *Weatherizing? For real? Why didn't she smack him?* But no, she looked as though she waited for him to say something else. He'd told himself that he wouldn't force himself upon her.

But this might be his last chance.

"God, you're wonderful, Tolly." Scott pulled her against his massive chest. "You might not know how much you mean to me, but I just can't bear the thought of losing you. Whenever you were with me, the nightmares stopped. Why is that?"

Tolly didn't answer. She did remember the way Scott twisted himself around her and held her so tight that first night in the motel. She had no explanation, but if he needed her, then by God, he had her.

"I didn't know how long I would have to beg to convince you to come with me, Tolly. But if it took me the rest of my life…"

"Oh, Scott." Tolly wrapped her arms around him. Waves of relief washed over her. She couldn't hold back the tears. At last, he opened his heart. At last!

"I don't want to live without you. You mean so much to me. I need you." He stroked her fluffy hair. "Could you leave the Lake City life for me, Tolly?"

"I'd leave Lake City for you and for me. My life is with you, Scott, wherever we are," she whispered.

He kissed her like a madman. "I need you back where you belong."

"And where's that?"

"By my side. In my bed. In my truck. On my bike."

"On top," she insisted.

"Anyway you prefer to have me."

Tolly giggled. The wicked gleam in his eye belied the humble tone of his voice.

Chapter 34

Wednesday morning, by the time they made the trip to Tolly's building, news vans had turned her street into a parking lot.

Scott circled the block so they could dash up the alley.

No, Bruce never cleaned Tolly's apartment. He was certainly too busy selling information on King to the highest bidder to bother now.

Tolly recognized the efforts Bill Martinez made to straighten the mess King's hired hand left behind but her apartment still tilted off-kilter.

"Tolly, I'm so sorry," Scott began, but she shushed him.

She gathered up the rent payments that Mr. Martinez stacked on a side table into a neat pile. But who cared?

The financial position of her building remained precarious. She'd fallen behind on almost every bill. In addition, several city departments sent notices for inspections and assessments, Kings final chips that he called in during the week she was away. The only remedy would be to raise the rents which meant breaking her word to Bill Martinez and her father.

She couldn't bear to do it.

Still apologetic, Scott got a box to pack up Tolly's kitchen with the same military precision he used to pack his condo. Tolly found a change of clothes scattered across her bed where Bruce threw them over a week ago.

"I am going to burn these khakis and this shirt," she called to Scott from the bedroom. "They're barely hanging by the threads."

"You look beautiful, Tolly," he called back.

She showered and then climbed to the first level to find Bill Martinez. After a ten-minute reassurance that yes, she was okay and no, he wasn't to blame for what happened, and no, no one else was in trouble, but yes, she appreciated his reaching out to her while she was way, Tolly interrupted him.

"Mr. Martinez, I wanted to let you know that I'm putting this building on the market."

"No!"

"Yes." Tolly smiled shyly. "I met someone. He and I are moving to Colorado." After more lengthy reassurances, she went downstairs to provide Scott additional packing instructions.

By Wednesday afternoon, Mr. Martinez's entire family had pooled their resources to purchase Tolly's building, equipment, and furniture. They paid her in cash. Everyone came down to meet Scott (and pick out rooms for themselves). They agreed to take care of the obligations to the city and would continue to rent the top floor to college students.

By the weekend, he and Tolly had readied themselves for the long return trip West, this time under more pleasant circumstances. Scott felt safe enough to breathe a sigh of relief. Too late for her to turn back now, he thought with quiet triumph.

They rode in Scott's pickup. Part of their combined households filled the bed. A large moving truck filled with the rest of their possessions and Scott's motorcycle would meet them in Calabasas.

They stopped overnight at a hotel in Omaha. The next morning, Scott gassed up at their favorite truck stop.

Before he pulled back on eighty, Tolly turned to him.

"We did meet before this Scott, didn't we?"

Scott didn't answer because the amazing forsight of fate rendered him speechless. He pulled onto the road.

"Was it you?"

Scott looked at her and waited.

"That day in the coffee shop, I felt... something. I saw a man with silver hair. Almost a year ago... it was you, wasn't it?"

The pickup gathered speed.

"Tell me," she insisted.

Scott smiled. "I couldn't take my eyes off you, Tolly. You sat in front of the window. You looked so warm and sweet when the sun shined through your hair."

"I always sit in front of the window."

"You took my breath away. And when you smiled, your whole face lit up. Everything about you, so fresh."

"If we actually spoke to each other that day, I wonder what we'd have said?"

Scott took a large hand off the wheel to give hers a quick squeeze. "Well, much as I'd like to think I was a smooth operator, I wasn't the same person you know now."

Tolly remembered Frank's grim description of Scott's despair that clashed with her impression of the joker and trickster. The Scott Windrunner that she knew made her laugh harder each day.

"You wouldn't have recognized me, Tolly," he told her. "I wasn't living a real life."

"Me neither," she admitted.

"So, maybe it all happened the way it was supposed to."

Tolly smiled. "I love you, Scott."

He looked at her. "I love you too, Tolly."

Her heart melted with relief to hear his love for her spoken aloud. Warmth washed over her. He kissed her, then returned his focus to the road that stretched all the way West before them.

After a heartfelt visit with Scott's family, Scott and Tolly trekked back to the cabin by the lake, more beautiful than Tolly remembered. The movers found the cabin. Tolly watched them open the big box truck and begin to unload. It was really happening. Her dreams were coming true.

"Do you think your father knew all along that this was how our story would end?"

"Well, first, it's only the beginning of our story, Tolly. But yes," he kissed her cheek, "James Windrunner will be sure to take full credit."

She laughed so hard that she almost missed it. Her father's ancient Ford pick-up truck rolled smoothly out the back of the larger moving truck. Someone had painted the old rusty classic a bright, shiny forest green.

"No!" Tolly's eyes filled with tears. "Scott!"

"Yashuda asked me to tell you that she is very thankful for your bravery, Tolly."

Tolly shook her head. It was too much.

"As a measure of her gratitude for your last-minute save of her campaign, she fine-tuned, detailed, ransomed, and paid for delivery to Calabasas."

"She did this?" Tolly asked, wonder in her voice. "And your motorcycle too!" Scott's motorcycle, returned to pristine condition, sat tied to the bed of her pick-up.

"Welcome home, Tolly," Scott said.

Chapter 35

"Our house is a home now."

Tolly watched Scott survey their shared office on the first floor of the pine log cabin with a satisfied expression. They often sat together in silence working on their start-up enterprises. She loved the laid-back Scott who smiled often.

He flashed a mischievous grin now. "Why don't you help me rebuild the old tree house? We can spend the night up there sometimes when we need to get away from it all."

Tolly burst into laughter.

"Of course I will," she replied, "After you build me a greenhouse."

Scott raised his eyebrows and waited, maybe for the punch line.

Without a word, she turned back to the computer and their business plans. When she looked behind her, he'd disappeared.

Her mind wandered.

Tina Yashuda had emerged as a fierce Lake City political contender and power player. She'd adopted Alexander King's green platform and then went on to win the general election. Tolly shook her head. Lake City seemed so long ago and so far away. Her fingers flew across the keyboard as she arranged for Mayor Yashuda to receive a bouquet of roses, signed, "Your friends, Tolly and Scott."

Jack remained CEO of Windrunner Security Company. His work samples had impressed Mayor Yashuda so much that she chose him to oversee computer and network security for her administration.

Through the window of their office, Tolly watched Scott walk back and forth across a field of grass. She'd paid for her past mistakes and so had he. Her life seemed like a dream come true these days. Scott was her dream come true—her silver fox.

Scott told her that he wanted to show other former members of the armed forces how to transfer their skills and experiences to build new career paths for themselves. He planned workshops on small businesses, sustainable building, the installation of small wind-turbines and solar heaters, and windbreaks.

Tolly frowned at the spreadsheet. Both she and Scott understood the value of second chances for themselves and others. They wanted to teach the vulnerable to be self-reliant. Even though they might have some lean years getting started, they could make it work, Tolly decided. She opened the curriculum proposals.

Nellie divorced Sonny. She decided to accept Valerie's offer of the assistant manager position at Canela Street. Scott and Tolly helped Nellie and her son and daughter to move to Patina. The kids assisted Nellie and Valerie as interns.

When Valerie learned of Scott and Tolly's plans for the future, she offered to join the roster and teach classes on grant writing.

After that, the offers to join the curriculum continued. Best of all, James requested Scott's permission to teach classes on the celebration of language and culture. Of course, Scott said yes.

She knew for a fact Scott loved her. She loved him. She would do anything for him.

Three hours later, he came inside the cabin with large sheets of rolled-up paper behind his back.

"Tolly," he said, "don't ever call my bluff."

With triumph, he unfurled the papers and showed her construction blueprints. "I'm going to build you the greenhouse to end all greenhouses."

"Scott!" She stared up at all six-foot, five inches of him. It would never be enough of him. Never. Sure enough, the waterworks started.

He pulled her gently towards him. "Just one thing in return, Tolly."

She agreed to his condition because she found it hard to refuse him anything, he asked so little of her. And because he asked her for so little, she gave him everything she had with joy in her heart.

Later that evening, in the warmth of the pine log office with its cedar fixtures, Tolly focused once again on her laptop. She opened a social media program.

As Scott suggested, the time had come for her to reconnect with her extended family, including Martina Butler, her cousin.

Acknowledgments

A common misconception is that writing is a solitary art. I wish to thank the following for their kind assistance and positive words: Mary McQueen and the McQueen family, Greener Homes National Summit, Arlene Guillen, Margo Seymour, Denver Tea Room, Crystal Sharp, Holiday Chalet Bed & Breakfast, Joe Cahn, Nate Stone, Denver Public Library, Rocky Mountain Micro Finance, Geoffrey Bateman, Eliana Schonberg, Anaa Mansouri, Rob Gilmor, University of Denver Writing Center, Denver March Powwow, Rocky Mountain Fiction Writers, Capitol Hill Fiction Writers, Cheryl Lucero, NEWSED, Leticia Tanguma, Bill Stowe, Dana Heath Battle, Jerry Hooten, Beaverdale Writers, Two Rivers Romance Writers, Go Green Warehouse, Red Cloud Renewable Energy Center, Lakota Solar Enterprise, Building Science Academy, Trees Water and People, The Gathering Place, Denver Department of Transportation, Metro Care Ring, Denver Urban Ministries, Father Woody's, Department of Energy's Tribal Energy Program, Rosebud Log Homes. Those countless individuals too numerous to name who spared me time energy, expertise, compassion, and random acts of inspiration, I thank you from the bottom of my heart.

Author's Note

Windrunner grew as an extension of the fictional world introduced in the corporate suspense *Celara Sun* [McQueen Press, 2010]. From that story of power and intrigue, Alexander King emerged as a J.R. Ewing-type villain for the green energy industry challenged by the protagonist Martina Butler along with a large supporting cast of characters that moved against the backdrop of Lake City and the Celara companies.

Two years later, minor characters from *Celara Sun* have come to the foreground of *Windrunner* to drive this romantic suspense across the western North American landscape. While green energy remains a theme, post-traumatic stress, domestic violence, and military service provide the supporting structure to Tolly Henry and Scott Windrunner's road adventure.

Works relevant to the creation of *Windrunner* include: *Medicine Bags and Dog Tags: American Indian Veterans from Colonial Times to the Second Iraq War; We Shall Remain: A Native History of Utah; The Ute Indians of Southwestern Colorado; A Century of Dishonor; The Everything Guide to Writing a Romance Novel; On Writing Romance;* and *Writing a Romance Novel for Dummies*. The many organizations relevant to *Windrunner* are listed on the Acknowledgements page. Thank you everyone for your time, energy, and support!

About the Author

Lee McQueen has a Master of Library Science from State University of New York at Buffalo, a Bachelor of Arts from Xavier University of Louisiana, and coursework in public affairs at the University of Texas at Austin. She has been both a librarian and a bookstore owner. Now editor and publisher at McQueen Press, she also takes on writing and research assignments. Lee is a member of Rocky Mountain Fiction Writers and meets regularly with University of Denver Writing Center. Other projects with McQueen Press include the novels *Kenzi* and *Celara Sun*, the screenplay *SUDAN: The Lion of Truth*, plus the non-fiction *Writer in the Library! 41 Writers Reveal How They Use Libraries to Develop Their Skill, Craft & Careers*.

Also from McQueen Press
Available via Amazon and other distributors.

978-0-9798515-9-9
2011
9.99

978-0-9798515-0-6
2006
11.99

978-0-9798515-6-8
2010
16.99

978-0-9798515-3-7
2007
Out of Print

978-0-9798515-4-4
2008
9.99

978-9798515-2-0
2007
13.99

Breakaway

Thinking about it everyday
Letting those thoughts slip away

Eternal Searcher waits for you.

You are the Sky.
I am the Blue.

Made in the USA
Charleston, SC
28 July 2012